D0433548

THE BROKEN CIRCLE

In the quiet Lancashire village that is home to forensic psychologist Jill Kennedy, the wealthy new owner of nearby Kelton Manor is found dead in the woods. As Jill and her sometime lover and colleague DCI Max Trentham hunt the dead man's killer, they are drawn ever deeper into the victim's dark past. When the name of prominent local businessman Thomas McQueen crops up in the course of their inquiries, Max finds himself adrift in uncharted waters; already facing suspension for harassing McQueen – believing him to be responsible for an unsolved murder a year earlier. Is McQueen really as innocent as he claims?

To my big sister, Linda,
with love

THE BROKEN CIRCLE

by

Shirley Wells

Magna Large Print Books
Long Preston, North Yorkshire,
BD23 4ND, England.

British Library Cataloguing in Publication Data.

Wells, Shirley
    The broken circle.

    A catalogue record of this book is
    available from the British Library   **4512529**

    ISBN   978-0-7505-3399-7

First published in Great Britain by Constable,
an imprint of Constable & Robinson, 2010

Cover illustration © Sally Mundy by arrangement with
Arcangel Images

Published in Large Print 2011 by arrangement with
Constable & Robinson Ltd.

Magna Large Print is an imprint of Library Magna Books Ltd.

Printed and bound in Great Britain by
T.J. (International) Ltd., Cornwall, PL28 8RW

Chapter One

HMP Styal doesn't look like Holloway's poor northern relation, but that's exactly what it is. Half the prisoners are housed in red-brick villas left over from Victorian times when the site was used as an orphanage. Waite Wing, where Jill was due in exactly twenty-eight minutes, is home to the most violent offenders.

Naming the wing after Terry Waite seemed like an act of madness to Jill, given that the man had spent years in solitary confinement, often blindfolded and chained to a radiator. But better that than Purgatory Wing, she supposed.

It was only the second time Jill had been to Styal and, as on her first visit, the sight of the place took her by surprise. It was deceptively peaceful so that few residents of the affluent, leafy Cheshire suburb even knew the prison existed.

Her drive down from Lancashire had been relatively traffic- and incident-free, and those precious minutes before she had to be inside the building would give her enough time to study the runners and riders. She reached over to the back seat for her briefcase, grabbed her newspaper, opened it at the racing page, spread it across the steering wheel and ran her finger down the card. She paused on Manor Boy...

As she'd driven through her village to come here, she'd seen a police car parked outside Kelton Manor. She'd wondered if perhaps Bradley Johnson had complained about youths throwing litter into his landscaped garden.

A couple of weeks ago, Jill had been walking past the manor when Bradley had been clearing up.

'A bloody condom now,' he'd snapped, holding the offending article high enough for her to see...

The Johnsons had been in the village a little less than a year. Americans, they'd lived in London for seven years then bought the manor at auction, an auction Jill had wanted to win, sixteen months ago. Renovation work had begun immediately and the family – husband, wife and two sons – had moved in six months later.

Jill couldn't claim to know any of them well, but she hadn't taken to Bradley on their first meeting. He'd been all over her like a rash, touching her arm on every sentence and gazing at her breasts and legs.

'Ah, the forensic psychologist,' he'd said, impressed. 'Gosh, honey, brains as well as beauty. Someone mentioned you and your work, can't think who, and I automatically pictured a flat-chested lady with thick ankles.' He'd touched her arm again. 'Not a flat chest or a thick ankle to be seen. What a delightful surprise!'

'The wonders of silicone,' she'd responded, smiling sweetly.

He hadn't known if she was joking or not, and had merely stared harder at her breasts in an attempt to satisfy his curiosity.

'And you write books as well, I hear,' he'd said. 'Self-help books, aren't they? Relaxation techniques and stuff like that? I must seek them out.'

'Do you need help to relax?' she'd asked.

'No. No, of course not,' he'd replied irritably.

He must have labelled her the mad forensic psychologist because any future meetings had been brief and a little wary on his part.

His wife, Phoebe, on the other hand, seemed a genuine, friendly woman, one who, when she first arrived in the village, had wanted to become part of the community. That had lasted about a month. These days, it seemed to Jill that she rarely left the solid stone walls of the manor.

The sons, Keiran and Tyler, were both studying at university and, although they'd be home soon for the Christmas holidays, they spent little time in Kelton Bridge...

Manor Boy. Jill had backed the horse a

7

month ago and he'd been going well until he ran out of steam a few lengths from the finishing post. Perhaps he was worth a tenner. He was a good price so perhaps she'd risk twenty pounds on him. Or maybe even thirty.

Her phone rang and she glanced at the display. It was her mother, and it would have to wait.

Seconds later, a message notification came through and she hit the button to play that.

'Now where are you?' her mother's plaintive voice demanded. 'Never mind. Give me a call as soon as you get this, OK? I've had another thought about the party and I need to tell you all about it. I've decided it's no good having a poky little hole-in-the-wall affair. Not when I've put up with the mad bugger for forty years.' Her mother laughed at that. 'Phone me the minute you can, love. Bye for now.'

Jill dreaded to think what 'thought' her mother had had about the party. In January, her parents would be celebrating their fortieth wedding anniversary and her mother, totally ignoring her husband's views on the matter, was determined to have the party to top all parties.

Forty years. As well as making Jill feel old, it was a reminder that her parents were no longer as young as she liked to think...

Pushing the thought aside, she phoned the bookie and placed her bets for the day. Then it was time to leave the sanctuary of her car and head for the building.

She should have prepared for this meeting, she really should. But how the hell did one prepare for a meeting with a woman who had murdered her own daughter?

Inside Waite Wing, the air was heavy with despair. It was also very noisy. Jill thought it had to be one of the most depressing places in the country. She wasn't surprised there were so many issues concerning suicide and self-harm. She knew the gloomy statistics. Around eighty-five per cent of the inmates had serious drug problems; many had been stealing hundreds of pounds a day to feed their addiction. Forty per cent of the women had mental health problems and, even worse, almost sixty per cent had suffered physical or sexual abuse.

Jill was shown to a small room that held a square table and half a dozen plastic chairs. She sat at the table to wait.

When Claire Lawrence was finally ushered to the room, Jill realized, and it came as a jolt, that she felt sorry for her. Sorry for every woman confined in this godforsaken place. She must remember the crime this woman had committed and remind herself that sympathy was misplaced.

Claire was thirty, but looked much older. Pale skin sat loosely on her thin body. Her hair, ginger in the photographs Jill had seen, was almost completely grey, and her eyes were a dull, lack-lustre green.

She was wearing a navy blue jogging suit that dwarfed her small frame.

'Hello, Claire.' Jill got to her feet and offered her hand. 'I'm Jill Kennedy. I believe you wanted to talk to me?'

Perhaps 'wanted' was too strong a word. Over the last eighteen months, various professionals had tried unsuccessfully to persuade Claire to tell them what she had done with her daughter's body. A month ago, during one of those interviews, Claire had said that she would talk to Jill.

Claire ignored the proffered hand and sat down. Jill sat opposite. And waited.

On her left hand, Claire sported a tiny tattoo showing a dove carrying the name Daisy in its mouth. A butterfly was just visible on her right wrist.

'Did you want to talk to me?' Jill prompted.

'Why not? I've talked to everyone else.' Her voice was a thin rasp from years of smoking heroin off aluminium foil. 'No celebrities like you, mind.'

Oh, for– This was to be a game. Claire wanted to pit her wits against her, to bring her down a peg or two.

'I'm no celebrity,' Jill responded.

'Saw you on the telly. They reckon you can get inside a killer's mind.'

'Then they're wrong.'

Claire stared at her for long, unnerving moments. 'You're younger than I reckoned,' she said finally. 'Are you married?'

'Widowed.'

That took her by surprise. It took most people by surprise. Something else it did was alter people's perception of her. If she'd been divorced, they would have seen her as a pushy, ambitious, career-driven bitch who was impossible to live with. If she'd been single, they would have labelled her sexually dysfunctional, someone who gained cheap thrills from delving into other people's minds. Knowing she was widowed threw them.

'Kill him, did you?' she asked with a thin smile.

'No. Someone else did.' Jill decided it was time she asked the questions. 'Why would I kill him? Were you ever tempted to kill your husband?'

Peter Lawrence hadn't been the catch of the century, but he was probably the best thing that had ever happened to Claire. Not that that was saying a lot.

'Many times.' Claire found the idea amusing. 'Every Friday night for starters. He were a right bastard when he got the drink in him.'

'Did you love him?'

'Love?' Claire repeated the word as if she'd never spoken it aloud before. Jill doubted if she'd ever considered the question. 'Love?'

she said again, and then her frown vanished and she laughed as if love was for idiots.

But what would Claire know of love? She had been born here at Styal Prison. Her mother, a prostitute with a drug problem, had spent so much time at Styal she probably gave it as her permanent address. Claire had been in and out of care until she was sixteen and old enough to sell her body to feed a drug habit. Like mother, like daughter – a full circle.

Claire was pregnant and homeless at seventeen and, when the child's father, if indeed he was the father, suggested they married and found themselves a council flat, she agreed. They lived there until Daisy, their daughter, was six years old. Then, when both Peter and Claire were drunk or high on drugs, they wrecked the place and were evicted.

Claire had a violent temper, and Peter was a drunk. It was an uneasy combination.

Peter was besotted with his daughter, however, as was Claire, and, for her sake, he took a variety of jobs. He worked as a taxi driver for three months, until he was sacked for being drunk. Next he was employed, for almost a year, as a builder's labourer but, again, he was dismissed, this time for absenteeism. Then he worked on a farm and, not only did he stick at it, he almost seemed to enjoy it. He still drank, but they had an income of sorts and they rented a flat in Harrington. Apart from the frequent squabbles, and the fights when they were under the influence of one drug or another, life seemed fairly settled.

When Daisy was ten years old, something, and no one knew what, went dreadfully wrong. The rows became more violent. Peter's drinking worsened. One day, he walked out on his wife and, more surprisingly, his daughter.

Claire and Daisy moved around after that, staying with whoever had a spare bed or, sometimes, even sleeping on the streets.

The council found her another flat, but she hadn't wanted to know. She'd simply kept on moving.

Then, almost a year to the day after Peter's departure, Claire killed their daughter.

'Did you love Daisy?' Jill asked.

There was no answer.

'I suppose you did,' Jill mused. 'Isn't that why you killed her? To save her from a life of poverty, drug addiction and prison?'

No answer.

'She was a pretty little girl, wasn't she?' Jill went on. 'I've seen photos that were taken at her school. She looks like you. The same nose and the same eyes.'

Still Claire didn't answer. She was curling a strand of her dull hair around the index finger of her left hand. And she was humming softly, almost inaudibly.

'You've been here eighteen months now, haven't you?' Jill murmured. 'Daisy would have been coming up to her thirteenth birthday. A teenager. What do you think she would have been like, Claire? Would she have done well at school? Do you think she'd have been into clothes and make-up?'

Even in this small room, there was no escape from the noise. Women outside were talking, laughing, shouting or screaming. Only Claire was silent.

'At thirteen,' Jill went on, 'I couldn't wait to grow up. I was desperate to be a teenager but then, the minute I was thirteen, I longed to be sixteen. Then I longed to be seventeen and learning to drive. Then eighteen so that people could no longer treat me like a kid.'

So much for Claire wanting to talk to her.

'Who was Daisy close to, Claire? You? Her dad? Who were her friends?'

There was no response from Claire. No comment, no change of expression, nothing.

Jill took a notepad from her briefcase and began writing. She was making a Christmas list, but Claire wasn't to know that.

'Do you like coming here?' she asked eventually, taking Jill by surprise.

'To Styal? No.'

'It's a shit hole, isn't it.' Claire smiled at that.

'So why don't you do something about getting out?' Jill put down her notebook. 'If you cooperated, if you talked to us and told us what you did with Daisy's body, you might get a reduced sentence.'

Claire shrugged as if escape from Styal was of no importance whatsoever. Perhaps it wasn't. After all, Styal was home to her. Where would she go? What would she do?

'No one's angry with you, Claire,' Jill lied.

Peter, when he heard what Claire had done, had vowed to kill her. He'd tried to visit her in Styal, but Claire had refused to see him. His anger had soon had him reaching for the bottle.

'All anyone wants is to be able to bury Daisy. People want to put flowers on her grave for her birthday and at Christmas. Is that really too much to ask?'

'People' was an exaggeration. Peter wanted that, or he had. He'd left Lancashire six months ago and Jill, who had wanted to speak to him prior to coming to Styal, had no idea where he was now.

'Her father wants to bury his little girl. Won't you let him do that?'

'No.'

'What has he done wrong?'

Again, Claire preferred to wind a strand of hair around her finger than answer Jill's question.

'D'you know how many killers get put away when no body's been found?' she asked instead.

'Very few,' Jill replied. 'Which makes you quite special, doesn't it?'

'Yeah.'

So Claire liked being in the minority. If she told them where Daisy's body was, she would be exactly like all the other killers out there.

'Where do you live?' she asked Jill.

'In a small village in Lancashire. Kelton Bridge. Do you know it?'

'Yeah, I know it.'

'I grew up in Liverpool, but I love Kelton. It's peaceful and everyone is very friendly.'

'I don't want to talk no more,' Claire said. 'I might talk to you next time.'

'Next time isn't good enough, Claire. I'm not–'

The sudden and almost deafening clamouring of an alarm drowned her voice.

Claire grinned smugly, as if she alone was responsible.

Either Styal was in danger of being razed to the ground or someone had decided it was the ideal time for a drill.

Jill hadn't learnt much, other than the fact that Claire was lonely, disliked being ignored and longed to be the centre of attention, but she wasn't sorry to end the interview.

Chapter Two

Max arrived at Manchester airport, went straight to the arrivals area, checked the screen and saw that Flight KL1073 from Amsterdam was delayed. Typical. Planes from all over the world were on schedule yet the short flight from Amsterdam was going to be an hour late.

He bought a newspaper, then went to the coffee bar to read it. All the while, he kept checking for updates on the ETA of Flight KL1073.

He didn't really have time for this. On the drive here, he'd had a call to say that Bradley Johnson, the lord of the manor, or Kelton Bridge manor at least, had been reported missing by his wife. Apparently, he'd left the manor on foot late yesterday afternoon and hadn't returned. As he'd been planning an early drive to London today for an important meeting, his wife was extremely concerned for his safety.

Max should really be looking into that. On the other hand, Bradley Johnson was a grown man and, although they might be short of coppers at the moment, there were more than enough to deal with a missing person inquiry. In any case, Max was always getting reprimanded about his lack of delegation skills.

He was reading about the government's latest harebrained scheme for reducing congestion on the country's motorways when an announcement was made. Flight KL1073 had landed.

Max nipped outside to smoke a cigarette and then stood to wait for the passengers to appear.

Beside him, an attractive girl, probably early twenties, paced impatiently. Max guessed that, any minute now, a handsome young bloke would appear to sweep her off her feet.

She checked her watch. Max checked his.

Finally, the double doors swung open and passengers, mostly businessmen and businesswomen, walked towards them.

Max was wrong. His companion suddenly raced forward and launched herself at a young, blonde-haired girl. Max watched them leave, arm in arm, talking excitedly and giggling.

Thomas McQueen was one of the last passengers to appear. Fifty-two years old, he wore his hair – long, lank and fair – in a ponytail.

Recognition and a brief flash of anger crossed his face as he spotted Max.

'Been taking a holiday, Tom?' Max greeted

him genially.

'As a matter of fact I have.' McQueen didn't slow his pace.

'Christmas shopping?' Max suggested.

'Expecting a present, Chief Inspector?'

'I am.' Max dodged a couple of people to keep pace with McQueen. 'You behind bars.'

'Behind bars for what?' McQueen asked, a half-smile curving his thin lips.

His lips were the only thin thing about him. His penchant for fine wines and top-class restaurants was piling on the weight and, as he was only around the five feet five mark, every pound added to the roly-poly image. Even his face was fat and bloated.

'Anything. I'm not fussy,' Max answered his question.

The murder of a certain Muhammed Khalil would do for starters. Once they had him for that, they could worry about the rest.

'You can't pin anything on me, as well you know.'

'Not yet.'

'Not ever.' McQueen stopped walking to look up at Max. 'You've had it in for me ever since that Khalil lad was killed. He happened to rent one of my properties, that's all. Thankfully, a lot of people do. If they didn't, I'd be out of business. I've committed no crime, Chief Inspector. None at all. In fact, the only lawbreaker around here is you. If I'm not mistaken, this is harassment.'

'Eh? Just because I happen to bump into you at the airport?'

'There's that. There's sitting outside my house for hours on end. There's following me into certain bars. It's harassment, plain and simple.'

Put like that, Max supposed he had a point.

'Do you know Bradley Johnson?' Max asked, changing the subject. 'Lives in—'

'Kelton Bridge. Yes, I know him. Why do you ask?'

'Seems he's been reported missing.'

'Oh?' McQueen's surprise seemed genuine.

'Yes, his wife phoned us early this morning.'

'He's a big boy.'

They reached fresh air and Max spotted McQueen's driver, minder more like, jumping out of a black BMW to open the passenger door for his boss.

'My car,' McQueen said unnecessarily. 'Be seeing you, Chief Inspector. But not quite so often in future, I trust.'

McQueen handed his two bags and a black briefcase to his minder, John Barry, and, leaving him to stow them in the boot, jumped in the car.

Unlike McQueen, Barry was in the peak of condition. An ex-boxer, he must still keep in training as his arms and shoulders were massive. His head, shaved and bullish, sat no more than an inch above those shoulders.

He wasn't the sort of bloke you argued with unless you had plenty of back-up.

By the time Max got back to his own car, McQueen would have been halfway to Harrington. There was no point even thinking of trying to catch up with him. In any case, Max had work to do. Until he could find some hard evidence linking him to Muhammed Khalil's murder, McQueen, sadly, was nothing more than a little extra-curricular activity.

Bad news was waiting for him at head-quarters.

'The boss wants to see you, Max,' DS Fletcher announced.

Fletch was sitting at his desk, pen in one hand and a bacon sandwich in the other. In fact, now Max came to think about it, he couldn't remember the last time he'd seen Fletch without food in his hand.

'OK, Fletch, thanks.'

'The second you arrive,' he added.

'So if he asks, I haven't arrived yet. OK?'

'OK,' Fletch agreed amiably. 'He doesn't sound terribly happy,' he added, 'so you might want a brew first.'

Max groaned. 'What's rattled his cage now?'

'Your guess is as good as mine,' Fletch said, licking melting butter from his fingers. 'Doesn't that lovely wife of yours feed you?'

'Not often enough. By the time the kids

have been fed, the day's gone.' His eyes took on the usual dreamy expression at mention of his daughters. 'It's OK, though. I won't starve.'

'I can see that.'

Fletch looked down at the amount of stomach that was hanging over his belt and sucked in a huge breath. 'It's all muscle.'

'Yeah, yeah.'

Max went to his office, but decided to save the brew till later. He was curious, but not particularly worried. His boss was rarely 'terribly happy'. No capacity for happiness, Max supposed. No sense of humour.

His phone rang and he was pleased to see it was Ben calling from France.

'Hi, son. How's it going?'

'It's dead boring,' Ben complained.

'You only arrived yesterday,' Max pointed out. 'Give it a chance.'

'But we've got to go and look round a boring old museum this morning. I hate museums.'

'It'll be fascinating.'

'You reckon?' Ben scoffed, and Max couldn't in all honesty say he did.

'Anyway,' Ben went on, 'I just thought I'd ring to see if the dogs are OK.'

'The dogs are fine, yes. I'm OK, too. Thanks so much for asking.'

'Ha, ha.' Max could hear the amusement in his voice, could picture the smile on his face.

They chatted for a couple of minutes, then Harry came on the phone. Max wondered why he worried about them so much. They were fine, not a care in the world, other than how they might escape the boredom of a museum, which was as it should be.

Half an hour later, unable to guess what today's bollocking would focus on, Max finally gave up. He didn't have a clue. So now he was extremely curious.

He took the stairs to Phil Meredith's office, knocked on the door and stepped inside.

'Where the bloody hell have you been?' Without waiting for an answer, Meredith spat out, 'You've really blown it this time. You've been warned countless times, but you take no notice whatsoever. A law unto yourself. Always bloody have been.'

Max still had no idea what he was talking about. One thing was certain, his boss was furious.

Meredith had recently taken to wearing contact lenses, probably because he thought they looked better for the TV appearances he loved so much, and they had a habit of making his eyes water. His brown hair was thinning on an almost daily basis so Max suspected the next thing would be a wig.

'Sorry, but you'll have to give me a clue,' he said.

'Don't you get bloody funny with me!'

'I'm not,' Max said patiently. 'It's just that

I don't have the faintest idea what you're talking about. I'm a detective. I work better with clues.'

'I'll give you clues all right. Thomas Mc-Queen.'

'Ah.' It was two months since he'd been warned – officially – to keep away from Mc-Queen.

'Ring a bell, does it? I thought it might. I will not have my officers harassing a–'

'Villain?' Max supplied helpfully.

'He's an innocent man. An innocent man who had dinner with the Chief Constable a fortnight ago.'

'You're kidding me?' Max had to laugh at the absurdity. 'God, I knew he was conning his way into polite society, but that's really taking the piss.'

'It's not funny. As far as we know, he's nothing more than a highly respected member of the community.'

'As far as we can prove,' Max corrected him. 'You know as well as I do that he's the biggest crook in Harrington.'

'If he was, he'd be behind bars,' Meredith snapped. 'You've got nothing on him, nothing at all. Khalil rented a property from him, that's all. Oh, yes, and his car was captured on CCTV in the area at about the right time. And that's it. Just because you dislike the bloke–'

'I do, but it's more than that and you know

it, Phil. He's mixed up in Khalil's murder. I know he is. And I intend to nail him.'

'That's where you're wrong. You've already had a written warning. I've had enough of you taking the law into your own hands. You're suspended from duty until further notice.'

Max opened his mouth to speak, but no words came out. Suspended? Hell, this was serious.

'Take a holiday,' Meredith suggested grimly. 'Do whatever it takes to get McQueen out of your head once and for all.'

'You're suspending me? Just because I had a five-minute chat with McQueen?'

'I'm suspending you because I'm damned if I'll have my officers disobeying orders and harassing–'

'Friends of your golfing chum, the Chief Constable.'

'I couldn't care less if he's bloody royalty,' Meredith yelled. 'I'm not having members of the public harassed by my officers. I won't stand for it.'

McQueen was guilty of many things, possibly even murder. Having no hard evidence didn't make him innocent. But there was no point arguing the case. It was time for a spot of grovelling.

'OK, you've made your point. I'll keep out of his way, but–'

'Damn right, you will, Max. As from now,

you're suspended. If you'd like to hand over–'

Meredith's phone rang and he picked it up to bark his name at the unfortunate caller.

Max was glad of the distraction. Obviously, he was out of practice when it came to grovelling. He'd have to try harder.

Meredith couldn't suspend him. What the hell would he do all day? Walk the dogs? Sort out his CD collection? Wash the car? He'd go mad.

Meredith banged down the phone. 'Christ, it never bloody rains!' He glared at Max. 'A body's been found in the wood out at Kelton Bridge. Presumably it's Bradley Johnson.'

Max, knowing it showed exceptionally bad taste when someone had died, bit back on the silent prayer of thanks. He was the duty Senior Investigating Officer and, although normally Meredith could turn to others, this week he was snookered. Don Cornwall had been rushed into hospital with appendicitis and Jerry was enjoying a well-earned rest in Mauritius.

'A suspicious death,' Meredith added. 'Wound to his head.'

Correction. Someone had been murdered.

'I see,' Max murmured. 'In that case, I won't take up any more of your time. You'll be busy. Shortage of officers and all that.' He turned to the door. 'Actually, this suspension couldn't have come at a better time. You know I'm staying at Jill's for a couple of weeks while my boys are in France? Yes, of course you do. The grapevine might take its time getting this far but–'

'You and Jill?' Meredith cut him off. 'Again? Bloody hell, Max, when you two were together last time, you treated her like shit and she walked out on you and the force. I'm damned if I'll have that happening again.'

Max winced. 'It won't.'

'It better hadn't.'

'Right.' Max had the door open, not sure if he was suspended or if Meredith wanted him to find Johnson's killer. 'I'll go and book a week in the sun then. Or perhaps I'll sort out my CD collection.'

'Max, I'm warning you, get bloody funny with me, and I'll have you back on the beat by lunchtime.'

'You mean...?' He assumed an expression of innocence, but the relief flooded through him.

'If it were up to me,' Meredith assured him, voice dangerously low, 'you *would* be back on the bloody beat by lunchtime. But with all this bad press we're getting...' He left the sentence unfinished. 'Get out to Kelton Bridge. The last thing we need right now is another unsolved murder.'

'What? You mean my suspension's over? That must be the shortest on record.'

Meredith looked on the verge of a coronary so Max decided against milking it

27

too much.

'Every damn day,' Meredith reminded him, 'the press have a bloody field day with us. The public are up in arms. People are convinced we haven't bothered to find Khalil's killer because we're racist.'

Max nodded. 'I do read the papers, you know.'

'My force? Racist? How dare they?'

Khalil had been murdered back in January, ten months ago, and they still had no suspects. Other than McQueen, that is.

'We'll find his killer,' Max said.

'Bloody right we will. Meanwhile, you'd better see what's been happening in Kelton Bridge.' He scowled at Max. 'It's handy you spending time with Jill as it turns out. This will be right on her doorstep. It shouldn't take you long to apprehend our man.'

'Indeed.'

Max didn't like to point out that, if they had Bradley Johnson's killer banged up before the day was over, there would be yet more accusations of the force not bothering to find the person responsible for Muhammed Khalil's death.

Ironically, the only people not crying racism were Khalil's family. A nicer bunch of people it would be difficult to meet and, for their sakes, Max was determined that Khalil's killer would be brought to justice.

Racism. God, that infuriated Max as

28

much as it did his boss. Max didn't have a racist bone in his body. He hated all scum the same, regardless of colour, creed or any other damn thing.

'I'll keep you informed,' he promised.

'You will, Max. And keep away from Mc-Queen!'

He would; he had better things to do with his time. For now.

Chapter Three

When Jill let herself into her cottage that afternoon, the Rolling Stones were complaining that they couldn't get any satisfaction. Loudly.

Why was it that Max couldn't do *anything* without background noise? And why was it so difficult for him to switch the radio off before he left?

She silenced the radio and shivered. The central heating should have come on an hour ago. Damn it, she really would have to get in touch with a reliable plumber.

Even her cats were feeling the cold. Sam, the laziest of the three, was curled up on top of the boiler, and no doubt wondering why it wasn't the warmest place in the cottage. Rabble, old and stiff, strode up to her and demanded food. Tojo, more inventive, had made herself a comfortable bed on Max's sweater. Served him right for tossing it on the sofa.

She hadn't had time to decide if inviting Max to her cottage had been a good idea as he'd only arrived last night. He'd come in useful when Sam had ambled inside and deposited a dead mouse on the sitting-room carpet, but she remained wary.

It was only a temporary arrangement while Max's sons, Harry and Ben, were away. They'd left for France yesterday for a fort-night's trip arranged by the school. The main appeal for Ben was the thought of a fortnight without lessons, and both boys imagined they would be spending their days skiing at Val d'Isère. Harry, especially, was spending hours at Rossendale Ski Centre and even Ben was becoming an accomplished snow boarder. Yet the trip wouldn't be all fun on the slopes. Far from it. They would be im-proving their French and learning about the country. At least, that was the plan.

Max was making the most of their absence by getting the decorators in. He'd given Jill a sob story and she, probably foolishly, had said he could have the spare bedroom for a fortnight.

She hit the reset button on the gas boiler and, very reluctantly, it groaned into life. She'd phoned a plumber last week, and he'd promised faithfully to take a look at her boiler on Wednesday. And then Thursday. A week later, there was still no sign of him.

And it was bitterly cold.

It was the last week of November, yet Lancashire had been threatened with heavy snowfalls before the month was out. So far, all they'd had were hard frosts and, yesterday, the temperature hadn't risen above freezing all day. So why were mice wandering into the jaws of cats? Or perhaps they were dying of cold and Sam was bringing in dead meat.

The sun was slowly sinking now and, as she gazed out at her garden, she thought it couldn't look more beautiful. Everything was dressed in white frost. Grass, shrubs, the shed, the bench – all white. A robin landed on the bench, his red breast the only splash of colour visible. She wished her camera was handy.

Her home was straight off a Christmas card. People had scoffed when she'd first decided to move to the small Lancashire village of Kelton Bridge, and they had seriously questioned her sanity when she'd told them that her new home, the quaintly named Lilac Cottage, was right at the end of a narrow, unlit lane. Yet Jill loved everything about it. The village was a world away from the rough Liverpool council estate on which she'd been raised and that suited her just fine.

31

The light on her answer machine was flashing and she hit the Play button.

'Hi, it's me,' Max's voice greeted her. 'Something's cropped up so we'll have to forget dinner. Better get yourself a take-away, kiddo.'

Damn. She'd been promised a meal out. Max was right; she'd have to order a take-away. There was no point looking in her cupboards and, from memory, her fridge contained nothing more than a carton of milk, a bottle of white wine, some orange juice and a lettuce that needed throwing out.

She went to her bedroom and undressed. She'd had a new shower installed, her toy of the moment, and she hit the button above the bed. The tiny light began flashing. She loved her shower. Every morning, she could stay in bed until the light stopped flashing, at which point the water would be at the right temperature.

Except it seemed to be taking a while this afternoon. She could hear the water running, but the light continued to flash.

Cursing to herself, she pulled on a dressing gown that Max reckoned Captain Oates would have killed for, and went to the bathroom. There was no hint of steam coming from the shower cubicle.

She padded downstairs in her bare feet, ignoring all thoughts of treading on a dead mouse, and went to the boiler. Sure enough,

32

the red light was on. Again. She hit the reset button and vowed that, come the morning, she wouldn't leave home until she'd extracted a promise from a plumber.

By the time she got back to the bathroom, there was steam, and she stepped beneath the deliciously hot jet and closed her eyes to allow the water to cleanse and soothe. When she finally stepped out and wrapped a thick towel around herself, she felt more or less human again. That was the thing about Styal; it stripped you of your humanity.

When she was dressed in jeans and a sweater, she went downstairs, touching radiators to check for warmth as she did so.

She put coffee on, and looked around her cottage. It would probably be OK having Max staying, and it was only for a fortnight anyway, but it was so long since they'd lived together that she had forgotten how untidy he was. He was incapable of returning things to their rightful place and she knew from experience that he didn't even notice the trail of clutter he always left in his wake. He'd obviously made himself a cup of tea before he left that morning. The milk hadn't been returned to the fridge, the empty cup sat on top of the dishwasher, a spoon and, worst of all, a tea bag had been abandoned in the sink.

The jacket he'd worn last night was slung over the back of a chair and a pile of loose change sat on top of the television.

She took her coffee into the sitting room and made a fuss of her cats. Max's dogs would be frequent visitors during the next couple of weeks and her cats wouldn't approve. Who could blame them?

Fortunately, Max's mother-in-law was looking after the dogs at the moment. After the death of her daughter, Kate had moved into the self-contained flat at Max's place and was always on hand to look after her grand-children, three dogs, the house or anything else. She was a true gem. And a good friend.

Knowing she could put it off no longer, Jill picked up the phone and tapped in her parents' number.

'About time,' her mother greeted her. 'I thought you'd emigrated.'

'Just busy working, Mum. So what's this big idea for the party?'

'We're having it at the Royal Hotel.'

'What? Good heavens.' Jill didn't know whether to laugh or cry. Her dad's idea of having a few pints at the working men's club had clearly been ignored yet again.

'As you know, I was quite set on the com-munity centre,' her mum rushed on, 'but–'

'It will probably have been razed to the ground again by then?' Jill suggested.

'Well, yes, there is that. But it meant get-ting caterers in and it was difficult to organ-ize the bar. So it'll be at the Royal Hotel.'

'Blimey, I hope Dad has some good win-

34

ners to pay for it. What does he think about it?'

'You can guess, can't you? But it won't hurt him to dress up for the day.'

Jill grinned at that. 'You mean he has to wear a tie?'

'Too right he does. Forty years I've had to put up with him. It's payback time.'

They spoke – at least, her mother spoke and Jill listened – for another half-hour. One thing was certain, Jill thought as she switched on her computer, this party would be an experience never to be forgotten.

She glanced at her watch. It was time to see how Manor Boy had done. Forgetting the notes she intended to write up, she opened the web browser and checked William Hill's site. It took a few minutes, but then she saw it. Her horse had won by a short head. At fourteen to one!

'Yay!' She scooped her lazy old tom cat into her arms and gave him a squeeze. 'Fourteen to one, Sam. That's saved him from cat food for a while. We're almost three hundred quid better off.'

She wished now that she'd invested a sensible-sized stake.

Feeling greatly cheered, she began typing up her notes on her meeting with Claire Lawrence. Claire might not be very communicative, but any visits broke up the monotony of her days and, given the

35

chance, she would play on this for months. Jill didn't intend to let that happen.

An hour later, no further forward on her impressions of Claire, she switched on the TV. She often put it on for company, but she rarely paid attention. She didn't today until, at six thirty, she heard Kelton Bridge mentioned.

Her head flew up and there was a picture of Bradley Johnson filling the screen. Not a very recent picture at that. He'd lost weight since it had been taken. A wiry man, with thick dark hair, a direct, unsmiling gaze at the camera–

The body, believed to be that of local business-man Bradley Johnson, was found in woodland in the village. Detective Chief Inspector Trent-ham of Harrington CID has confirmed that a murder investigation has been launched and has appealed for witnesses.

The shock had Jill's heart racing.

On leaving Styal, she had thought how lucky she was to live in a sleepy Lancashire village where everyone had a friendly word and residents looked out for each other. No one had looked out for Bradley Johnson, had they?

Bradley Johnson dead. Murdered.

'Something's cropped up,' Max had said. It certainly had.

It was no use, she couldn't concentrate on Claire Lawrence now.

At a little after nine that evening, she heard Max's car pull on to the drive. He came inside, bringing a blast of icy air with him, and she saw that his hair, thick, dark and swept back from his face, was dotted with rapidly melting snowflakes.

'Whatever's happened, Max?'

'Someone's murdered the lord of the manor.' He shrugged out of his jacket and threw it over the back of a chair.

'I do possess coat hooks, you know.'

'Sorry?'

'Never mind. I don't suppose you can teach an old dog new tricks. So what happened to Bradley?'

'His wife reported him missing at about seven this morning. He'd gone out yesterday afternoon and, when he hadn't returned in the evening, she assumed he'd stopped off at the pub. She went to bed and only realized he hadn't come home when she woke up this morning.'

Max gave her a quick, absent peck on the cheek as if they'd been married for a quarter of a century, and headed for the kitchen.

'Drink?' he called over his shoulder.

'Please.' She followed him. 'Have you eaten?'

'Post-mortem,' he said as if that explained everything.

Jill supposed it did. She knew Max could never face food after – or before – attending a post-mortem. Knew, too, that he would soon be complaining about the smell cloying his nostrils and sticking to his clothes.

'How was he killed?'

'Three blows to the head.' He took two glasses from the cupboard and filled them with generous measures of whisky. 'Meredith had suspended me when the call came through, too.'

'What?'

'Yeah.' He grinned at her astonishment.

'Whatever for?'

'Harassing a friend of the Chief Constable's.'

'Good grief.' She chuckled at that. 'You mean he has friends?'

'Few and far between, I'm sure, but unfortunately, Tom McQueen happens to be one of them.' He handed her a glass of whisky and took a swig from his own. 'I met McQueen at Manchester airport this morning and he must have been straight on the phone to make a complaint. Funny that,' he added thoughtfully. 'I'd just heard that Bradley Johnson was missing so I asked McQueen if he knew him. Coincidental, don't you think? I ask about Johnson and he makes sure I'm warned off.'

'I expect he's just tired of you dogging his every move.'

'Perhaps,' Max agreed. 'Anyway, I came straight out here and pulled a team together.

Thankfully, Melissa did the post-mortem. And Yvonne Drever is back from leave so she's one of the family liaison officers assigned to the Johnsons.'

'How's Phoebe holding up?'

'Very well,' he answered, looking deep in thought. 'She may have been expecting the worst – having reported him as missing, I mean. She's quite calm. It's a job to tell. Yvonne's with her, though. And she's good.'

Jill knew Yvonne. She was a young WPC with a natural instinct for the job. She would watch and listen.

'So that's my day,' he said, throwing himself down in an armchair in the sitting room. 'How's yours been?'

Instead of sitting next to him, she sat on the floor by the fire.

'Awful. I hate Styal.' She took a big swallow of whisky and felt the warmth in her throat. 'Claire's very uncommunicative. She's also been put on suicide watch. I'm there again tomorrow.'

She shuddered at the memory of Styal and turned her thoughts to other matters.

'What do you think about Bradley Johnson, Max? Was it premeditated or was he in the wrong place at the wrong time?'

'I don't know. His wallet was in his jacket pocket untouched. There was two hundred and forty quid in that.'

'Not a mugging then.'

'It's hard to say. He was also wearing a money belt, and that was empty.'

'So someone could have emptied the belt and left the wallet?'

'It's possible. Two hundred and forty quid is a lot to leave behind though.'

'It is. Almost as much as I won today,' she added with a small smile.

Her winnings didn't seem quite so exciting now.

'When I drove past the manor this morning,' she explained, 'there was a patrol car parked outside. I had a quick look at the horses when I got to Styal and saw that Manor Boy was running. Now that was a coincidence, wasn't it?'

'It was,' he said, amused. 'And you mean it won?'

'Easily. It's netted me three hundred quid.'

'Aw, hell. You could have bought me dinner out of your ill-gotten gains.' He sniffed his shirt. 'Do I smell like a mortuary?'

'No.' And Jill didn't want to think about it.

'Hm. I'd better go and have a shower.'

Before he could move, the doorbell sounded. Jill's good friend, Ella Gardner, was standing on the doorstep brushing snow from her coat before removing a blue hand-knitted hat.

'What a surprise,' Jill greeted her. Ella was usually in bed by ten and, like many pensioners, didn't venture far after dark. 'Is everything all right?'

'Fine,' Ella replied, stepping inside. 'I would have phoned but – well, it didn't seem the sort of thing to discuss on the phone. Oh, Max, am I glad to see you.'

Ella wasn't a typical pensioner. In her late sixties, and a widow, she dressed conservatively, but she had more energy than a lot of teenagers and often had Jill in gales of laughter with her colourful accounts of life in the village.

'Let me take your coat,' Jill offered, but Ella was having none of it.

'I can't stop.' She went to the fire and held out her hands to its warmth. 'I've been in Manchester all day so I've only just heard about Bradley Johnson. What a dreadful business. The thing is, I think I must have been one of the last, if not *the* last person to see him alive.'

'Oh?' She'd got Max's interest.

'I nipped up to the shop for a loaf of bread yesterday,' she explained, 'and decided to do a detour through the wood as it was such a lovely afternoon. It was bitterly cold, of course, but bright and sunny. Or it was when I started out. I was just coming out on to Ryan Walk when I met him.'

'What time was that, Ella?' Max asked.

'The sun was almost set so, oh, about four o'clock, I suppose.'

'How did he appear?'

41

'In a bit of a hurry, to be honest. I had the impression he was meeting someone.' She grimaced. 'After we'd passed the time of day and chatted about the weather, he looked at his watch and said he must be off. Of course, he might not have been meeting anyone at all, he might just have been bored. It wasn't the most scintillating of conversations. I was bored stiff myself.'

'Which way did he go?' Jill asked curiously. 'Through the wood? When it was almost dark?'

'He did.' Ella nodded. 'It wasn't that bad so he would have been through it before it was really dark. He was probably heading for the pub. People often use the wood as a short cut.'

Jill nodded at the truth of that.

'I didn't think anything of it at the time,' Ella went on, 'mainly because I had other things on my mind. I heard a dog barking and I thought it might be that yappy little ankle-biter of Olive's. She often takes the thing for a walk through the wood. As you can imagine, the last thing I wanted was to bump into her, old gossip that she is. She saw me coming out of the doctor's surgery a couple of weeks ago, and ever since, she's been fishing for information. It was only a routine check-up, but I'm sorely tempted to tell her I've caught something unpleasant from too much unprotected sex.'

Jill spluttered with laughter. She, too, had been on the receiving end of Olive's interrogations in the past.

'Did you see anyone else?' Max asked, and Ella shook her head.

'I walked on to the shop, bought a loaf, and walked home without seeing anyone out of the ordinary. There were a few children hanging about in the high street, but that was all.' She sighed, impatient with herself. 'I've always considered myself fairly observant but, no, I can't think of anyone else.'

'That's OK,' Max told her. 'You might find that you remember something else in a day or so.'

'If I do, I'll be sure to let you know. I'm sorry I can't be more helpful.'

'Don't worry about it,' Max told her. 'That's great, thanks.'

'I'd better be getting home,' she said, adding a rueful, 'It's way past my bedtime.'

'I'll walk with you,' Max offered.

'Thanks, but there's no need, Max. Don't worry, if I bump into any murderers, I'll scream loud enough for you to hear me.'

'It's no trouble.' Max was already putting on his jacket. 'I'll nip into the pub on my way back and have a chat with the landlord.'

Not wanting to be left out, Jill grabbed her coat. 'I'll come with you.'

By the time they reached the end of Jill's lane, it was snowing heavily. Very little was

43

sticking, but it could be a different story in the morning. With luck, Kelton Bridge would be cut off and she wouldn't be able to get to Styal...

They soon reached Ella's bungalow and, once they'd seen her safely inside, they headed for the Weaver's Retreat.

One of the best things about the pub was the landlord's passion for roaring log fires. There were two huge fires, one at either end of the main room, and Ian tended them with a dedication that bordered on obsession. Customers could never complain about being cold. Everything in the pub was well looked after. Ian was never idle. If he wasn't pouring pints, he was dusting the old jugs that hung above the bar, wiping down tables, or polishing the long mahogany bar.

If the building was impressive, however, trade this evening certainly wasn't.

'It'll be this weather keeping people at home,' Ian grumbled. 'I don't remember the last time it snowed in November.'

The pub was deserted apart from a couple that Jill didn't recognize sitting at the table nearest one of the fires.

'Either that,' he added in a voice low enough not to put off his customers, 'or this business with Bradley Johnson is too close to home. Any idea what happened?' he asked Max.

'It's early days. Two double whiskies,

44

please, Ian,' Max added as an aside. 'We were wondering if you'd seen or heard anything.' He handed over a twenty-pound note. 'It's possible that he was on his way here to meet someone.'

'Oh?' Ian put their drinks and then Max's change on the bar. 'If he was, he didn't make it, and I can't think of anyone who looked as if they were waiting for him. Trade wasn't exactly brisk in the afternoon, but it did get busy early evening. A gang of people came on here from a funeral.'

'What did you think of him, Ian?' Jill asked, perching on a stool.

'To be honest, I didn't know him that well. It seemed to me – and this is only my opinion – that you were either in favour or out. I was never in.'

'Me neither.'

The other customers left and Ian collected their glasses.

'He threw extravagant parties, I gather,' he said, 'but I was never invited.'

'I saw him in here once or twice,' Jill said, 'but he wasn't a regular, was he, Ian?'

'No. He'd call in two or three times a month for a couple. He always drank brandy. He was pleasant enough, I suppose, and made a point of speaking to everyone.'

There was nothing Ian could tell them so, when they'd finished their drinks, Max took their coats from the pegs.

'If you two are off, I may as well lock up for the night,' Ian grumbled. 'Who'd be a publican, eh? First it was the drink-drive thing, then the smoking ban – as for the price of beer, soon there'll be none who can afford a drink.'

'And on that cheerful note,' Jill grinned.

'I'll be seeing you,' Ian said, chuckling.

In the short time they'd been inside, the temperature must have risen because the thin layer of snow had already turned to wet slush. It looked as if Jill would have no excuse to keep her from Styal after all.

'Someone will be talking to Olive Prendergast tomorrow,' Max remarked as they walked home. 'We'll need to know if it was her dog barking.'

'It's a good place to start,' Jill said, smiling. 'What Olive doesn't know about the comings and goings in this village isn't worth knowing. She loves to talk, and what she doesn't know she'll invent and add her own personal touch of venom.'

'Bloody villages,' he muttered.

Max's dislike and distrust of village life was legendary. He was a townie through and through. Apart from his large garden which was mainly lawn, he couldn't see a blade of grass from his home on the outskirts of Harrington and Jill knew that was just how he liked it. He preferred a view of lights, people and traffic to bleak, frost-covered hills.

'Who else in the village owns a dog?' he asked, and Jill laughed.

'It'll be easier to tell you who doesn't own one. I don't, Ella doesn't, Ian doesn't. Oh, and the Johnsons don't. Apart from that–'

Max groaned.

Chapter Four

Sunday brought another sharp, crisp frost. October had been wet, dull and grey and November had started in the same damp, miserable way, yet now, as it neared its end, it was turning into a gem of a month. The bright sunshine drew the eye to every white-coated blade of grass, hedge and tree. Nature at its most impressive.

Max knew Jill's usual routine on a Sunday was to spend a lazy morning in bed with the newspapers. Most of the time, that would suit Max, too. Not today, though. He needed to be at headquarters later and he couldn't abide the thought of wasting a single moment of the day.

Having been out of bed early and driven home to collect his mail, he'd put the dogs in the car and returned to Jill's cottage, determined to drag her out for a good walk. Mayhem ruled for a few minutes as the dogs

47

made themselves at home, and Jill's cats wisely raced outside, but things soon settled down.

'Come on, lazybones,' he said, as she was about to make her third coffee of the day. 'Let's take the dogs for a run. It's gorgeous out there.'

'It's gorgeous in here,' she retorted. 'The boiler's working for once, and I have coffee.'

However, she pulled on another sweater, her thick coat, scarf and gloves. Max grabbed his own jacket and put it on over his shirt.

'What is it about men?' she asked, shaking her head in amazement. 'Is it a macho thing to freeze to death? The temperature out there is, well, it's freezing.'

'It'll be warmer than you think in this sunshine,' he said confidently.

The dogs ran around in circles as they tried to get out of the front door, slowing everything down considerably, but, when it was open, they raced off down the lane.

'What a bunch of misfits,' Jill said with amusement.

Max had to smile. He hadn't really wanted one dog, his erratic and unpredictable lifestyle didn't suit animals, and he still found it hard to believe that he'd been conned into homing three. Holly, the faithful, quiet collie, had belonged to a man currently serving time for murder. Fly, the manic half-Labrador and half-collie, had been rescued by his son and, it had to be said, had been exceptionally well trained by the boy. Muffet, the old black crossbreed with his grey muzzle, another dog rescued by Ben, was the grumpy old man of the trio. For all that, the dogs were the greatest of friends and Max wouldn't have been without them.

Despite the temperature, and it was a lot colder than Max had anticipated, and although they were squinting against a low sun, it was good to be outside.

They were heading towards the church and even Max, who'd been born with a deep dislike of village life, had to admit that it was the stuff of postcards. It didn't come more picturesque than Kelton Bridge, and he could see the appeal for Jill.

Difficult to believe this quaint, sleepy village could be a setting for murder.

As they drew level with the church, a woman and her dog rounded the corner.

'Olive Prendergast and the ankle-biter,' Jill warned him.

Even allowing for the thick blue coat, boots, hat, scarf and enormous fur gloves, she was a stocky woman. She strode out like a drill sergeant.

Max's three dogs ran on ahead to investigate.

'Fly will think it's edible,' he said beneath his breath and Jill grinned.

Fortunately, Olive had the foresight to

scoop the animal into her arms before Fly got a taste.

'Morning, Olive,' Jill greeted her. 'What a beautiful day!'

'It is,' Olive agreed. 'Not that many people will see it. I've just walked through the estate and they're all lazing in their beds. The only thing that gets them out of the house is going to collect their dole money. That and a trip to the bookmaker's,' she added with a sly look at Jill.

While Jill struggled through a gasp of shock at Olive's last comment, Olive turned her attention to Max.

Max had never had the dubious pleasure of meeting Olive, ex-postmistress of Kelton Bridge, but he'd heard all about her from Jill. He knew Olive rarely had a good word for anyone. Correction. She never had a good word for anyone.

'I thought you'd be busy looking for the person who did for Johnson,' she said, and the criticism of Max, of Harrington CID and of the whole of the UK police force was evident.

'Even I have a few hours off now and again,' Max told her.

'You're none the wiser then,' she decided with satisfaction.

'We're following several leads.' That was a blatant lie, but it sounded impressive.

'Oh, yes?' Impressive or not, Olive wasn't

taken in. 'You'll have your work cut out. There must be plenty of suspects. There's not many round here who'll be sorry to see him gone. He wasn't popular, was he, Jill?'

'People are wary of newcomers to the village,' Jill agreed.

'Did you ever go to those parties he gave?'

Jill shook her head and Olive made a sucking sound through false teeth.

'Drugs,' she confided in a whisper. 'And sex.'

'Really?' Jill said. 'I didn't realize you'd been on the guest list, Olive.'

'Huh. You wouldn't catch me mixing with the likes of him.' Olive clutched the ankle-biter closer to her chest. 'It was a well-known fact, though. All those who thought they were someone were there. The holier than thou set. But oh no, you wouldn't catch me mixing with the likes of those.

'A young policeman, name of Benson, visited me on Friday,' she rushed on, 'and I told him the same thing. I had nothing to do with that family. I expect she'll move away now and the manor will be up for sale again. Perhaps someone local will buy it this time. Mind, that's not likely, is it? Apart from those on the estate–' she nodded towards the small social housing complex – 'people in Kelton are honest, hardworking folk. That sort can't afford places like the manor.'

Max thought Olive was set to gossip all

51

day but, eventually, she hurried on her way, putting the dog back on the ground when she was a good fifty yards from them.

'What a delightful woman,' he said.

'Cheeky cow. Did you see the way she looked at me? To hear her talk, people would think I spent all my days at the bookie's!'

'I know,' he said, feigning outrage. 'What nonsense, when everyone knows you've got a phone account with William Hill.'

'It's just as well I have. Bloody woman!'

'She's certainly one of a kind. And the dog that Ella heard barking didn't belong to her. She and the ankle-biter were on a bus coming back from Burnley at the time.

'I'll tell you something else, though – no one's talking.' Hour after frustrating hour spent on house-to-house inquiries had given them nothing of use. 'People might not have liked Johnson, but no one's talking. It's a village thing, isn't it? They clam up. They stick together. They'll speak ill of the dead all right, but only to each other, not to out-siders. Take Olive, for instance. If you hadn't been here, I bet she wouldn't have said a word about him.'

'I bet she would. She'll talk to anyone. Old gossip.'

'He wasn't popular though, was he?'

'Not really. It's true that villagers are wary of newcomers and the crime they might bring to the area, but with Bradley it was

52

more than that. I don't really know why. I suppose some were jealous of his lifestyle, not that they'd admit it.'

They walked on.

'I know you're busy right now,' Max said, 'but you'll have to help me out on this one, Jill. You know the people. They'll trust you.'

'You forget, Max, that I'm a newcomer, too. I'm still the fancy psychiatrist who lives in Mrs Blackman's old cottage. You need at least three generations living in the village before you're considered a local.'

'Bloody villages,' he muttered, and she smiled.

They walked on and ended up on Ryan Walk, where Ella had met Bradley Johnson.

'It gives you the creeps, doesn't it?' Jill said. 'Awful to imagine how poor Connie Walker must have felt when she walked into the wood and found Bradley Johnson's body.'

'A shock to the system, yes.'

'It's no longer sealed off,' she noticed.

'No, we finished here last night.'

He took the path and Jill, a little reluctantly he thought, followed. It was much colder beneath the trees where the sun couldn't penetrate. In fact, it was freezing. Why the hell hadn't he worn something warmer?

'Not that we found a lot,' he went on, pushing his hands deep in his pockets. 'Johnson was killed on the main path – here. His body was dragged to the base of that tree.' He nodded at a spot five or six yards away.

'So whoever killed him wasn't bothered about someone finding him.'

'Apparently not. Believe it or not, we also got a couple of footprints that may reveal something. Mind you, given the number of people tramping through here, that's doubtful. Other than that, nothing. No murder weapon.' He kicked at a pile of dead, frost-covered leaves. 'We've no idea of the motive. No idea who he was meeting. If indeed he was meeting anyone. But if he wasn't meeting them at the pub...' He shrugged. 'Well, you wouldn't set up a meeting in this place, would you?'

'You might,' Jill said, 'if you wanted to keep away from prying eyes. In fact, in Kelton Bridge, it's about the only place you could meet if you wanted to do that.'

Not only was it colder beneath the trees, it was dark and eerily quiet. The ground crunched under their feet as they walked on, but no birds sang out.

'What are you doing tomorrow morning?' he asked.

'Nothing I can't get out of. Why?'

'I'm calling at the manor to see Phoebe Johnson. Apparently, one of Johnson's infamous parties was given last week and she's promised to provide me with a list of guests. I'd like you along with me.'

'OK.'

They weren't alone in the wood. Twigs were crackling and someone coughed. Max sensed Jill edge closer.

The dogs had been chasing each other in circles but they ran ahead to check it out. An elderly man appeared and then Max noticed that instead of three dogs running around there were four. The addition was a young border collie.

Jill relaxed and had a smile on her face as they met up with the man.

'Morning, Jack,' she said. 'How are you today?'

'Mustn't grumble, Jill. Yourself?'

'Very well, thanks. Max, this is Jack Taylor. Jack, this is—'

'I know who he is.' He looked Max up and down and clearly found him wanting.

Max looked at him, too. He was possibly in his seventies, maybe even his eighties, with thick white hair. Tall and upright, there was no spare flesh on him. His waterproof coat was grubby, his trousers had a small tear at the knee and his heavy boots were caked in dried mud that had to be days old.

'I recognize you from the telly,' Mr Taylor said. 'You're looking into the murder of him from the manor.'

'That's right. Did you know Mr Johnson?'

'Pah!' He spat on the ground to his right. 'All I know is that the world's a better place without him. Men like that – a wrong bugger, that's what he were.'

'What makes you say that?' Max asked curiously.

'He were a wrong 'un, that's all.'

'A witness thought he might have been meeting someone,' Max told him. 'You wouldn't know anything about that, would you?'

'Why the hell should I know what he was doing?'

'Is that a no?'

'I had you coppers knocking on my door yesterday,' he snapped. 'Why the hell am I being singled out, eh? There's a word for that.'

'Harassment, probably,' Max said, 'but I can assure you that you aren't being singled out. We're speaking to everyone in Kelton Bridge.'

'That's as maybe. I'll tell you what I told them. He were a wrong 'un, that's all I know about him. Deserved all he got. And that's all I know.'

'It's possible that he was meeting someone with a dog,' Max put in, his gaze resting on the man's young collie.

'Bugger me!' Jack Taylor exploded. 'Some folk have got nothing better to do with their time than talk.'

'We find it helpful,' Max said drily. 'Do you often walk your dog here?' he asked, changing tack.

'Yes. Most days.'

'Were you here on Wednesday afternoon?'

'No.'

He hadn't even stopped to think.

'Are you quite sure, Jack?' Jill put in. 'It was a nice afternoon, a day very much like this one.'

'Look,' he said, fixing bright eyes on Jill and then Max. 'If I said I weren't here, I weren't here, right? I might be getting on a bit, but I'm not bloody senile yet. Good day to you both.'

He stalked off, stiff and erect. A whistle to his dog and the collie was immediately following her master.

'So much for the community spirit,' Max said grimly.

'It's funny,' Jill said, 'but I've always found him quite pleasant and approachable. I know he doesn't suffer fools gladly, but he was certainly a bit wound up about Bradley Johnson.'

'What do you know about him?'

'Let me think.' They walked on through the wood. 'He used to be a miner, I gather. He's a widower with a son and daughter-in-law living in the village. He has two or maybe three grandchildren and one of them is Hannah Brooks. You know her, yes? She lives in Kelton and she's standing as Conservative candidate.'

'I know of her,' Max agreed.

'He's a keen gardener,' she went on. 'He has a large garden and wins prizes for his stuff – vegetables mostly – at the village show. His granddaughter, Hannah, is expecting what, as far as I know, will be Jack's first great-grandchild. But really, that's all I know about him.'

'And the fact that he's a cantankerous old sod,' Max muttered.

She grinned. 'Well, yes. That, too.'

Chapter Five

At a few minutes after eleven o'clock the following morning, Jill was stamping her feet on the doorstep to Kelton Manor and trying to bring some warmth back to them. It was another bitterly cold day and, so far, she'd spent most of the morning on the phone to plumbers. For some inexplicable reason, they couldn't accept that a boiler only working when it felt like it – as in on the occasional mild day – was an emergency. Wasting time on that, and getting nowhere, had meant she'd been unable to study form and, in the end, she'd phoned her bet through without having a good look at the runners or riders.

The manor was one of Jill's favourite buildings, but it had lost a little of its charm since the Johnsons moved in. There had once been an impressive Victorian conservatory but that had gone, and a double garage, clad in stone, had replaced the old stable block. The main building, however, was listed and, standing square in its tree-lined and stonewalled garden, taking centre stage in the village, it was in a class of its own.

There was no bell, but the heavy wooden door swung open in answer to Max's knock, and Jill pinned a smile in place for Phoebe Johnson.

Although they'd only spoken half a dozen times, Jill had found her to be a friendly, easygoing, relaxed sort of person. That, of course, was before her husband had been murdered. Jill hadn't seen her since. She'd popped a condolence card through the letterbox, but, as they were almost strangers, she hadn't wanted to intrude.

'Hello, Jill,' she said, 'good to see you. You, too, Chief Inspector. Thank you for calling. I don't suppose you've found anything?'

'I'm sorry,' Max said.

'It's early days, I know. Please, come inside.'

They stepped into the vast hallway and Jill knew immediately that, despite the problems being thrown at Phoebe right now, a temperamental boiler wasn't one of them.

'Come through to the sitting room,' Phoebe said, leading the way.

It was the first time Jill had been inside the

manor since her unsuccessful attempt to buy the place at auction, and it had changed considerably in the relatively short time the Johnsons had been in residence. Changed for the better, too. Where once had been many old, dark paintings, there were now pastel-coloured walls dotted with vibrant, modern works of art and rich tapestries.

The sitting room, which took up almost the same floor space as Jill's entire cottage, boasted a deep pile cream carpet, sofas and chairs in a warm russet colour and, best of all, a log fire. A pile of condolence cards lay on a small, round table.

'How are you coping, Phoebe?' Jill asked.

'Oh, you know.'

Jill didn't. As she hadn't mixed in the same exalted circles, she had no real idea of the relationship that had existed between Phoebe and her husband. Phoebe's expression didn't give much away, either. She looked pale and tired, and her eyes were a little bloodshot, but her blonde hair was as immaculately groomed as ever and her face bore just the right amount of make-up.

'By the way, thank you for your card, Jill. It was kind of you. Everyone's been so kind.'

'It was nothing,' Jill murmured. 'I'm so sorry about your loss. It's a shocking thing to happen.'

Phoebe nodded at the understatement. 'The boys – my sons, Keiran and Tyler – are suffering dreadfully, too. They've always thought Kelton Bridge a terribly dull place where nothing ever happens. And now this. Their own father.' She indicated chairs near the fire. 'I'm sorry. Please, sit down. Can I get you anything? Tea or coffee?'

They declined the offer.

'Were Keiran and Tyler close to their father?' Jill asked.

'Very close,' Phoebe replied, 'and my heart breaks for them. Like all of us, I suppose, they expected him to live for ever. You do, don't you?'

'You do,' Max agreed.

Phoebe was in her late forties, and a very attractive woman. Tall and slender, she wore black trousers with a red blouse that was nipped in at the waist by a wide, black belt. She was graceful. Her hands, long, thin and expertly manicured, moved a lot as she spoke. From what Jill had heard, she'd been born to a fairly affluent family in New York but, perhaps because she'd lived in England for ten years, her American accent was diluted.

What struck Jill as strange was the way that, on moving to the village, Phoebe had been out and about wanting to meet the locals and become involved in things. Yet all that had stopped abruptly. About a month later, she withdrew completely and rarely seemed to leave the manor at all. Perhaps village life wasn't all she had expected. Perhaps she found it boring after London.

'You were going to provide us with a list of guests for the party,' Max reminded her.

'Yes, I've got it here.' She walked over to a low, modern unit, pulled open a drawer and took out a few pieces of paper. 'That's the lot,' she said, handing them to Max.

They were sitting on opposite sides of the fire so Jill couldn't see the list. She couldn't move, either, as Phoebe sat down next to Max and looked at it while he did.

'Thomas McQueen,' he remarked. 'Were you and your husband good friends with him?'

Jill didn't know how many names were on the list, but she wasn't surprised that, from what had to be quite a few, Max singled out McQueen.

'I'd never met him until the party. I'm not sure if Brad had, either. Having said that, they seemed to get along well,' she answered thoughtfully. 'I'm not sure you'd describe them as good friends, but they enjoyed a few jokes at the party. I've no idea how they met, though.'

'McQueen's a local businessman,' Max told her, 'mainly dealing in property. Is it likely, do you think, that he and your husband had business dealings?'

'I can't think why. If they did, I don't know anything about it.'

'Your husband wasn't planning to buy property in the area?'

'No.'

One by one, they went through every name on Phoebe's list. There were thirty-six in total. It was a time-consuming job but it did show them that the guests had been present at Bradley Johnson's invitation. His wife, apart from organizing the invitations and the catering – outside caterers had been employed – had little to do with it. She had hardly known the guests.

'If your husband had been on his way to meet someone on Wednesday afternoon,' Max asked her, 'is it likely that he would have told you about it? Is it the sort of thing he would have discussed with you?'

Jill noted a flush on her cheeks. What was that about?

'I think so, yes,' she said, but Jill wasn't convinced. 'Of course, it would depend who he was meeting. If it was business, he'd probably think it would bore me.' Her smile didn't reach her eyes. 'He always assumed that I couldn't be expected to understand his business deals.'

Was she bitter about that? Did she feel excluded from his life? Had he treated her as if she were the dim blonde?

'He was a good husband,' Phoebe broke into her thoughts, 'and a good father. He worked too hard, that was his only fault. His

63

folks came from Texas and struggled to put food in their children's mouths. He was always–' she paused, searching for the right word – 'adamant that his children would have the best. I think he lived in fear of ending up with no money, of having to start all over again.'

'That's understandable,' Jill murmured.

'Oh, I know what you're thinking,' Phoebe rushed on. 'You think it was my money, my family's money at least, that attracted him to me.'

Jill shook her head, surprised. 'I didn't realize your family was wealthy.' She'd heard rumours to that effect, but that was all.

'It had nothing to do with that, you know. We fell in love. Twenty-six years we'd been married and he still loved me. He was a very loyal man. He wouldn't have left me,' she whispered.

'I'm sure he wouldn't,' Jill murmured.

What the hell had brought that on? Jill quickly reassessed the situation. Phoebe had loved him. Or hated him. Either way, she'd felt passionately about him. There was such a thin line between love and hate that it was difficult to tell.

Was it possible that, contrary to what Phoebe claimed, Bradley had been on the point of leaving her?

If so, would she have let him go?

There was a huge difference between a

loyal husband and a loving one. A loyal husband stayed out of a sense of duty whereas a loving one stayed because he belonged.

Three blows to the head had killed Bradley Johnson. Presumably, anyone could have delivered those blows. Although fairly tall, he'd been a lean man without a spare ounce of flesh. Not a heavy man. It would have been easy enough for Phoebe to follow him, hit him over the head to knock him senseless, hit him again a couple of times to make sure he never drew another breath, drag his body a few yards, walk home, wait a few hours and then report him as missing. That way, he'd never leave her.

'May I?' Jill took the guest list from Max and glanced at the names. She knew very few of them, but that wasn't surprising. 'None of the guests are from the village,' she pointed out. 'Did any stay over?'

'Only two couples,' Phoebe said. 'Ed and Martha Cooper – Ed's been a friend of Brad's for years, ever since we moved to England. He owns a hotel chain, and they live in Cheltenham now.'

'And the other couple?' Max asked.

'Peter and Brenda Driver. I can't say I know much about them, other than the fact they live in Manchester. I don't know how Brad knew them.' She pointed to the list, still in Jill's hand. 'Do you think the party is relevant? Do you think one of the guests

65

might have – you know?'

'We've no idea,' Max said frankly. 'At the moment, we have no leads at all. But if we talk to these people, they may give us something.'

'I see.'

'Are your sons here?' Max asked. 'We'd like a word with them, if we may. It's possible that they might be able to tell us something.'

'They've gone to Rawtenstall. Asda,' Phoebe explained. 'Life goes on, doesn't it? They need to eat.'

'Of course.'

Jill and Max were preparing to leave when a car was heard slowing to a stop outside.

Phoebe went to the window. 'Here are the boys now,' she said, and she sounded resigned, as if she didn't want her sons involved in any of this.

Doors opened and banged shut as the two boys – adults, Jill reminded herself – brought in bags from the car. They were laughing. Their father had been bludgeoned to death five days ago, and they were laughing.

Phoebe left the room to talk to them and, a couple of minutes later, they followed her into the sitting room. 'Haven't you arrested anyone yet?' Tyler demanded of Max.

Tyler was twenty-one, older than Keiran by two years. Both were tall, dark-haired, good-looking boys, but Tyler was a couple of inches taller and he was the one you noticed. Keiran would blend in a crowd; Tyler was too forceful, and too handsome to be ignored.

'We're doing all we can,' Max assured him. 'We think your father may have been meeting someone on Wednesday afternoon. Would you know anything about that?'

'No.' Tyler answered for both of them.

'Keiran?' Jill prompted, but he shook his head.

'What would we know?' Tyler demanded of Jill and Max as if they were idiots. 'We weren't even here. We only came home when Mum called us with the news.'

'When does the term finish for Christmas?' Jill asked.

'A fortnight on Friday,' Keiran told her. 'But because of – everything that's happened, we'll stay here until the new year now.'

Jill nodded her understanding.

'I believe you were intending to spend Christmas here anyway,' Max said pleasantly. 'What were you planning to do with your time? Had you decided? Had your father spoken to you? Were you going anywhere or doing anything special?'

'We'd nothing planned,' Keiran said.

'We wouldn't have seen anything of Dad,' Tyler added. 'He'd have been in London. Working. He was always working.'

'Over Christmas?' Jill asked doubtfully.

'Yes. Over Christmas.'

Tyler was the angry young man. Keiran

67

was quieter, and more difficult to fathom. Yet neither seemed as grief-stricken as Jill had expected.

They were no help whatsoever and, half an hour later, Jill and Max stepped outside and left the residents of Kelton Manor to their grief.

'You'll let us know as soon as you have something?' Phoebe called after them.

'Of course,' Max promised.

'I'm out all day tomorrow, but you have my mobile number, don't you?'

'Don't worry, we'll keep you informed of any developments,' Max assured her.

Satisfied, Phoebe closed the door.

'We'll call in again tomorrow,' Max said when they were in his car. 'I want to speak to those boys alone.'

'We?' Jill queried.

'Yes, it won't take long.'

Max drove them out of the village and they were almost at headquarters when Jill reached into the back seat for the list of guests that Phoebe had given them.

'I'm surprised Hannah Brooks wasn't invited. Over the last two or three months, I've seen photos of her with Bradley Johnson. They would have been in the Burnley paper, or maybe the *Rossendale Free Press*. She was planting trees or opening supermarkets or some such thing and Bradley was there, smiling for the camera and telling everyone how marvellous she was and how everyone should make sure she was our next MP.'

'Perhaps she had something else on that night,' Max suggested.

'Yes, that's possible. She's pregnant, too, so perhaps she's not doing much socializing at the moment.' Her earlier thoughts came back to her. 'Could a woman have killed him? I mean, would you have to be particularly strong or anything?'

'It's possible. A good blow from behind, so long as it had the element of surprise, wouldn't have needed all that much weight or force. Then a couple more for good measure. Yes, it could have been a woman, I imagine.' He took his eyes from the road briefly to look at her. 'Are you thinking of Phoebe?'

'It was just a thought.'

'Yes. I had the same one.'

Chapter Six

Jill grabbed the bouquet of flowers from the back seat of her car, held them close against her chest in an attempt to protect them from the wind, locked the car, and ran up the drive to Hannah and Gordon Brooks' house.

The doorbell was answered almost immediately by a tired-looking Gordon.

'Jill, how lovely to see you. Come in.'

'No, thanks, Gordon, I don't want to intrude. I just wanted to say how very sorry I am for your loss. I only heard this afternoon. I'm so sorry.'

'Thank you. But come in, please. Hannah would love to see you.'

His hand was on her arm and she had the feeling that, if she resisted, he would pull her inside by force. She guessed they were struggling to come to terms with the tragedy and finding it difficult to be in each other's company for long stretches.

'Thank you,' she said, stepping inside.

Although Jill didn't know him well, she'd always liked Gordon. Their first meeting had been at a lecture to Kelton Bridge's local history society. Jill had only gone along because Ella had organized the event and had begged as many people as possible to support it. Gordon was a stalwart member of the society and had welcomed Jill and introduced her to several people.

He worked in Manchester for a firm that specialized in buying foreign properties, mostly in Spain and France, for people wanting to retire to the sun. He was quietly spoken, friendly and unassuming, and Jill had gained the impression that Hannah made all the decisions in their household.

'Hannah's in the lounge,' he told her, ushering her through the hallway.

Hannah had been lying on the sofa, a duvet wrapped around her, but she stood when she saw Jill and went forward to give her a hug.

'Are these for me?' she asked. 'Oh, Jill, you shouldn't have. They're gorgeous.'

'They're nothing,' Jill told her. 'I'm sure you could open a florist's by now, but I always think flowers cheer a house. I'm so sorry, Hannah.'

'Thank you.'

Hannah couldn't quite meet her gaze. She was a strong character and Jill suspected that she could cope admirably until people said a kind word. That was often when people lost the tight control they had on their emotions.

'I do have a few,' Hannah went on, nodding at three floral displays in the room, 'but you're right, they do cheer the place up. Everyone's been so kind,' she added. 'Let me see to these.'

Jill followed her into the kitchen where Hannah set about arranging the flowers with great care. Perhaps it helped to take her mind off everything.

'I was speaking to Ella this afternoon,' Jill explained, 'and she mentioned that you'd come home from hospital this morning. She was horrified to learn that I didn't know. News might travel fast in Kelton, but it didn't reach me.'

71

Hannah carried on arranging her flowers. In her early thirties, she was conservative in everything, from her dress sense to her politics. Jill suspected she would love to break out of the constraints imposed by being the local Tory candidate and go wild for a few hours or days. She was attractive, and usually took great care with her appearance, but this evening she looked as bad as she must feel. Her hair was unbrushed, her face was devoid of make-up, and her eyes were red from crying and surrounded by dark circles from lack of sleep.

'I saw Jack yesterday,' Jill said. 'I hope he didn't think I was being rude, but of course, I hadn't heard. Strange that he didn't mention it.'

'Not really,' Hannah said, standing back to assess her arrangement. 'It's hit him hard. He was really excited about the birth of his first great-grandchild.'

'That's understandable,' Jill said.

All the same, she thought Jack would have mentioned it.

'And people don't talk about mis-carriages,' Hannah added bitterly.

'It's difficult,' Jill said, taken aback by her tone.

'Will you stay for a drink?' Hannah asked. 'We were just about to open a bottle of wine.'

'Thanks, but no. I'm sure you don't want company.'

'Please stay,' Hannah implored her. 'Company is exactly what we need.'

'Well, if you're sure. I rarely turn down a glass of wine.'

Hannah smiled at that. 'White or red?'

'Whatever you were planning to open.'

Hannah carried the flowers into the lounge and placed them on a table beneath the window.

'They're gorgeous,' she said. 'Thank you so much, Jill.'

She turned to Gordon. 'Are you going to open that bottle of wine then?'

'Of course.'

He smiled, sheepishly Jill thought, and went off to the kitchen. When he returned, he carried three glasses of red wine.

The atmosphere in the room was heavy with tension. Jill wasn't surprised. People often said that grief brought people together. In her experience, it was more likely to tear them apart.

Hannah knocked back her glass of wine and immediately went to the kitchen for the bottle and a refill.

'Gordon thinks it's my fault,' she said as she filled her glass. 'He says I overdid things.'

'Hannah!' Gordon was as appalled as Jill was embarrassed. 'Of course it wasn't your fault, sweetheart. Yes, I think you overdid things but–'

He broke off before he said anything

more. He blamed her for overdoing things, but not for losing the baby.

'I went out for a walk on Wednesday afternoon,' she explained, 'and yes, I was tired when I got home.'

'Where did you go?' Jill asked casually.

Bradley Johnson had been murdered that afternoon but, after an inner debate, Jill decided it showed an appalling lack of taste to ask if she'd seen Bradley Johnson or anyone acting suspiciously.

'Oh, all over,' she replied vaguely. 'Into Bacup, into the park there.'

'I should have taken her to hospital that night,' Gordon said, his expression bleak as he stared into the depths of his red wine. 'Hannah would have none of it, though.'

'I felt fine,' she muttered.

'And on Thursday morning—' Again, Gordon left the sentence unfinished.

On Thursday morning, Hannah had been rushed into hospital where she had lost her unborn child.

'As tragic as it is,' Jill said calmly, 'it's no one's fault.'

'It's my fault,' Hannah retorted. 'We're all agreed on that. But hey,' she added, raising her glass, 'at least now that I'm no longer pregnant, I can have a drink.'

Moisture glistened in her eyes as she spoke and Jill took a large swallow of her wine. She had to get out and leave these people to

74

their grief.

'We were talking about Bradley Johnson before you arrived,' Gordon said, changing the subject. 'What a dreadful thing to happen.'

'*You* were talking about him,' Hannah corrected him.

Jill thought it wise to ignore that.

'It's awful, isn't it?' she said. 'I didn't know him well, but I always liked Phoebe. It's just dreadful. A terrible shock for her.'

'Yes.' Hannah's voice was clipped.

'You must have known him well, Hannah,' Jill went on. 'He was going to help with your campaign, wasn't he?'

'He was,' Gordon said, 'and it's just impossible to accept what's happened. He was a great support to Hannah.' He patted his wife's hand and smiled. 'Still, with or without him, we'll have you elected, darling.'

The doorbell rang and Jill took another swallow of her wine as she sensed escape beckoning.

Jack Taylor came into the room, preceded by his collie. The dog ran up to Hannah and licked her face.

'Sally! Get off!' Laughing affectionately, she hugged the dog.

'Well?' Jack said. 'Oh, hello, Jill,' he added.

'Hello, Jack.'

'Take your coat off, Granddad,' Hannah said.

'No, I'm not stopping,' he said. 'I'm on my way up to Archie's. I just thought I'd check to see as you got home OK.'

'Safe and sound, as you can see.'

'Good.'

'You'll at least stop for a drink, won't you, Jack?' Gordon asked, his hand on the bottle.

'No, thanks. Not now.'

'What's the weather doing?' Hannah asked him. 'They've promised snow.'

'Ay, and I wouldn't be surprised if we don't get some. Not that we have proper snow these days. I remember the days it were up over the walls on the Burnley Road. And that were nothing unusual.'

'It'll be this global warming,' Hannah teased him.

'Stuff and nonsense,' he retorted. 'Global warming? Pah. These politicians do dream up some rubbish.'

'Scientists have dreamt that up, Grand-dad.'

'And they're just as bad,' Jack retorted.

Jill was intrigued by the exchange. Hannah was teasing; Jack couldn't meet her gaze. What was all that about?

'We were just talking about Bradley Johnson,' Gordon put in. 'Have you heard anything, Jack?'

'No, and I can't say as I'm interested in it, either.' He clicked his fingers and Sally ran to his side. 'Right, I'll be off now then. I'll

76

maybe pop in tomorrow, Hannah.'

'Take care, Granddad. And thanks for calling. Maybe you'll manage to stay for a few minutes tomorrow,' she added drily.

'I will,' he called over his shoulder.

Gordon showed him out and then returned to the lounge.

'Is he all right, do you think?' he asked, looking to both of them for an answer. 'He seemed a bit off.'

'He'll be fine,' Hannah told him. 'He'll be more upset than he lets on about losing his first great-grandchild.'

'I realize that. It's one reason I asked about Bradley Johnson, so that we could talk about something else.' He sighed. 'Stupid idea, I suppose. He wasn't Johnson's biggest fan, was he? He's never liked the idea of foreigners moving into the village.'

'He'll be fine,' she said again. 'Archie will cheer him up.'

'They're close, aren't they?' Jill said, smiling. 'Jack and Archie.'

'Almost joined at the hip,' Hannah replied. 'They went to school together, worked down the pit together, walked every inch of the hills together. They're as thick as thieves, those two.'

Jill emptied her glass.

'Thanks so much for the wine,' she said, getting to her feet, 'but I'll have to get off now.'

'Stay for another,' Hannah said.

'I'd love to, but I can't. Really.' She gave Hannah a quick hug. 'Take care of yourself, Hannah, and if there's anything I can do, anything at all, just call in or give me a ring.'

'Thanks, Jill.' Again, Hannah couldn't quite meet her gaze.

Jill was glad to escape into the bitterly cold wind. She was still standing under the canopy above the front door, hunting in her pocket for her car keys, when she heard Hannah's voice raised in fury.

'For Christ's sake, Gordon, can't we talk about something else?'

Shivering, Jill dashed to her car.

Chapter Seven

The following morning, Max was back at Kelton Manor.

'Let's make this quick,' Jill muttered. She was standing by his side as he hammered on the door, rubbing her chilled hands together for warmth. 'I want to see Ella before I head off for Styal.'

Today, the door was opened by Tyler Johnson and Max thought he looked surprised, and far from happy to see them.

'Mum's out,' he explained.

'Yes, she mentioned that yesterday.' Which was why Max was there. 'It's you and your brother we'd like to talk to.'

'Us? About what?'

It looked as if, given the choice, he would have slammed the door in their faces.

'May we come inside?' Max asked.

With some reluctance, Tyler held open the door and they stepped inside. Max was grateful for that as it was another bitterly cold day. According to the weather forecasters, it was actually warmer today, but the strong north wind was simply making it feel colder.

He had expected to be taken into the sitting room but Tyler, his hands in the back pockets of his jeans, swaggered towards the kitchen.

Max was aware of Jill gazing in wonder at the furnishings and array of appliances. Not that she could have used any of them – the kitchen was a foreign land to Jill. This room was vast, though. The table at which Keiran sat was a long, oblong mahogany one with eight chairs lined up. The rest of the kitchen featured a huge picture window, green Aga, walk-in freezer–

'Is everything all right?' Keiran asked, and Max dragged his attention from the wine rack that held thirty bottles of exceptionally fine red.

'Just a couple of questions,' he told him. 'What I'm trying to do is eliminate as many people as possible. Now, we know you arrived here on Thursday morning, yes? What time would that have been?'

'It was just after eleven,' Tyler said.

'That's right,' Keiran agreed.

'The thing is,' Max said, 'your mother said she called you to let you know your father was missing at nine thirty that morning. You're at Lancaster University, Keiran, is that right?'

He nodded.

'And you're at Sheffield, Tyler. Now what I can't understand is how you could speak to your mother, pack a few things, drive from Sheffield to Lancaster to pick up your brother and then drive down here in an hour and a half. While I can appreciate that, with so much on your mind, you might have ignored the odd speed limit or two, you still couldn't do it in an hour and a half. It's about a hundred miles from Sheffield to Lancaster so that's getting on for two hours. Then, from Lancaster to Kelton would take you another hour.'

'OK.' Tyler sighed heavily as if all this was far beneath him. 'I'd been staying with Keiran in Lancaster for a couple of days.'

'Mum wouldn't have minded,' Keiran put in quickly. 'It was Dad who would have objected.'

No invitation was forthcoming but Jill pulled out a chair and sat down.

'Why's that, Keiran?' she asked. 'I suppose he would have expected you to be studying, yes?'

She addressed herself to Keiran and Max had to agree that, if there were problems in this family, Keiran would talk far more freely than his older, more arrogant and confident brother.

'He'd have expected Tyler to,' he said.

'Oh? Not you?' she pressed.

'I'm studying linguistics,' he said and it was impossible to miss the trace of bitterness that curved his top lip. 'If you'd known Dad, you'd have known just what a waste of my time and his money he considered that.'

'Ah. Did you argue about it?'

He smiled at the question. 'Many times.'

'What about you, Tyler?' she asked. 'Did you argue with your father?'

'Of course he didn't,' Keiran muttered. 'He was golden boy. Got his head screwed on properly, that one,' he mimicked Bradley Johnson.

'Shut up, Keiran,' Tyler warned.

'Everything I did was a waste of time,' Keiran went on, ignoring his brother. 'He belittled me. Everything I did was wrong – my clothes, my friends, my conversation, my studying. Everything.'

'Keiran, for God's sake!' Tyler looked at Max. 'So there were a few arguments in this house. So what? Every family has them. It

81

means nothing.'

Tyler was tapping his foot, his gaze on the door as if he couldn't wait to be rid of them.

'If one of us was going to kill him,' he added sarcastically, 'we would have done it long ago. So you can eliminate us all, OK? Keiran and I were in Lancaster, and Mum was the one to report him missing.' He paused, looking at Max. 'So we're eliminated, yes?'

'It seems like it,' Max agreed.

'Good,' Tyler said. 'Now, was there anything else?'

'Your mother couldn't think of any enemies your father might have had,' Max said. 'Can you?'

Tyler laughed at that. 'How long have you got? Look, he was a successful man and, to be that, you have to be ruthless. In business, he didn't care how many toes he stepped on. Of course he had enemies.'

'To do with his business?'

'Yes.'

'Is the world of electronics so cut and thrust?' Jill asked.

They were giving the impression of a typical successful businessman but Max knew of the setbacks Bradley Johnson had suffered over recent years. Apparently, he'd pinned his hopes on a revolutionary piece of software, invested in it heavily, and had almost been put out of business when a rival had unveiled an almost identical product a couple of months before Bradley's proposed launch.

'Any business is cut and thrust, as you put it,' Tyler said.

'I see,' she murmured.

Max smiled inwardly. Jill would let him treat her like the village idiot. She wouldn't like it, but she would allow it. For now.

'And can you think of anyone else who disliked him?' she asked.

'Well, no one in this godforsaken village liked him. Why would they? The Yank coming and throwing his money around? They were jealous of him.'

'Does anyone spring to mind who might have been jealous enough to kill him?' Max asked.

'No. No, of course not,' Tyler snapped.

'We'd love to help,' Keiran said, 'but we can't. We were both in Lancaster at the time and, besides, we've hardly spent any time in the village. We didn't really know much about Dad's life.'

'OK,' Max said briskly. 'That will be all for now. If you think of anything, will you let me know?'

'Of course,' Tyler said, striding for the door to show them out. 'And thank you for calling,' he added.

A few flakes of snow were falling as they stepped outside. They had walked to the manor and now, heading back through the village, they strode out before the biting wind had a chance to penetrate their bones.

'They're both a bit uneasy,' Jill remarked.

'Yes, and despite their alleged closeness, they're not exactly grieving for their father, are they?' Max murmured.

'They're not. I'm sure Tyler knows more than he's saying. Mind you,' she added drily, 'that wouldn't be difficult. And what about Keiran? Usually, he's nothing more than a parrot to his brother. Today, he was very talkative.'

'And bitter.'

'Yes, he was.'

As they walked on, Jill glanced at her watch. 'Are you off to headquarters?'

'Yes. You?'

'I need to see Ella, then I'm off to Styal again,' she said, and he saw the way she shuddered at the prospect. 'Oh, and before that, I'm going to see if I can blackmail a plumber to come out and look at the boiler...'

Chapter Eight

Jill had intended to go straight to Ella's but, first, she nipped into the Co-op in Bacup, and as she'd managed to find a parking spot, no mean feat, she thought she'd take a walk into Stubbylee Park. She had plenty of time to call on Ella before she had to be at HMP Styal.

Several people were walking with dogs and making the most of the sunshine.

She walked on, past the aviaries, then crossed the track at the top to walk into Moorlands Park. This smaller area was deserted apart from someone sitting, quite still, on one of the children's swings and a stiff, elderly lady walking with an equally stiff Jack Russell terrier. The only sounds to be heard were the distant rumble of traffic passing through the valley below and the caged birds singing joyfully.

As she walked around the edge of the football pitch and up the side of Olive House, she wondered just where Claire Lawrence had buried her daughter's body. She was still no closer to knowing. Claire, she suspected, would have chosen somewhere tranquil and beautiful, somewhere that held happy memories for Daisy. But where?

According to expert opinion, Claire had truly believed she was Daisy's saviour. There were no religious beliefs behind her thinking; she simply thought that it was better to be dead than to exist in this world. Sadly, given Claire's world, there was a certain logic to that thinking.

But still that theory didn't sit comfortably with Jill.

She walked through the formal, circular

garden and towards the children's play area, and recognized the man sitting on the swing. It was Gordon Brooks.

She pushed open the gate and walked over to him.

'Hello, Gordon,' she said quietly.

He'd been so lost in his thoughts that he hadn't heard her approach, and was startled by the sound of her voice. 'Oh, Jill. Hello, there.'

He blinked rapidly, and she wished she hadn't intruded.

'How are you?' she asked. Stupid question. It was clear that he was suffering.

'Fine, thanks.' He forced a smile. 'You?'

'Yes. Just enjoying this weather. I should be working really, but it's too nice to be sitting in front of a computer. No doubt we'll soon have our usual winter weather of rain, rain and more rain.'

'No doubt.'

'How's Hannah?' she asked, sitting on the swing next to his.

'Fine, thanks. Yes, fine.' He sighed. 'She had a little too much to drink last night. I'm sorry about that.'

'I don't blame her,' Jill replied. 'If I'd lost my baby, I'd want a damn good drinking session, too.'

'Yes.' He smiled gratefully.

'It's going to be difficult, Gordon.'

'Yes. Yes, I know it is. Some things are just

too painful to talk about, I suppose.'

'They are,' she agreed.

Gordon didn't seem to be coping at all well and, if he felt unable to talk to Hannah, it would be a long time before he got over this. Tall and thin, with wispy fair hair, he could never be described as robust, but today he looked tired, drawn and defeated.

'We all deal with grief in our own way,' she reminded him, 'and the loss of a child is particularly difficult to accept. It goes against the natural order of life. It seems so cruel. Senseless. Unfair. People are torn by so many conflicting emotions.'

'A colleague told me that it was unlucky to make preparations,' he confided. 'Apparently, his wife wouldn't allow so much as a disposable nappy in the house. I told him that was nonsense. Superstitious nonsense.' He reached into the pocket of his thick sheepskin coat for a handkerchief and blew his nose. 'I did the lot,' he went on. 'I wanted it all to be ready for my little girl. We were having a girl, you know. Nothing was too much trouble. No expense was spared. The nursery is decorated, mobiles are hanging from the ceiling, and dozens of expensive toys are sitting on the shelves. My little girl will never play with those, will she?' He turned slightly to look at her. 'It seems that my colleague was right.'

'No,' Jill said, and she could have wept with

him. 'You were right, Gordon. It is superstitious nonsense. I'm no doctor, but I know for a fact that having a room decorated in a certain way isn't a cause for miscarriage.'

He scuffed his shoes on the soft, impact-absorbing surface at their feet. 'Put like that, it sounds silly,' he agreed.

'When tragedy happens,' she went on, 'we need someone to blame. If there's no one, and there really isn't, Gordon, we look for something else. And that can be anything from walking under a ladder to stepping on a crack in the pavement.'

'I suppose so.'

Jill had a sudden longing to push her swing into action and see how high she could go. It was years since she'd been on a swing. Years. She'd better not, though. There was sure to be some law about adults on swings

'Jack called in,' he said, 'so I thought I could get some air for a while.'

'That's good. They're close, aren't they?'

'Yes. Mind you, he won't talk about it, either. He's of the old school and keeps his feelings to himself. Stiff upper lip and all that.'

Jill nodded her understanding.

'It's affected him badly, though,' Gordon added. 'You can't say anything to him without having him jump down your throat.'

Jill had noticed.

'Hannah's the same,' he said after a while.

'She's not a great one for showing her feelings, but I get the impression that she's angry with me, that she blames me in some way.'

Jill had gained the exact opposite impression. She had thought that Hannah blamed herself.

'I'm sure she doesn't.' Jill leaned across and patted his arm. 'She'll be hurt and angry because she's lost her baby, but not angry with you. She'll need you far more than you'll know.'

He didn't comment on that.

'I sometimes feel angry with her,' he admitted instead.

'Oh?'

'Like she said last night, I told her time and time again that she was overdoing things, but she took no notice. "Women are giving birth every minute of every day," she'd tell me. Her stock phrase was "Stop fussing". Perhaps I did fuss, but only because I felt she was overdoing things.'

Jill decided to let him talk. It might help to get it out of his system.

'I'd give everything I have to put the clock back. I should have taken her to hospital on the Wednesday night,' he said, his gaze on the distant hills. 'She'd really overdone things that day. When I came in from work, she told me she was tired because she'd been out walking all afternoon. She hadn't wanted anything to eat and then decided

89

she'd go for a lie-down. She was exhausted.'

Once again, Jill wondered if, during that walk, Hannah had seen anyone or anything that might help with the investigation. She had only come out of hospital yesterday morning so perhaps she hadn't been questioned yet. But she would be, and Jill couldn't probe. Not now.

'And then,' he said, clearly thinking along the same lines, 'Bradley Johnson from the manor was murdered. Everything seems to be – oh, I don't know, just awful at the moment.'

'It is,' she agreed. 'That will have upset Hannah, too.'

'Yes. They'd done a lot of work together lately. You'll have seen the photos in the paper. They were pictured together at that new hotel in Harrington, the one with the conference facilities, and the spa, the one that's going to bring so much business to the area.' He rolled his eyes as if the idea was ridiculous. 'Then there was one taken at the library in Rawtenstall and another of them both collecting for the hospice outside Tesco.' He gave her a weak smile. 'He was seeing more of Hannah than I was.'

He got off his swing. 'I'd better be getting along, Jill. I only came out to escape Hannah for an hour or so. I can't talk to her, I can't even look at her, but I know I have to.'

'Try talking to her, Gordon. Start by telling

her how you feel. It will help you both.'

'I suppose.' He rubbed weary hands across his face. 'Who would have thought it would come to this? Me and Hannah, I mean. When we were both at Warwick – we met at university there – we could talk about everything under the sun. We were as close as two people could be. But now...'

'Just pretend you're both young students again,' she urged him. 'Try to recapture those days and that closeness.'

He looked as if she had suggested he book a luxury weekend break on Mars.

'I'll try,' he said without conviction.

'I'm truly sorry, Gordon.'

'Thank you. And thanks for listening.'

'Any time,' she said, meaning it. 'If ever you need to talk, you know where I am.'

'Thanks. I appreciate that.' He nodded a little awkwardly, obviously embarrassed about saying so much. 'Be seeing you, Jill.'

He strode off, heading down towards the main road, leaving Jill feeling thoroughly depressed. A man had been murdered in her village, Hannah and Gordon had lost their baby, and soon she had to set off to interview a woman who had murdered her own daughter.

'To hell with it!'

She pushed back her swing and launched herself into the air. The swing's chains creaked ominously, but she didn't care. She

91

had forgotten how exhilarating it was to swing back and forth, legs kicking out at the air…

Jill drove home, had a quick coffee, then set off at a brisk walk for Ella's bungalow.

Typically, Ella was out. As it turned out, though, it didn't matter because the raffle ticket stubs that Jill had promised to hand back were in the pocket of her other coat.

As she trudged back home, a huge dark cloud blocked out the sun. A cloud hung over Kelton Bridge, too. Jill loved her village, and couldn't bear the misery that surrounded it now. A murder, a miscarriage – all was doom and depression.

'My, someone's looking glum!'

Jill had been too wrapped up in her thoughts to spot Ella.

'I was miles away.'

'So what are you up to?' Ella fell into step with her.

'Taking raffle tickets back to you,' Jill told her drily. 'Raffle tickets that are in the coat that's hanging up at my cottage.'

'Ah, a senior moment.' Ella grinned at that. 'Don't worry, I have them all the time.'

'I'll drop them in this evening,' Jill promised.

'No need. I'll walk back with you and collect them if you like.'

They walked on, chatting about this and

that, and Jill's spirits lifted. Ella's good company always cheered her.

'I need to collect Jack's tickets,' Ella said as they neared The Terrace. 'Are you in a rush, Jill, or can you spare five minutes?'

'It's fine by me, although he's probably at Hannah's. I met up with Gordon and he said he'd escaped for a bit of air while Jack was with Hannah.'

They walked up the path to Jack's house, and Ella, without hesitating, walked round to the back door. She hammered on that, and shouted, 'Are you in there, Jack?'

There was no response.

'He might be in his shed.' Ella strode off down the path. 'The old fool practically lives in there.'

Jill followed her and, sure enough, Jack was in his shed. Ella yanking the door open must have startled him, but he didn't seem bothered.

He was sitting in a wooden chair. Well-worn and with a slatted back, the chair looked to be older than Jack. It had pride of place in his garden shed and, from it, he would be able to see the long, tidy length of his garden and the house.

'My,' he said, 'I don't often entertain visitors in here.'

'It's just as well.' Ella pointed at several cobwebs and pulled a face. 'Look at the state of the place.' She tutted. 'I well remember Mary saying you'd live in here given the choice.'

'Why not? This chair is the most comfortable one in the village.'

Outside, to the left of the shed, was an incinerator from which a thin wisp of smoke curled skywards.

'Have you been having a bonfire?' Ella asked, wrinkling her nose at the smell.

'I have.'

'Old love letters?' Ella teased.

'It wouldn't matter if it were. You can burn stuff but memories – and truth – remain.'

Ella nudged Jill and winked. 'You didn't know Jack was a philosopher, did you?'

'Away with you, woman,' Jack said irritably.

Reluctantly, it seemed to Jill, he left the comfort of his shed and stepped outside.

'You'll be here for those raffle tickets,' he guessed. 'They're in the kitchen.'

His dog trotted by his side as they walked up the path to the house and, a few minutes later, Ella was putting the ticket stubs in her pocket and they were on their way again.

'Him and his shed,' Ella said, shaking her head.

'How long has he lived there, Ella?'

'He was born in that house. What is he now? My, he must be seventy-eight.'

'He looks good on it.'

'He does,' Ella agreed. 'I think it was in 1952 that he married Mary. Around that time anyway. Shortly after that, their son, James was born. They wanted more children, Mary did especially, but it wasn't to be.'

Ella thought for a moment.

'We were good friends, me and Mary. You would have liked her. It's hard to believe that twenty years have passed since she died. Cancer,' she added grimly.

Ella, who had lost her beloved Tom to cancer, hated the disease with a passion.

'I remember when James married Emily,' she went on, her frown clearing. 'Mary was beside herself when they went to live in Manchester. "Good God, woman," Jack used to say, "Manchester's not the other side of the world, is it?" It might as well have been for Mary. But they had the phone put in and, besides, James and Emily were only in Manchester a few years before they moved back to the village. And they had three children – Hannah, Adam and young Luke.' She laughed at herself. 'Hark at me. Young Luke is twenty-eight now.'

Just like Jack, Ella and her husband spent their lives in Kelton Bridge. Ella, fascinated by the history of the area, knew all there was to know about the place.

'It was Hannah who claimed Jack's heart, though,' she murmured. 'He'd always longed for a daughter, not that he would have admitted as much, but Mary always knew that, and I suppose Hannah filled an

95

empty space in his heart. And, of course, Hannah worships him.'

'He must be so upset for her and Gordon,' Jill said.

'Dreadfully. Far more than he'll let on. But he and Archie will set the world to rights over a couple of pints. Archie will help him get life into perspective.'

Jill hoped so.

They carried on to Jill's cottage and she handed over those raffle ticket stubs.

And then it was too late to waste yet more time on a plumber. She needed to be on the road.

HMP Styal was as depressing, noisy, cheerless and smelly as ever. Jill tried to block out the background din and concentrate on the woman sitting opposite her.

'I hear you've been upset, Claire.'

Jill had been told that, while watching television with several other inmates last night, Claire had 'gone berserk'. She'd upended a table and thrown one of the metal-legged chairs at the set. She was quiet now, but possibly only because, once again, she'd spent the night sedated.

'Was it something you saw on the television?' Jill asked.

Claire gazed back at her, her expression more vacant than ever. She was still hungover from the medication they'd given her.

What else could it have been? According to one inmate, Claire had been laughing with her and then, suddenly, she had thrown that chair.

'I often feel like throwing things at the telly,' Jill went on. 'Sometimes, for me, it's when I'm watching the news and I hear that the government have come up with yet another madcap idea. More often than not, though, it's when my horses lose.'

Claire managed a small smile at that.

HMP Styal was even more smelly than usual. 'What was on the lunch menu today?' Jill asked, pulling a face.

Claire, finally, managed a real smile. 'It doesn't matter. Whatever you pick, it all smells the same.'

'That bad, eh?'

'Disgusting,' Claire said, nodding.

They could talk about the weather, the food, music and suchlike all day but Claire wouldn't, or couldn't, talk about anything on a deeper level.

According to that inmate, there had been nothing more interesting than the local news on the television when Claire had hurled a chair at the set. The girl had been adamant that nothing distressing or even thought-provoking had been shown. Jill would watch a recording of it for herself. There must have been something shown to produce such a dramatic reaction.

'A man from my village, Kelton Bridge, was murdered last Wednesday,' Jill said. 'I suppose you saw that on the news?'

It was the only thing she could think of that would have been on last night's news bulletin.

'Yes. Some American, wasn't it?'

'That's right. Someone clearly took a dislike to him. It's very sad for his family. It's always those left behind who suffer, isn't it?'

'Sometimes. But he won't be suffering, will he?'

'I don't suppose he will. Not that he was suffering before,' Jill pointed out. 'It seems as if he had the perfect life. A beautiful wife, two clever sons, a lovely home in a village, plenty of money – a happy life.'

'The beautiful wife and clever sons will be able to bury him. That's all people care about, isn't it?'

'Not all,' Jill said, 'but yes, it helps if you can bury your loved ones. It brings closure. It allows you to move on. People like to visit the grave and feel close to those who are gone.' She paused. 'Wouldn't you like to visit Daisy's grave?'

'What grave?'

'You laid her to rest somewhere, Claire.'

'Did I?'

'Wouldn't you like to visit the spot? Yes, I'm sure you would.'

Claire just smiled at that.

'You're very lucky if you don't need to visit Daisy's resting place.' Jill leaned back in her seat, watching every expression that flitted across Claire's face. 'You've been lucky all along, though, haven't you? You were able to say goodbye to her. Her dad didn't have that chance, did he?'

'I didn't say goodbye to her. And what does he care? He never cared about her like I did.'

She meant he didn't love her as much, but Claire couldn't say the word love. It was alien to her.

'Maybe not, but he did love her in his own way. Can't you tell him where she is, Claire? Would it really be so awful if he could go and say goodbye to her?'

Claire's lips tightened into a thin line.

'What do we have to do to find her, Claire? Dig up the whole country? Because we will find her, you know.'

She smirked at that.

'Of course, it wouldn't be the whole country,' Jill said casually. 'You won't have left her alone in a cold, dark building and you won't have left her in a stretch of icy water. She'll be somewhere peaceful. Somewhere beautiful. In death, you'll have given her beauty. You couldn't do that in life, could you, Claire?'

'You don't have a clue, do you?' Claire scoffed.

She was right about that.

'Then tell me,' Jill said urgently. 'Explain it to me, Claire.'

There was a long silence and Jill, breath suspended, thought that Claire might actually be thinking about telling her where she'd buried her daughter.

'I thought I could tell you,' she said finally, 'but I don't want him going near her. He'll never touch her again.'

'Who? Peter?'

'It's hours since the grub came and you can still smell it, can't you?' Claire said vaguely.

Jill didn't give a damn about the smell. She was intrigued by Claire's last statement. *Never touch her again*. What the devil did she mean by that?

'Tell me about Peter and Daisy,' Jill pleaded.

'What's there to tell?'

'He loved Daisy, didn't he? He wouldn't have harmed her.'

'Peter? He'd have belted her when he got the drink in him. Just like he belted me.'

Jill was going round in ever-decreasing circles. She'd talked and talked, yet she was no further forward. She knew that Claire had loved her daughter like she'd never loved anything in her sad life before. Jill assumed that, by killing Daisy, Claire thought she had saved her from the only life she was capable of giving her.

Jill didn't like assuming anything. She liked to approach every case with an open mind but, with Claire, all she was doing was relying on psychiatric reports. Worse still, she couldn't even get close to understanding Claire. Try as she might, she couldn't see Claire as a woman capable of killing her own daughter.

'I thought about you and Daisy this morning,' she said casually. 'I walked into Bacup and up through Stubbylee Park. I even had a go on the swing.' She smiled at the memory. 'I bet Daisy loved it there, didn't she? You know the paddling pool? They've filled that in. It's a shame, isn't it? Health and safety, I suppose. They must have worried that a child would drown. Sometimes I think this country is health and safety mad, don't you?'

'If you say so.'

'It wasn't used very often, though,' she went on, 'so I don't suppose people will miss it. The dogs might. Whenever I've been there in the past, dogs have been splashing around in it or having a drink.' She paused. 'The council are doing a lot of work round there at the moment. They must have money to burn. If it stands still, dig it up, seems to be their motto.'

Claire didn't look unduly worried at the prospect of an unsuspecting council worker stumbling across a child's body.

'They're digging up by Lee Quarry, too,'

Jill went on. 'They've put mountain bike trails in. It's proving very popular.'

No reaction.

'How did you get along with Peter's parents, Claire?'

These days, the couple couldn't find a good word to say about Claire but that wasn't surprising. 'Hanging's too bloody good for her!' they'd chanted in unison.

'I only saw them twice,' Claire said. 'They didn't want much to do with Peter or me. They thought Peter had gone mad when he married me.' The idea seemed to amuse her. 'Perhaps he had.'

'Didn't they see much of Daisy?'

'No.'

Much more of this and Jill would admit defeat.

Yet there was something here that intrigued her. Something wrong, something she couldn't pinpoint.

Claire had walked into the local police station very early one morning clutching a pillow and an empty bottle. She claimed she had given Daisy a few Diazepam tablets to swallow before suffocating her and disposing of her body. She had adamantly refused to say how or where.

'You never learned to drive, did you, Claire?'

'No. Why should I?'

Because it would make it easier to move a

body around. Without a car, just how did she move Daisy's body? She must have moved it because a massive police search of the house and vicinity hadn't revealed anything...

'No reason. Given the traffic chaos I endured coming here today, I can't say I blame you.'

Claire smirked at her. 'You're not doing very well, are you?'

'Sorry?'

'You're no closer to finding out where Daisy is.'

Unless Jill was mistaken, that was the first time Claire had uttered her daughter's name.

She was right though; Jill wasn't doing very well.

'I can't do it on my own,' she pointed out. 'I need your help, Claire. If you're not prepared to help me, I'll never do very well, will I?'

'Perhaps next time,' Claire murmured.

And perhaps not.

'OK.' Jill looked at her watch. 'I've got another half an hour,' she said, 'so we can talk about anything you like. Unless you'd rather be on your own,' she added.

Claire shrugged as if it didn't matter one way or another, but Jill knew it did. These sessions were a lifeline to her, simply because they broke up her long, empty days.

'Right,' Jill said, taking that as agreement to talk about something. 'Pick a subject.'

Claire smiled. 'Funerals.'

'OK,' Jill said thoughtfully. 'I want to be cremated. I can't bear to spend my days underground being eaten by worms. And I want a single spray of white flowers on my coffin from someone who loves me. That's all, just a single spray. What about you?'

'I don't want to be burned.'

'You'd rather be in the dark with the worms?' Jill pulled a face.

'It doesn't matter when you're dead, does it?'

'Perhaps not. OK, next subject?' Jill prompted.

'Dogs.'

Funerals and dogs...

'Dogs are the bane of my life at the moment,' Jill told her. 'My – boyfriend–' Ridiculous to class Max as a boyfriend, but still. 'He's spending a few days with me at the moment and he has three dogs. I have three cats so you can imagine what it's like. I do like dogs, but having three about the place is mayhem. What about you, Claire? Do you like dogs?'

'They're OK.'

'Have you ever lived with any?'

'No.'

'Didn't you ever want one?'

'No.'

'Cats?'

'No.'

'What do you think about dogs then?' Jill asked.

'They're OK.'

'Next subject then,' Jill said.

'You choose.'

Jill thought for a moment. 'Houses,' she said. 'Where would you live if you had all the money in the world?'

'On a boat on the canal,' Claire answered without hesitation, and she was staring at a spot behind Jill.

'Really? Yes, I'd like that, too. You'd be free to move around whenever the mood took you.'

Claire nodded.

'Canals are straightforward, too,' Jill went on. 'You can't get lost. Well, I probably could, but you know what I mean. No traffic jams. A quiet, leisurely pace of life. Yes, that appeals to me, too.'

Claire was still gazing at some spot past Jill's shoulder.

'Have you ever lived on one, Claire?'

'No.' She began scratching her arm, a sure sign that she was upset. 'I'm tired of talking now,' she said, standing up.

'OK.' Jill gathered up her things. 'I'll see you next time then.'

As she left Styal behind, Jill thought about the long stretches of the Leeds and Liverpool Canal and the Rochdale Canal. Daisy's body wasn't at the bottom of one, she was sure of that, but it might be in some quiet spot *near* a canal and both canals rolled through some of the most rugged and beautiful scenery in the country...

Chapter Nine

When Max got to his office the following morning, DS Warne wasn't far behind him.

'It seems as if Johnson might have met someone with a dog, guv,' she said, waving a report in the air. 'They've found white dog hairs on the victim's trousers and, better still, a dark hair that might, just possibly, belong to our killer.'

These days, when disillusionment echoed around every corridor, DS Grace Warne was a gift from the gods. When she'd first joined them, Max had attributed her tireless energy and enthusiasm for catching bad guys to her youth. He'd guessed that one of her brothers had been given a policeman's outfit one Christmas and Grace had taken to playing with it. She'd been with him for four years now, though, had even married, yet her enthusiasm hadn't waned. He'd never heard her complain about the endless paperwork or the many ridiculous rules and regulations. She loved her job.

Max took the report from her and skimmed through it.

'Let's not get too excited,' he warned her, guessing it was too late for that. 'The body was lying in that wood for hours so any dog could have investigated it. It seems to me that the world and his bloody wife walk their dogs there. And Johnson had walked from the manor so he could have stopped to chat to anyone with a dog before entering the wood. We have to accept, Grace, that almost everyone in Kelton has a blasted dog.'

'There's still the unidentified human hair.'

'True.' Unlike Grace, Max couldn't get too excited.

'It's something.'

'Yes, and the way things are going, we should be grateful for anything, I suppose.' The truth was, they had no real leads at all. 'Considering everyone walks through the wood,' he said, 'someone should have seen something.'

Grace shrugged. 'They didn't, though. And there are no cameras in the village. Well, that's a lie – there are some in the shops and the bank and one at the filling station. We don't think he went anywhere near those, but we're getting them checked just in case,' she added.

'Yes, I know,' he replied drily. 'I saw Doug struggling to stay awake on that particular job.'

'Yes, well.' She grinned at that. 'It's a thankless job, guv. Not a lot happens in that village.'

'Apart from the occasional murder,' Max pointed out.

'Apart from that,' she agreed.

'Anything on that blue van yet?'

Two people had reported seeing a blue van parked in a lay-by a hundred yards from the wood.

'Not yet, guv, no.'

'We've only just gone public with that so I suppose it's early days. Let's just hope he comes forward.'

When Grace had gone, Max read through a pile of witness statements again. So far, the blue van was the only lead they had. That and a white dog.

His mind went back to his meeting with Jack Taylor. He had a black and white dog and, when they spoke, he'd been less than complimentary about Bradley Johnson. Even Jill had been puzzled by his rudeness.

It was difficult to see him as a killer, though. He was knocking on eighty and had lived in the village all his life. He'd be demanding more coppers on the beat and complaining about the amount of crime in the area, not committing it.

All the same, he might have seen or heard something that he wasn't telling. Max decided that another chat with him wouldn't go amiss.

Dog hairs apart, there was something about the old man and his hostility that didn't feel right.

He could send Grace or Fletch or any one of a number of officers to speak to him but, as he was working on hunches rather than anything significant, he didn't want to waste their time. Besides, his lack of delegation skills would give his boss something to moan about...

He drove out to Kelton Bridge and parked his car a few yards past number four, The Terrace so that Jack Taylor wouldn't see who it was. Given advance warning, Max suspected he'd ignore any unwanted callers.

There was no bell so Max hammered on the door and then, more gently, on the thin glass pane. There was no response. He would have expected the dog to bark, too, so it seemed likely that Jack wasn't at home after all.

Number four was on the end of a row of terraced houses, and had a large garden at the side. Max walked around and stood for a moment gazing at the long length of garden at the back. It was narrow, just the width of the house, but it had to be at least a hundred and fifty feet long. Considering winter was upon them, it was well stocked. Max saw Brussels sprouts, leeks and turnips, and large patches had been dug over, presumably in readiness for the spring. Jill had said he was a keen gardener. He must also be very fit for his age. At the bottom of the garden was a shed, in front of that an incinerator and, to the side, a small greenhouse. On the stone-flagged path, a red, white and blue rope dog toy lay abandoned.

Max was about to head back to his car when the shed door opened and the collie raced up to him. Its tail wagged joyfully and it was more than willing to make friends. Sadly, its owner wasn't as welcoming.

'What the hell are you doing snooping around?' Jack Taylor demanded in astonishment.

'Mr Taylor, good morning. I wondered if I might have a word.'

The dog ran around Max's legs a couple of times and then raced off, picked up the rope toy and brought it back to him.

'Have you got a warrant?' the old man snapped.

'A warrant? For what? I only want to ask you a couple of questions.'

Max grabbed hold of the rope and had a quick game of tug with the dog. 'A lovely animal,' he said.

Jack Taylor ignored that. 'What questions?' he demanded, standing directly in front of Max now.

He was a tall man and, despite his age, held himself very erect. Unless Max was mistaken, he was wearing the same clothes he'd been wearing when he and Jill had met him in Black's Wood.

'I'm still trying to unravel the events of last Wednesday,' Max said. 'As you know, we believe Mr Johnson may have been meeting someone with a dog. We've found white dog hairs on his clothes.'

'Well, well, well. By God, you lot are bloody clever, aren't you?' It was rare to see him smile, but that brought forth a chuckle.

'I know you've been asked if you were in the wood on that particular day–'

'I have, and I've told you – as well as every bugger else that I weren't.'

'You're quite sure about that?'

'Of course I'm sure.'

'A dog like this must need a lot of exercise,' Max remarked, stroking the dog's head. 'I have a collie and, although she's getting on a bit, she'll run all day. You must have taken this one for a good walk on Wednesday.'

'I must have.'

'If you didn't go through the wood, where would you have gone?'

Jack Taylor shrugged and stared off into the distance. 'I can't rightly remember.'

'Yet you can remember that you didn't go through Black's Wood that day?'

'Oh, yes, I can remember that.'

'And you're quite sure you didn't meet Mr

111

Johnson at some point during the day?'

'Quite sure.'

Max thought how much more useful bashing his head against the dry stone wall would be.

'Why didn't you like the man?' Max asked, changing track.

'What's there to like?'

'Your granddaughter was quite a fan, I gather. I seem to recall her having her photo taken with him a couple of times.'

'What the bloody hell does my Hannah have to do with anything?' Jack demanded furiously. 'If folk know what's good for them, she'll be our next MP so she's had her photo taken with all sorts of simpering idiots.' He shook his head in amazement. 'Bloody hell!'

'I'm sure she has,' Max said pleasantly, 'but she seemed quite happy to be with him. How come you dislike him so much?'

'I took a dislike to him, that's all. Now, is that it?'

'I thought your granddaughter might have been on his guest list. He threw a party a couple of weeks ago,' Max explained, 'and all the local celebrities were there. I'm surprised your granddaughter wasn't.'

'Perhaps she's got more sense than mix with the likes of him.' He glared at Max as if he'd like to physically toss him aside. Given the amount of digging he'd been doing, he was probably capable of it too. 'Right, I've had enough of your questions so you can bugger off. Come on, Sal.'

Max either had to turn around and walk back up the path or risk being mown down by Jack Taylor. He decided it would be wise to get out of the man's way.

'If you remember where you went last Wednesday,' he said, walking back towards the house, 'or if you recall seeing anyone at all, I'd be grateful if you'd let me know.'

'I'm sure you would, Sherlock,' Jack muttered.

Max returned to his car and, seconds later, Jack Taylor, with the collie trotting along beside him, headed down the lane in the direction of Black's Wood.

Max was walking out of headquarters that evening when Jill drove into the car park. He stood for a moment, bracing himself against the strong wind, and watched as she stopped the car and gathered up things from the passenger seat.

He walked over and opened the door for her.

'Hiya,' she said, smiling. 'Are you going or coming?'

'Going. Fancy coming with me? I'm off to see our good friend, Thomas McQueen.' He glanced up at his boss's window as he added, 'And it's legit. We're talking to all those who attended Bradley Johnson's last party.'

She was out of her car, clutching a leather briefcase in her arms. 'I'm nothing to do with Bradley's case,' she reminded him, and she, too, glanced up at Phil Meredith's office window. 'As Meredith would be happy to tell you, I've loads of things to do.' She paused. 'But yes, OK. I'll come along.'

Although the thought of suspension had filled him with dread, Max had been hoping for a quiet fortnight. He'd hoped that, while his sons enjoyed themselves in France, he and Jill would manage some quality time together. It had taken all his powers of persuasion to get her to offer him the spare bedroom for a couple of weeks, and he'd hoped to convince her that they could be an item again – a more serious item. They were hardly seeing each other at all at the moment, though.

All the same he must be doing something right. As yet, that spare bedroom hadn't been used.

'What's amused you?' she asked, regarding him suspiciously.

'Nothing.' He banished the smile from his face and unlocked his car.

'How was Styal yesterday anyway?' he asked as he drove them out of the car park. 'You didn't mention it.' And he'd forgotten to ask.

'That'll be because I'm getting nowhere.' She gave a rueful smile. 'I knew it would be a long, hard slog, but I really am getting nowhere. Except, if I had to hazard a guess, I'd say that Daisy's body is somewhere near a canal. Not in a canal, but somewhere close by. Somewhere pretty. A peaceful spot.'

'Great. And how many miles of canal are there around here?'

'A lot,' she admitted. 'But, although I wouldn't put much money on it, it's currently my best guess. I'm thinking about Peter Lawrence, too. Has there ever been any hint of him being interested in children sexually?'

'No. Why?'

'Something she said about him not touching Daisy again.' She leaned back in her seat, slipped off her shoes and wriggled her toes. 'I don't know. I'm working completely in the dark. There's something about Claire that just doesn't ring true and I'm damned if I know what it is.'

A lorry was reversing into King Street and Max sat in the queue of traffic that had built up.

'What about you?' she asked. 'Anything new?'

'Not really. The driver of the blue van has been in touch, but nothing exciting there. He claims he parked in the lay-by near the wood because his girlfriend phoned him. It's feasible, I suppose. We're getting his phone records checked.'

'What's he like?'

'As clean as the proverbial.' He sighed. 'He's worked for the same delivery company for twelve years, no form, not even an unpaid parking ticket. I think we can rule him out.'

'So what about Tom McQueen? Is he expecting you?'

'He's expecting someone.' Max nodded. 'Meredith's not happy about us questioning him, but we can't exclude him. We're talking to everyone who was at that last party.'

'That's fair enough. Even Meredith can't argue with that.'

'Don't you believe it. McQueen's a friend of the Chief Constable's, remember?'

Thomas McQueen lived in a large, detached stone house on the outskirts of Harrington and Max was soon stopping the car in front of metal, electronic gates. He pressed the buzzer, and a disjointed voice said something. God alone knew what.

'DCI Trentham, Harrington CID,' Max replied. 'Mr McQueen is expecting me.'

After a couple of clicks, the gates whirred open. Very slowly. Max inched his way in, almost losing a wing mirror in his impatience to get to the front of the house.

'Have you been here before?' he asked, and Jill shook her head.

'You're in for a treat then.' Max had conned his way in once before and the overall tackiness had almost left him speechless.

116

A slim, attractive woman opened the front door and, although he'd only seen her once before, and then from a distance, he recognized her as Mrs McQueen. Panting by her side was a big, mean-looking Rottweiler.

'Don't mind Ernie,' she trilled. 'He's far too fat to do any damage.'

Jill didn't look convinced. Max wasn't either. The animal was overweight, yes, but, as he panted, it was impossible to miss the size of his yellow teeth. He wore a wide, leather, studded collar. Max returned the dog's stare and noticed that there wasn't so much as a single white hair on him...

'Mrs McQueen,' Max said pleasantly, 'I'm DCI Max Trentham, Harr–'

'I know who you are,' she said. 'I'm Barbara, but call me Babs, for God's sake.' She looked at Jill.

'Jill Kennedy, Harrington CID,' Max added.

Barbara McQueen nodded, but took little notice of Jill.

It was true what they said, Max thought. Money was a huge attraction for some women. Barbara wasn't much above thirty-five years old. She had dark hair, was extremely curvaceous and attractive, beautiful even, but Max gained the impression she didn't have the highest IQ in Harrington. From what he'd found out about her, she did little with her time other than visit beauty

117

salons and hairdressers.

There was something about her that had Max mentally scratching his head. They hadn't met before, of that he was almost certain, and yet there was something – familiar about her. Max rarely forgot a face and, if they had met before, it would come to him sooner or later.

'Come inside,' she said. 'Tommy's in the pool.'

As they walked along a thickly carpeted hallway, Max was aware of Jill gaping at the furnishings. Someone, either Tom or Barbara McQueen, had appalling taste. They had money, more than enough to employ an interior designer, but instead, seemed to prefer a mix and match of all sorts of furniture. The carpet was white, and a few chairs scattered around were bright red. That would have looked fine, but it was the pictures, all in odd, mismatched frames, the green paintwork, the garish jukebox, the rotating mirror ball and the stone statue of a naked boy peeing by the door that caught the eye.

A visit to the McQueens' home was certainly an experience.

Double doors barred their entrance to the pool. Barbara pushed them open and the steamy atmosphere took Max's breath away for a moment.

The swimming pool, with its dark blue tiles, looked extremely inviting. Chairs of

118

every different colour were scattered around and there was another stone boy urinating.

'Tommy!' Barbara McQueen shouted. 'The police are here!'

Tom McQueen completed his length and then hauled his considerable bulk from the water.

'Well, well, well,' he said, climbing the steps and grabbing a towel. 'DCI Trentham no less. I was expecting that nice young sergeant.'

'DS Warne was busy,' Max told him.

'Nice pool,' Jill said, looking around her.

Max introduced her again, and McQueen looked impressed. His ponytail hung down the back of his neck like a dark snake.

'My dear, you're welcome any time you fancy a swim.' He was still breathless from his exertions.

'I might take you up on that.'

Max, keen to get on to more important matters, tapped his foot impatiently.

'I'd like to ask you a few questions about Bradley Johnson,' he said.

'So I gathered.' McQueen rubbed at the ponytail with a towel and then draped a white robe around himself. 'I'm not sure I can tell you anything. Let's go into the drawing room. I'm getting myself a drink.' He grinned. 'What a pity you're on duty, Chief Inspector.'

Tosser.

They followed him to the drawing room where McQueen took a glass from an oak cabinet, grabbed a bottle from a beechwood cupboard, poured himself a glass of brandy, and set it down on a pine coffee table.

In this room, the walls were painted in a colour that Max thought would probably be described as lavender. The carpet was green. One wall was fitted with bookshelves but, on closer inspection, it was possible to see that the 'books' were for display purposes only. That came as no surprise because he could not imagine Mr or Mrs McQueen reading the latest Booker prizewinner. Thankfully, there were no urinating boys in this room.

'Bradley Johnson,' Max said, reminding McQueen of the purpose of their visit. 'I gather you and your wife attended a party at Kelton Manor the Friday before Johnson was murdered.'

'Did we? It's possible.' He shrugged. 'Damned if I can remember when it was. Babs!' he hollered.

When they were seated, the door opened and Barbara joined them.

'That party at the Johnsons' place,' he said to her. 'When was it?'

'God, Tommy, it was only a week ago Friday.' She grinned at Max as she perched on the arm of her husband's chair. 'I keep telling him his memory's going. His dad went senile quite young, you know.'

'It wasn't exactly memorable,' McQueen said in his own defence. 'In fact, it was bloody boring.'

'Really?' Jill said. 'I live in the village and, although I've never been to a party at the manor, I was led to believe they're very lavish affairs.'

'He's a bit of a show-off,' Barbara told her. 'He might just as well hand everyone a list with the price of the wine and the food on it. His wife's OK, I suppose. A bit mousy, but OK. He was too flash for my liking. I mean,' she gushed, 'me and Tommy have money, but we don't throw it in people's faces, do we?'

Max and Jill smiled in agreement.

'Chief Inspector,' Barbara asked curiously, 'have we met before?'

The question took him completely by surprise. 'Not that I'm aware of.' And yet, the more he looked at her, the more he was convinced that they *had* met.

'Is there anything you can tell us about this particular party?' Max asked Tom McQueen, putting his mind to more important matters. 'Did you see or hear anything that, with the benefit of hindsight, might be unusual?'

'Like someone threatening to kill him?' McQueen asked, grinning. 'Er, no.'

A phone rang somewhere in the house and Barbara skipped off to answer it.

'How did you get along with Johnson?'

Max asked.

'OK,' McQueen told him.

'Did you do any business with him?'

McQueen's eyes narrowed. 'No.'

'I heard that Johnson was looking to buy property in the area,' Max lied. 'I hope he wasn't going to tread on your patch, Tom.'

'My patch? Look, Trentham, just because I own a few properties–'

'How many is it now?'

'Enough. And they're all legal and above board.' He took a sip of brandy. 'You can check everything with my accountant if you can be bothered. Oh, silly me. I was forgetting. You've already done that, haven't you?'

Max ignored that. 'Why would anyone want Johnson dead? Do you think he was treading on someone else's toes?'

'Nah. I'll bet there was a woman involved.'

'What makes you say that?' Jill asked curiously.

'Because he couldn't keep his trousers on,' McQueen told her. 'Had a bit of a thing for other men's wives, I gather.'

'I hope he wasn't after your wife, Tom,' Max put in.

'He wasn't. She's got more sense. Besides, what could he offer a woman like my Babs, eh?'

Max could think of a few things.

'If he had been, though,' McQueen added slyly, 'then I would have been topping your

122

list of suspects.' He swilled brandy around his glass. 'All the same, I bet there's a jealous husband involved.'

'Are you saying he wasn't happily married?' Jill asked.

'Nope.'

'But you know he had affairs?'

McQueen shrugged. 'I don't know for sure,' he admitted, 'but yeah, I reckon so.'

'So what makes you say he couldn't keep his trousers on?' Jill persisted.

'That's what people reckoned.'

'People? For God's sake, Tom, name names!' Max snapped.

'I can't remember names,' McQueen told him. 'It was just something I heard a couple of times when he first came to the area.'

Barbara came back into the room.

'Perhaps your wife can remember,' Max said patiently.

'Remember what?' She sat on the arm of McQueen's chair.

'Mrs McQueen – Babs – your husband seems to believe that Bradley Johnson had extramarital affairs,' Max explained. 'Have you heard anything?'

'No, but I'm not surprised.' She leaned towards Max and whispered, 'The man was an outrageous flirt.'

'Really? Did he try it on with you, Babs?'

'Yes, but he didn't get anywhere, I can tell you. I told him not to let Tommy catch him, too.' She trilled with laughter. 'My Tommy wouldn't stand for that, would you, sweetheart?'

'No,' McQueen assured her.

'I'm sure he wouldn't,' Max replied smoothly. Damn it, they must have met before. 'Any idea who else he might have tried it on with?' he asked her.

'Not really. Have you, Tommy?'

'No.'

They stayed for another fruitless half-hour. Just as they were being shown out, a small, yappy West Highland White Terrier raced along the hall heading for their ankles. Fortunately, Barbara scooped it into her arms before it could inflict damage.

'Now, now, Hamish,' she scolded. 'You can't go biting policemen, can you?' She held the dog at arm's length and gave it an adoring shake. 'You're a far better guard dog than Fat Ernie, aren't you?'

While Barbara showered kisses on the dog, Max and Jill stepped outside into a blizzard. They dashed to the car and, by the time they'd fastened their seat belts and Max had started the engine, those huge metal gates had swung open to allow them to escape.

'You reckon Bradley Johnson was a bit of a one with the ladies?' Max asked doubtfully.

'I don't know. Could be. The first time I

met him, he flirted with me. Mind you, I was instantly forgotten.'

'Why was that? Because he didn't fancy you, or because he was doing dodgy deals and you're too close to the force?'

'I hadn't thought of that.'

'Looks like it's time for another visit to the manor...'

Chapter Ten

It was getting late, and Jill was starving. Added to that, she hadn't had a chance to check the racing results yet. What she really wanted was a long, hot soak in her bath followed by a meal out. Beef and Yorkshire pudding. Or maybe a Chinese. Instead, she walked up the path to Kelton Manor with Max.

She'd known, though, as soon as the McQueens had mentioned affairs, that they needed to speak to Phoebe Johnson and satisfy their curiosity.

As ever, Phoebe looked hopeful as she opened the door. It was a week since she had last seen her husband alive and it was almost as if she expected him to be knocking on the door.

'We've no real news,' Max told her, 'but

we'd like to ask you a couple more questions, if we may.'

'Of course. Come in. What an awful night,' she said absently, as they followed her into the sitting room.

'Dreadful,' Jill agreed.

Thankfully, their drive back from Harrington had been without incident but, according to the radio, roads in the north-west were in chaos with fallen trees and lorries blown over.

They were offered seats, and Jill grabbed the chair nearest to the fire. She wondered who had bothered lighting it. Perhaps this duty fell to Molly Turnbull, the Johnsons' cleaner. She couldn't imagine raising enough enthusiasm to light a fire if she was grieving for her husband.

They chatted for a few minutes about Keiran and Tyler – 'they're coping well and have driven up to Lancaster this evening to collect a few things' – and about the vicar's earlier visit – 'so very, very kind of him'.

'You said you wanted to ask me questions?' Phoebe said at last.

'Yes,' Max began. 'First, and I know it sounds silly, can you tell me if your husband was fond of dogs?'

'He was, yes.' She was frowning, clearly wondering why he would ask such a question. 'Mad about them, in fact. For as long as I've known him, he's always stopped to make

126

a fuss of them. I used to warn him about approaching strange dogs, but he just laughed at my fears. He would have liked one, but I'm – well, to tell the truth, I've always been a little afraid of them. With Brad away so much, it would have been left to me to look after it.' She looked at them both. 'Why do you ask?'

'White dog hairs were found on his trousers,' Max explained.

'Really? Well, that doesn't surprise me. He was always fussing them.'

Which didn't help at all.

'Thanks for that,' Max said. 'We need to ask something else, too.'

'Yes,' Jill said, 'and it's a little delicate, I'm afraid.'

'Oh?' Phoebe was wary now. Too wary. She looked worried that they had dis-covered something, yet what could that be?

'We need to know everything, and I mean everything, about your husband, Phoebe.' Jill took a breath. 'We need to know if he was seeing, or if he had been seeing, another woman.'

'Oh!'

'I'm sorry,' Jill said quietly, 'but if you know anything at all...'

Phoebe stood, went to the fire and fiercely prodded the coals with a brass poker. Even-tually, she straightened.

She was good at keeping her emotions in

check. All she needed was a few moments, and she had herself under control again. Yet in that split second, she'd been angry.

'Yes, he's had an affair,' she said at last. 'Affairs,' she corrected herself. 'I suppose it was only a matter of time before someone talked,' she added bitterly. 'People love a bit of malicious gossip, don't they?'

'What can you tell us about the women involved?' Max asked, ignoring her last comment.

'Not a lot. Only that they meant nothing to him. In fact, they were just a joke as far as he was concerned.' She sat down again and her shaking fingers played with a button on her skirt. 'I have to admit that I'd hoped all that was over,' she said at last. 'When we moved here, he said he wouldn't play around again. They meant nothing to him,' she informed them urgently. 'These women were just – well, you know what some men are like.'

'Yes, of course,' Jill said. 'But since you moved to Kelton, has there been someone?'

'Yes,' Phoebe said.

'Can you give us a name?' Max asked.

'I can.' Yet she seemed reluctant to do so. 'As I said, when we first moved to the village, he said he wouldn't play around, and I believed him. Oh, I knew what he was like, but I thought he would at least confine any affairs to London. He was often staying there, you see. So coming here was going to be OK. As he said, the twin set and pearl brigade didn't appeal to him. Anyway, when we'd been here, oh, about a month, I suppose, I saw him with someone.'

That explained a lot to Jill. When Phoebe had first come to the village, she'd tried to get involved in the community. Suddenly, all that had stopped.

'You saw him?' Jill prompted.

'Yes.' She took another deep breath, and Jill felt for her. She was icy calm, but how painful to have to broadcast your marriage's problems to strangers. 'In the pub car park of all places,' Phoebe added with a weak smile. 'I didn't recognize the woman he was with, but they were all over each other. He didn't see me.'

'Did you ask him about the woman?' Jill asked.

'Yes. He said he was ending it and I believed him.'

'Did he tell you the woman's name?'

'I didn't ask,' she said. 'I couldn't have cared less. You see, I knew he saw them as a joke. He laughed at them and their big ideas of happy ever afters.'

She was lying. Bradley's betrayal had wounded her deeply.

'I saw her the following day and I recognized her immediately,' Phoebe explained. 'She recognized me too, of course. She couldn't look at me and I didn't bother to exchange the time of day with her.'

'Do you have her name?' Max asked.

'I saw her in the baker's,' Phoebe said, hanging on to that name, 'and asked about her. I was told her name was Joan Murphy and that she lived in one of the new houses at the top of the village.'

Max looked at Jill, and she gave a brief nod. Yes, she knew Joan Murphy.

'Are you sure it was her?' Jill asked.

'Oh, yes. Quite sure.'

'Has there been anyone else that you know of?' Max asked.

'No. As I said, it was nothing more than a joke to Brad. I never gave it a second thought.'

'I see,' Max murmured.

'Brad is – was,' she corrected herself, 'different. His upbringing–' She broke off and looked at Max. 'His father died in prison. Did you know that?'

Max shook his head.

'Yes,' she said. 'Brad had a very difficult childhood and it scarred him. Because of that, he pushed himself too hard. He was afraid of ending up with nothing, you see. Because he worked so hard, I suppose he had to play hard, too.'

'Of course,' Jill said.

Phoebe got to her feet again and stood with her back to the fire.

'Will any of this have to get out?' she asked.

'It's the boys, you see. I wouldn't want them to know certain things about their father. It would be difficult for them to understand.'

'Hopefully not,' Max said, rising to his feet.

But Jill hadn't finished.

'Do you know how the affair between your husband and Joan Murphy started, Phoebe?' she asked.

'According to Brad, she was all over him. Flirting with him. He said that because she was young and pretty he felt flattered. He only saw her a couple of times, he said, before he realized what a fool he was being. I don't know where they met, or where they went when they saw each other. No doubt, the woman in question will be able to tell you.'

'Yes, of course.' Jill rose to her feet and gave Phoebe's shoulder a sympathetic squeeze. 'I'm sorry we have to ask such questions.'

'That's all right.' But Phoebe's smile belied the hurt and anger...

Claire Lawrence was wrong, Jill thought, as she and Max battled against the wind to get back to her cottage. Claire believed that, once a person was dead, their suffering was over. And so long as those left behind could visit a grave, they were able to get on with their lives.

Death wasn't like that. There were too many repercussions. Phoebe, for example, not only had to cope with her own grief, she had to deal with her husband's infidelity, too. The questions would always be there. Had he really loved her? What had those other women been like? Had they been cleverer, wittier, prettier, sexier? Had they been more exciting sexually? Had he come to her bed straight after making love to them? Had he made love to her and wished he was with one of the others?

On top of that, she had to try to protect his memory for their sons' sakes and that wouldn't be easy. Once the police were involved in a murder inquiry, the press became hungry for gossip. All sorts of details would come out.

'Young and pretty,' Jill murmured as they walked away from the manor. 'Joan is neither of those things.'

'Oh?'

'No.' Jill thought about it. 'She's nice enough, but quite plain. I'd always thought she was happily married, too. She's an artist – a painter. She has that small shop on the corner, next to the bank. I suppose she must sell a few of her paintings, but they're too – blue for my taste.'

'Blue?'

'Yes. She seems to be having her own blue period. She paints huge flowers and they're always blue.'

'Well, it's too late to see her this evening,' Max decided. 'We'll go out for something to eat instead, shall we?'

'OK.'

'Cheer up. I'm even offering to pay.'

She smiled at that. 'In that case, lead on, because I'm starving!'

Chapter Eleven

When Jill woke up, she felt shattered. She and Max had stayed up, talking through this case long into the night. The one good thing was that, unlike Max, she hadn't been knocking back whisky in large quantities. She wouldn't have wanted a hangover as well.

Max was already up and dressed, and he brought her a coffee and put it on the bedside table.

'Right, I'm off,' he said, adjusting his tie. 'As soon as I can get away, we'll go and see Joan Murphy. OK?' She sat up and pulled the quilt up under her chin. 'Fine.'

She had offered him the spare bedroom, but as yet, she hadn't insisted he actually use it. Lust, she decided grimly, had a lot to answer for.

'Are you OK?' she asked. 'No hangover?'

'A hangover? No.' He sounded astonished. 'Why on earth should I have a hangover? I didn't have that much to drink.'

'Only enough to slay an elephant. If I'd had that much, I would have been unconscious for a week.'

'Ah, but you don't get enough practice.'

'Ha.' She reached for her coffee. 'Thanks.'

'You see? Having me around has a lot of advantages.'

'True.' She knew from painful experience that it also had a lot of disadvantages. Like, just when she started to believe they had something good, something strong going for them, he'd go off and sleep with someone else...

He dropped a quick kiss on her forehead. 'See you later.'

He'd been gone less than five minutes when Jill's phone rang. She saw from the display that it was one of her parents and, knowing it was far too early for either of them to call for a chat, she quickly hit the button.

'Hello?'

'A bloke's been done in on your doorstep and you don't say a word. Not a word!'

'Oh, hi, Mum.' Relief flooded through her. She'd thought it was some sort of family crisis.

'Well?'

Jill took a swallow of coffee. 'Well what?'

'Why didn't you tell us?'

'Because I didn't think to mention it. Because you don't know him. Because I hardly knew him.'

'Max is in charge,' her mother said. 'We saw him on the telly.'

'He is, yes.'

There was a pause as her mother waited for something from Jill. She'd have a long wait. Jill had nothing to say. If she so much as hinted that Max was staying at her cottage, her mother would be taking out a subscription to *Brides* magazine and choosing her mother-of-the-bride outfit. As for sharing the same bed—

'I don't know much about the case,' Jill said. 'I'm busy working on something else.'

'You do see him now and again, I suppose?'

'Who?' But she didn't need to ask. Her mother's interest in the murder of Bradley Johnson was nothing compared to her obsession with Max and Jill's relationship.

'Max, of course.'

'Now and again, yes.'

'Getting on all right, are you?'

'We're getting on fine,' Jill assured her.

'Good. It's high time you learned to forgive and forget, my girl.'

Jill had forgiven a long time ago. Given the stress their relationship had been under at the time, perhaps it wasn't too surprising that Max had looked elsewhere for a little light relief. She'd forgiven, but she hadn't forgotten. Just as Phoebe Johnson wouldn't forget her husband's infidelity...

135

'Yes, Mum. Anyway, it's time I was getting on.'

'Before you go, I'll have to tell you what happened here last night. You know that Terry Hunter? Chap who got put away for death by dangerous driving?'

It was so long since Jill had lived on the estate that she'd forgotten most of her un-savoury neighbours. Terry Hunter, however, was difficult to forget.

'Yes.'

'He's out now. Came home, saw that Lisa was living with her new bloke – don't know his name and it won't be worth remembering because she changes men more often than she changes her knickers – and did no more than smash the place to bits. The council are round there now trying to replace windows. Well, it's not the council, it's the housing association. Same thing, though.'

Jill wasn't in the least surprised. The only thing that amazed her was that her parents refused outright to budge from the estate. Jill had given up trying to persuade them to do just that. It's home, they'd say.

'And what happened to Terry?' she asked.

'He's back in custody.'

'How long was he out?'

'Less than twenty-four hours, daft sod. Anyway, I suppose I'd better let you go. You'll let me know when – well, when there's something worth knowing?'

'About what?' Jill asked innocently. 'The murder of Bradley Johnson?'

'About anything that's worth knowing,' her mother retorted.

Jill had to smile at that. 'You'll be the first on my list, Mum. Promise.'

Still smiling to herself, she got out of bed. Three cats needed feeding, sulking cats probably because Max had kicked at least two of them off the bed during the night. She also wanted to write up notes on her last meeting with Claire Lawrence.

It was getting on for eleven o'clock when she heard Max's car pull on to the drive.

'Joan Murphy's shop is closed today so we may as well walk up to her house and see if she's there,' he greeted her.

Jill agreed. The more they were out and about, the higher the chance that someone would say something of use.

This morning, however, people hurried on their way, keen to get behind closed doors and out of the biting cold. Jill didn't blame them.

'If she's not at home,' Max said, seemingly oblivious to the temperature, 'we'll pay Jack Taylor another visit.'

'Jack? Why?'

'I thought we agreed he wasn't being particularly cooperative.'

'We did, but I'm sure it's nothing.' She

rolled her eyes. 'He's an awkward bloke at times but other than that–'

'There's his dog–'

'We'd agreed to forget the dog. You said yourself that we were fixating on the creature. One thing's certain, no dog killed Bradley Johnson. True, he might have been killed by someone who owned a dog, but it's more likely he just brushed past one.'

'Not necessarily. He walked into the wood at the exact time that Ella heard a dog barking. And we think he was meeting someone. It makes sense to think that he might have been meeting someone who owned a dog. Besides, Jack Taylor knows something, I'm sure of it. He's a difficult old sod.'

'He is,' Jill agreed, smiling at the description, 'but he's no lawbreaker.'

'I'm sure he knows something.'

As much as she hated to admit it, because she liked Jack and had a great deal of respect for him, Jill shared the same feeling. Yet what could he know? And why would he keep that information from them?

'I expect he's out of sorts because of Hannah's problems,' she said. 'It's a difficult time for them all.'

'Perhaps,' Max agreed.

They walked up the driveway to Joan Murphy's house and were about to ring the doorbell when a car pulled up in front of the garage.

A slightly uneasy-looking Joan climbed out.

'Hello?' There was a question in her voice. 'Jill?'

'Hello, Joan,' she said. 'This is DCI Trentham. We'd like to ask you a few questions if we may.'

'Me?' She stood at the door to her car, keys in her hand and a startled expression on her face. 'Why me?'

'Shall we go inside?' Max suggested.

She was clearly nervous. If what Phoebe had told them was true, though, and Joan had been involved with Bradley romantically, Jill supposed that wasn't surprising. She wouldn't want the world to know of the affair.

Jill had never considered Joan a particularly attractive woman, or indeed a woman who might be looking for passion in another man's arms. Having said that, she didn't know her well. They stopped for a chat if they met up in the village, or at the pub, but that was all.

She was younger than Bradley, around the forty mark, but no one would describe her as 'young and pretty'. One wouldn't call her frumpy exactly, but she was certainly plain.

This morning, she was wearing a long, brown woollen skirt topped with a jumper and cardigan in matching blue. A thick scarf was wrapped around her neck and, as she unlocked the front door and let them in, she removed it to reveal shoulder-length hair that was showing signs of grey. She wore no make-up and her skin, red from the cold, looked in dire need of moisturizers. Apart from a watch that was more practical than fashionable or attractive, she wore no jewellery.

Seeming to grow more nervous by the second, she showed them into the lounge and offered them seats.

The room was warm and very comfortable. Much of the furniture looked to be almost new, even the carpet showed no signs of wear, but, from a quick glance, Jill noticed signs of recent neglect. No dusting had been done for a while, the windows needed cleaning and an outing with the Hoover wouldn't have gone amiss.

'Is everything all right?' Jill asked her. 'I expected you to be at your shop.'

'Oh, no, everything's fine. I've started closing on Thursdays and opening Sunday mornings. People amble around on Sundays and are grateful to see a shop open.' She perched on the very edge of an armchair, poised for flight. 'What can I do for you?'

'We believe you knew Bradley Johnson well,' Max began.

'Who said that?' Her skin turned an even deeper shade of red. 'I wouldn't say I knew him well.'

'So how would you describe your relationship with him?' Max asked.

'We met socially a couple of times, that's all. With his wife and my husband,' she added quickly.

'We heard you were a little closer than that,' Jill said. 'We're sorry to have to pry, Joan, but we do need you to tell us everything.'

Joan looked from one to the other of them, conflicting emotions flashing across her face.

'Mrs Murphy, did you have an affair with Bradley Johnson?' Max asked at last. 'Yes or no?'

'Oh, God.' Joan promptly burst into tears.

She was on her feet, dashing from the room, and returning seconds later with a handful of crumpled tissues.

'There's nothing to worry about,' Jill assured her, mentally crossing her fingers. 'None of this will go beyond these four walls.'

'Oh, God,' Joan said again. She took several deep breaths, then whispered, 'Yes.'

'It's OK,' Jill said. 'Can you tell us about it?'

Joan was still mopping tears from her face, but she nodded.

'I should have told you, I suppose, but I didn't think it would come out. And, even if it did–' She broke off. 'I was too scared to say anything in case the police thought it was me who killed him.' She fixed large, frightened eyes on Max. 'It wasn't. I swear

141

to God that I know nothing about that.'

'Just tell us what happened,' he said patiently.

Another deep, shuddering breath.

'I'd been in the churchyard tidying up Dad's grave. I'm always upset when I do that. But I thought I was OK so I went into the post office,' she said. 'It was so embarrassing. One minute I was queuing up at the counter, the next I was in floods of tears because I missed my dad so much. I rushed out of the shop and bumped straight into Bradley. He saw how distressed I was, and he invited me to sit in his car while I pulled myself together.'

Jill nodded encouragingly.

'I was in such a state that I blurted it all out. How I'd been up to tidy Dad's grave, how I still missed him even though it had been two years since he died, how we'd all been planning to go to Australia together to visit my brother and his family, how I'd thought Dad would be around for ever, how I never made it to Australia but instead had to sell his house. Brad was – understanding,' she finished. 'Kind, patient and understanding.'

'What happened next?' Jill asked.

'He drove me home,' Joan said. 'A couple of days later, he called to see me, to make sure I was all right. Steve was away that week and–' She bit her lip. 'Brad was flirting with me, and I was flattered. You'd think I'd know better, wouldn't you? But I didn't. I fell in love with his charm, his good looks, his ways.'

'And that's how the affair began?'

'Yes. It lasted about a month.'

'Who ended it?' Jill asked. 'You or Bradley?'

'He did.' She dried her face on a couple of tissues and then pushed them up the sleeve of her cardigan. 'I'd better explain,' she said shakily.

'That might be best,' Max agreed, and Jill could sense his impatience.

'As I said, our affair lasted a month. Then he went quiet. We'd agreed to meet but he didn't turn up. I couldn't believe it was over – especially without him telling me. I kept trying to contact him, but it was difficult. He didn't answer his phone and I didn't like to call the house. I did once, but his wife told me he was away in London. Eventually, after about three weeks, he finally called me.'

She gave a rueful, embarrassed shrug.

'We arranged to meet,' she explained, 'and, although I was relieved to hear from him, I was terrified of what he might say to me. I thought I knew what that was, of course. I assumed he wanted to tell me that things were over between us, and that he was going to be faithful to his wife. You know the sort of thing.'

'Is that what he said?' Jill asked curiously.

143

'Oh, no.' She was growing more confident now that she'd started her story. The distress was lessening and she was becoming harder and colder. 'I'd been a fool. Such a stupid fool. He'd never been interested in me. That first time we met? Outside the post office? I'd mentioned selling my father's house and, from that, he assumed I had money. I did have a bit put by, of course, because the proceeds of the sale were split between my brother and me, but nowhere near as much as he imagined.'

Were they talking blackmail?

'What did he want?' Jill asked.

'Five thousand pounds. Cash,' she said bitterly. 'If I didn't hand over the money, he said he'd tell Steve about us.'

'So you handed over the cash?' Max asked.

'Yes.' That word came as little more than a whisper.

'And he came back for more?' Max guessed.

'Three times.' She dabbed at her eyes with the tissues. 'I gave him fifteen thousand pounds in all. I gave him the last five thousand just a week before he was killed.' Eyes, filled with fear once more, turned on Max. 'But I had nothing to do with his murder,' she said urgently. 'I can't say I'm sorry about it because he was a lying, cheating...' The sentence was left to hang in the air.

'It's OK,' Max said.

'I wish I hadn't paid him,' Joan said bitterly. 'That first five thousand – I was so shocked when I realized what he was up to, I just handed it over. The thing was,' she went on, colouring, 'I'd told him things about Steve, personal things, and I didn't want Steve knowing. I trusted Brad, you see.' She shook her head at her own stupidity. 'You must think me very naive and foolish.'

'Not at all,' Jill told her.

Foolish or not, Joan had given them their first real lead. If Bradley Johnson was blackmailing Joan, it was likely that he'd been blackmailing others.

'When things were going well between the two of you,' Max said, 'did he mention past affairs? Did he mention any other women?'

She thought for a moment and shook her head. 'That was just it, you see. He made me feel as if I was the only woman in the world. God, how pathetic does that sound? At my age, too.'

'We believe,' Jill said, 'that he'd had several affairs in the past.'

'Quite probably,' Joan said. 'He was an attractive man and he knew how to turn on the charm. I don't think,' she added vehemently, 'that I've ever hated anyone like I hated him.'

Jill nodded sympathetically.

'The irony is,' Joan added shakily, 'that Steve left me anyway. All the time I'd been seeing Brad, before that even, he'd been with someone else. He's left me for her.'

'Steve's left you?' Jill asked in astonishment.

'Last night,' she said. 'He'll be here for his stuff at the weekend.'

'Oh, Joan, I'm so sorry.'

'Thanks,' she murmured, before she took a deep, shuddering breath and broke into uncontrollable tears.

Jill tried to comfort and calm her, but she was inconsolable.

'How will I cope without Steve?' she asked repeatedly. 'How will I cope?'

'Things will work out,' Jill told her. 'You'll see.'

Jill held her close and continued to offer platitudes, but she despaired. Did any married couple have a good relationship? A relationship based on trust and respect? It seemed that, everywhere she turned, it was to see rocky marriages and infidelity.

Chapter Twelve

Max left Jill at her cottage, jumped in his car and drove down the lane. A hint of blackmail changed the direction of the whole investigation and Max needed to get back to headquarters and update the team.

They knew Johnson was a ladies' man. What did he do? Seek out wealthy women, work his charm on them until they were smitten, and blackmail them? That's exactly what he'd done with Joan Murphy. Perhaps she wasn't wealthy in the accepted sense, but Johnson had known she had money from the sale of her late father's house.

'Would all his victims have been vulnerable women?' he'd asked Jill.

'Oh, no,' she'd replied confidently. 'He would have grown increasingly ambitious. He would have sniffed out the dirt on anyone. Everyone has skeletons. No one would have been safe from him.'

Thomas McQueen must have more skeletons than most. Had those secrets earned him an invitation to Kelton Manor? It would take a very rash and foolish person to blackmail McQueen. They'd be lucky if their fate was no worse than being bludgeoned to death in a wood.

On his way out of the village, Max drove past Jack Taylor's house. Then, on an impulse, he stopped the car.

He didn't really have time, but the old man intrigued him. Perhaps a mention of blackmail would jog his memory about his whereabouts on the afternoon in question.

Surprisingly, Max's knock on the door was answered almost immediately. It was clear, however, that Jack Taylor had been expecting someone else.

'Oh, it's you,' he said grimly.

'Fraid so,' Max said. 'I'd like another chat. May I come in?'

Just as he thought Jack was going to refuse, the old man shrugged. 'Suit yourself.'

Max followed him into the cottage and into a small kitchen where another man, one Max didn't recognize, was sitting at the table. With the three of them, plus the dog, there was no room to move.

It was a clean room, but, owing to the small windows, quite dark. At least it was warm, though.

'DCI Trentham, Harrington CID,' Max introduced himself to the stranger.

'He's in disguise,' Jack Taylor muttered to his friend. 'Must have left the deerstalker and pipe at home.'

'Ah,' the other chap said, eyeing Max up and down.

'No doubt Dr Watson will be along in a minute.'

Max bent to stroke the dog while the two men enjoyed their little joke.

'Do you live in Kelton Bridge?' Max asked the stranger.

'I do, yes.' He looked about the same age as Jack Taylor, just as tall but – less healthy. He was pale, and his breath came in short rasps as if he'd got bronchitis.

148

'And you are Mr...?'

'Archie Weston.'

The name meant nothing to Max but, as he lived in the village, one of the many uniformed officers doing the house-to-house inquiries would have questioned him about the day Bradley Johnson was murdered.

'I'm sure you've both been asked about–'

'We have,' Jack Taylor cut him off. 'Bloody hell, you lot are hopeless. I thought you had all sorts of clever ways of tracking down killers these days. What about DNA and stuff like that? You want to watch more telly, my lad.'

My lad? Max might be half their age, but even so, they made him feel like a raw recruit.

'We do,' he said, 'and that's why we're particularly interested in people who own dogs.' He turned to Mr Weston. 'I don't suppose you own a dog, do you?'

'As a matter of fact I do,' he said. 'The sister of this one.' He nodded at Jack Taylor's collie. 'She's in Rawtenstall being bathed today.'

Max made a mental note not to mention blasted dogs again. Everyone in Kelton Bridge had one.

'Is Jess a suspect?' the man asked with a chuckle. 'If I've told her once, I've told her fifty times that she can't go round bashing people over the head.'

Max chose to ignore that.

149

'There's a possibility that Bradley Johnson may have been blackmailing someone,' he said.

'What the bloody hell does that have to do with us?' Jack Taylor demanded.

The simplest of statements had his blood pressure raised. Max was convinced he knew something.

'Word gets around these villages,' Max explained. 'Someone will have heard something.'

'Not us,' Taylor assured him.

'What about you, Mr Weston?'

'Nope. I can't say as I've heard anything.' A sudden coughing fit had him gasping and it was several moments before he was able to continue. 'You get newcomers to the village,' he said when he could draw breath again, 'and you get trouble. That's a fact.'

Jack's collie began licking Max's hand and, as he looked down at her, her tail wagged joyously.

'I suppose your dog needs a lot of exercise, too, Mr Weston,' Max murmured.

'Jess? She does weightlifting,' he answered with amusement. 'It comes in handy when she wants to bash people over the head.'

'The afternoon Bradley Johnson was murdered,' Max said, tired of playing games with them. 'Where were you both?'

'I've told you countless times,' Jack exploded.

150

'No, you haven't. You've told me you can't remember. This is a murder investigation, and can't remember isn't good enough.' He let that sink in. 'What about you, Mr Weston? Where were you?'

'Ah, well, I had a very nice young policewoman asking me that same thing. A young blonde girl from Gloucestershire. Needed fattening up a bit, but a nice lass.'

'PC Williams,' Max guessed, recognizing the description of one of the newest recruits.

'Yes, that's her. As I told her, I can't rightly remember.'

'At the hospital probably,' Jack suggested.

'Ah, yes, I might have been there.' He rubbed at his chin. 'So perhaps I have an alibi, after all. Alibi, that's what you call it, don't you?'

'It is,' Max said, his patience wearing thin.

'I might have been there,' Archie Weston said. 'You can see my appointment letters if you like.'

'Thank you. I'll do that.'

'You'll what?' Jack demanded. 'What the bloody hell do you want to do that for? If Archie says he were at the hospital, that's where he were. Good God, I remember a time when a man's word were worth something.'

'If only we could return to those times,' Max agreed pleasantly. 'However, as things stand, I need to eliminate as many people as

151

possible. And Mr Weston hasn't said he was there. He's merely offered it as a possibility.'

There was a knock on the door and Jack went to see who it was.

Seconds later, an exceptionally well-groomed border collie bounded into the room, leapt over Archie Weston as if they'd been parted for years, jumped up at Max and tried to lick his face, then began pawing Jack Taylor's dog and barking with sheer joy.

'You'd best let 'em out, Jack,' Archie suggested. 'And don't wander off, Jess,' he warned the exuberant dog, 'because you're a murder suspect. They'll be taking your paw prints next.'

He laughed at his own joke until he was coughing and gasping for air in a way that would have floored most men. Max wouldn't have been at all surprised to find he'd been at the hospital getting that checked out.

While Archie fought for breath, Max stood at the window to watch the two dogs chasing each other up and down the long length of the garden.

'Right,' he said, turning to face Archie Weston. 'I'll see that letter. When will you be home?'

'In about an hour. Probably. I'm stopping at the butcher's and I need to get some milk from the shop – yes, I might be home in about an hour.'

And he might not, Max suspected.

152

'You'll be there this evening, will you?'

'I might be.'

'I'll call in about seven.'

Away from Jack Taylor, Archie might be more approachable. God, he felt like a headmaster splitting up two naughty schoolchildren.

It was getting on for seven thirty that evening when Max knocked on Archie Weston's door.

As Weston had said, PC Williams had spoken to him last week and, at that time, he hadn't been able to remember where he'd been on the day in question. Max wasn't surprised that Jack Taylor had suggested the hospital as his possible whereabouts. If ever there was a candidate for urgent hospital treatment, it was Archie. Assuming the NHS was doing its job properly, which Max wouldn't put money on, he would be having tests to make sure that cough wasn't connected to something serious.

The door swung open and Archie Weston, far more welcoming than his friend, stood back to allow him entry. As soon as Max stepped into the hall, the border collie launched herself.

'Sorry about the dog,' Weston said. 'I've not been well lately so she hasn't had the exercise or the training she needs. I did walk her into Bacup this afternoon, but you'd never know it.'

That was a good walk for someone in the peak of condition and Archie Weston wasn't that. Max guessed though that he was as stubborn as Jack Taylor. It would take more than ill health to stop him doing exactly as he pleased.

'It's the training she needs more than anything,' he added.

Max was reminded of the first time that Ben had brought Fly home. The dog had been manic. Yet now, thanks to Ben's patience, he was a well-behaved, obedient dog. This one, however, was quivering with pent-up energy.

'Come into the front room,' Archie Weston offered. 'It's warmer. Would you like a brew? I can't offer you coffee because I don't drink it.'

'A cup of tea would be very welcome. Thank you.' A large whisky would be even better but, as soon as he'd finished here, Max was meeting Jill at the pub and the whisky could wait till then.

It was kind of him to offer and Max wanted to keep on the right side of him.

Being careful not to trip over the dog, Max followed Archie into the kitchen. 'Shall I make it?' he offered.

'No, you're all right. I might look like I'm totally buggered, lad, but I can still manage to boil a kettle.'

The kitchen was even smaller than Jack Taylor's, but the furnishings were very similar.

'Have you known Mr Taylor long?' Max asked casually.

'We've been friends all our lives. Good friends,' he added. 'Let me think, we started school seventy-three years ago and we were friends before that. It's a long time.'

'It is. The two of you must be very close.'

'We are.' Archie moved slowly about the kitchen, putting the teapot to warm, getting cups from the cupboard and milk from the fridge. 'We were to have been married on the same day. Had it all planned. Do you take sugar?'

'No, thanks.'

The cups were finally put on a tray that Max offered to carry. An offer that was turned down.

'I'm not an invalid,' Archie told him quietly.

It was no mean feat getting the tray to the 'front room' without the dog knocking it from his hands, but finally he set it down on a table next to a pile of newspapers and correspondence.

This room was warm, cosy and cluttered. Several framed photos were on a table next to the small television.

'You said you were to have been married on the same day as Mr Taylor,' Max reminded him when they were seated and

155

had their cups in their hands. 'Was it to have been a double wedding?'

'Ay, it were.' Archie pointed to one of those photos. 'That's my Gladys,' he said fondly.

The black and white photo had been taken in the forties or fifties and showed a laughing girl with blonde hair in the style of the day.

'I remember how jealous Jack and me were when her uncle invited her to stay with him. Had money, her uncle did. He thought she'd like to visit the Farnborough Air Show. I don't think she were bothered one way or the other,' he added with a small smile, 'but she knew me and Jack would have given our right arms to be there.

'There were twenty-seven people killed that day, and a lot more injured. A fighter plane – a De Havilland 110, it were – broke the sound barrier and then disintegrated over the spectators. Gladys died two weeks later.'

The story had the hairs standing up on Max's arms.

'I'm sorry,' he said, wishing the words didn't sound so inadequate.

'Life goes on,' Archie said. 'So Jack and Mary were married, and I were Jack's best man.'

'You never married?'

The question seemed to surprise him. 'No.'

'Jack – Mr Taylor and his wife – they were happily married, were they?'

156

'Lord, yes. When she died, cancer it were, he were devastated. It's been the two of us ever since. Well, there's young Hannah, of course.' He nodded at the photos again.

'Ah, Hannah Brooks. Of course, she's Mr Taylor's granddaughter, isn't she?'

'My goddaughter, too,' Archie said proudly. 'When Jack and me worked in the pit,' he added, 'we were paid-up members of the Labour Party so it goes against the grain to vote Tory. Mind, they can't be any worse than this lot, can they?'

'Probably not,' Max agreed with amusement. 'So you worked in the mine together?'

'We did. Of course, they're all gone now.' Tea sloshed into his saucer as he began coughing. 'That's probably just as well,' he added breathlessly when it was over.

'Not the healthiest of occupations,' Max agreed. 'Or the safest.'

'You're right at that. Jack and me lost a few friends to the pit.'

Jack Taylor and Archie Weston were as close as two men could be. Archie would know his friend's every thought.

'Jack didn't like Bradley Johnson, did he?' Max said casually.

'He didn't. I didn't either.'

'Why's that?'

'As I said, you get new people in the village and you get trouble. That's a fact.'

'Oh, I don't know about that. A friend of

mine, Jill Kennedy, is fairly new to the village. She hasn't caused trouble.'

'Jill? Oh, she's a lovely girl. Lovely.' A twinkle appeared in his eye. 'Ah, yes. There's been a rumour that she's seeing some copper. That'll be you then.'

'It will.'

'I suppose you're one of these who don't believe in marriage?'

'On the contrary, Mr Weston–'

'Call me Archie, lad. Everyone does. Now, what were you saying?'

'Just that I'm having a hard time persuading Jill that I'm a good risk.'

'Women today.' Archie shook his head. 'Ever since they decided on this equality thing, they've been nothing but trouble.'

Max laughed at that. 'Chain them to the kitchen sink, I say.'

'That's not a bad place for them,' Archie agreed with a chuckle.

'Jill has nothing but praise for Jack so he's obviously treated her with respect. Why's that? If he's so against newcomers, why is he OK with Jill and not with Bradley Johnson?'

'Jill didn't come here throwing her money around. She didn't make out she were better than any of us.' His lips were a thin, angry line. 'She didn't – push people around. She's different, that's all.'

Max could understand that.

'You were going to show me a letter from

158

the hospital,' he reminded Archie.

'Yes. I've got it ready for you.' He got to his feet, moving stiffly across the room to take a folded piece of paper from behind the clock on the mantelpiece. 'It shows the times of my appointments if you can make any sense of it.'

Max was shocked to see from the letter that Archie was having radical radiotherapy treatment that involved visit after visit to the hospital for several weeks.

'Lung cancer,' Archie said unnecessarily. 'It's a bit of a bugger.'

'A bit of a bugger is about right, Archie. The treatment isn't very pleasant, is it?'

'It's not, but I'm free of that at last. Between us, we've decided it's a waste of time.'

'I'm sorry.'

'Don't be, lad. Some days I feel as if I could run a marathon.' He gave a wry smile. 'And some days I struggle to get out of bed in the morning. Still, I'm seventy-eight so I've had my quota. It's flown by, though. One minute I were thirty, the next I were seventy. Flown by it has.' He glanced down at the dog that had just that second settled at his feet. 'Jack'll look after her when I'm gone.'

'I'm sure he will.' Saddened, Max handed back the letter and stood up. 'It's time I was off, Archie. If you hear anything, you'll let me know?'

'I will. And if I see young Jill, I'll put in a

159

good word for you.'

'Thanks. I need all the help I can get in that direction. And thanks for the tea.'

Max stepped outside into a blizzard. Nothing was sticking, it was too windy right now, but it was snowing heavily.

He dashed to his car and, once inside, wondered why he wanted a cigarette so badly. Only that morning, he'd decided to quit. Again. And Archie Weston's laboured breathing should be enough to put off anyone for life.

He drove towards the Weaver's Retreat and passed the newsagent's. It was still open. One cigarette wouldn't hurt, would it? He'd just buy ten. Then, when they had gone, that would be it. No more.

He doubled back at the roundabout, parked outside the shop and dashed inside. There was a queue, people buying lottery tickets mostly, and Max almost changed his mind and walked out. But then he was at the counter and he soon had ten cigarettes and a box of matches in his hands.

Back in his car, he lit the cigarette, inhaled deeply, and then called himself all kinds of an idiot. He should throw them away. Now. But that would be a waste. He'd keep the remaining nine in the car, just in case...

He drove off, intending to go straight to the Weaver's Retreat, but he did a detour round the back of Bacup. He wondered if

Jill knew that Archie Weston was being – or had been – treated for terminal lung cancer. Probably not. Archie wasn't the type to broadcast the news...

He rounded the sharp bend on Greave Road and there, parked outside the Crown Inn, was Tom McQueen's car.

The Crown was one of Max's favourite pubs so dropping in to sample a pint of one of their excellent guest beers could hardly be classed as harassment.

He stepped inside and the warmth hit him.

Walking into the Crown, with its stone-flagged floors, was like stepping back in time, and that wasn't a bad thing. He went up to the bar, ordered himself a pint and then, when it was in his hand, turned around to see who was about. It was crowded, but Tom McQueen, sitting alone at a table in the corner, was easy enough to spot.

'Tom, what a surprise!' Max carried his pint to the table and, without waiting for an invitation, sat down. 'I didn't know you came here. I often call in. You get a good pint, don't you?'

'Don't tell me this is a coincidence, Trentham.'

'What? Hey, I'm off duty.' He took a swallow of his pint. It was a pity he was driving. 'You're a long way from Harrington, Tom. What brings you out to this neck of the woods?'

'I was out this way and thought I'd call in for a quick one. That's not a crime, is it?'

'Not yet. On your own, are you?' Max asked, looking around. There was no sign of the minder.

'I am.'

'It's a nice place to stop, isn't it?' Max looked at the oak beams, the jugs and horse brasses, and the roaring coal fire. 'I only stumbled across it when I came out to watch the Nutters last Easter.'

The famous Britannia Coconut Dancers performed their folk dances with blackened faces that were supposed to reflect either a pagan or medieval background, or their mining connections. No one seemed to know for sure. One theory was that the dances had originated with the Moorish pirates who settled in Cornwall and were employed in local mining. Then, when the mines and quarries opened in Lancashire in the eighteenth and nineteenth centuries, it was only natural that they should bring their expertise north. Whatever, the spectacle of the men with their black faces, and their red, white and blue arched garlands, was well worth seeing.

The subject clearly didn't interest McQueen, however. Perhaps he had other things on his mind.

'I don't suppose you've heard anything about Bradley Johnson?' Max asked. 'Anything that might interest me?'

'Not a whisper.'

'I've heard he wasn't averse to a spot of blackmail. Would you know anything about that?'

McQueen's gaze sharpened at that. 'No.'

'He wasn't blackmailing you, was he?'

'Me? God, man, what do you take me for? Blackmailed by a tosser like him? Besides,' he added, 'I've got nothing to hide. He'd have nothing on me.'

'Come on, Tom. Everyone's got something they'd rather keep private.'

'Not me.' He gave Max a smug smile. 'As pure as the driven white stuff, that's me.'

More like the filthy black slush out in the gutter.

'What would you have done if he'd tried it on?'

Grinning, McQueen leaned across the table to whisper, 'I'd have told him to fuck off.' Sitting back in his seat, he added, 'Then again, I might have bludgeoned him to death in Black's Wood. Who knows?'

He'd glanced at his watch five times in as many minutes. He had to be meeting someone.

'Does the name Claire Lawrence mean anything to you?' Max asked.

Jill had watched the local news programme from the evening that Claire had gone berserk and, other than a mention of

163

Bradley Johnson's murder, and a quick shot of McQueen and several others at a fund-raising event for the local hospice, it was all sport and weather.

'Why should it?'

Unless Max was mistaken, the question had touched a nerve.

'I just wondered. She's currently behind bars for murdering her daughter. I'm sure you remember the case, Tom.'

'No, I can't say I do.'

Liar.

McQueen emptied his glass – he'd been drinking whisky – and got to his feet. 'I'd have another but I don't want to be caught drinking and driving. Night, Chief Inspector.'

When he'd gone, Max walked to the window and gazed at the car park opposite. It was pitch black out there but, when McQueen opened his car's door, the courtesy light came on. Max could see enough to know he was making a call on his mobile phone.

He was tempted to follow him, but McQueen would be wise to that. With Max on his tail, he'd go straight home and cancel any meetings he might have had.

Max wondered if his sharp exit had been prompted by talk of Claire Lawrence. Max would look into that and see if Claire had ever rented one of McQueen's properties.

Come hell or high water, Max would have

McQueen behind bars for something. If not for murder, then for dealing. All he needed was a bit of hard evidence.

And for how long had he been saying that?

Claire had been on drugs for most of her life so she would have been an ideal candidate for one of McQueen's properties. There was no proof, but Max was convinced he preyed on the vulnerable and Claire would have been a gift to him. Not only could he squeeze rent from her, she'd soon become a valued heroin customer.

Chapter Thirteen

Jill walked out of the bookie's on Saturday morning, having wagered a small fortune on what, hopefully, were promising horses, and was heading for the newsagent's to buy her lottery ticket, when she bumped, almost literally, into Hannah Brooks. She would have to get her ticket later. It was a rollover this evening so she didn't want to forget. Still, if those horses came good, she'd be quids in.

'Hannah, hello. How are you?' She had the distinct impression that Hannah would have avoided her given half a chance.

The miscarriage had taken its toll and Jill was shocked by her appearance. Although three or four inches shorter than Jill, she always seemed larger than life, one of those with boundless supplies of energy. This morning, she looked small. Or perhaps that was because her coat, a long and navy woollen one that she wore with the collar turned up and her shoulder-length fair hair tucked inside, swamped her small frame. The blue and yellow hand-knitted mittens she wore would have suited a young child.

'Hello, Jill. I'm fine, thanks.'

'And Gordon?'

'Oh, you know.'

Jill didn't, but she could guess. 'It sounds trite, I know, but things will get easier.'

'Yes. Yes, you're right. And everyone's been so kind.'

They were blocking the narrow path cleared of snow on the pavement.

'Good to see you, Jill, but I'd better get home.'

Jill was right; given the choice Hannah would have ignored her.

'I'll walk with you. It's nice to get out in this weather, isn't it? Anything's better than all that rain we had.'

'Yes.' Hannah looked resigned to having to make conversation. 'I'm sorry about Monday evening,' she said at last. 'I don't drink often and I'm afraid it went to my head. I just wanted to get – merry,' she said. 'Fat chance, eh? It was foolish of me.'

166

'Not foolish at all. Quite understandable, in fact. In the same circumstances, I would have wanted to get totally legless.'

Hannah smiled, grateful for the understanding.

'I haven't been far this morning,' she said, 'only up to Granddad's. He was out at the crack of dawn with his dog.'

'Jack's a keen walker, isn't he? How's he taking things?'

'Nothing fazes him. Disasters come and go and he takes them in his stride.'

'I saw him the other day and we were talking about Bradley Johnson,' Jill said. 'He didn't care for him, did he?'

Hannah shrugged that off. 'He didn't care for foreigners as he called them. No matter that Mr Johnson had lived in England for so long,' she added lightly. 'As far as Granddad was concerned, he was a foreigner.'

'Strange though, don't you think? To take such a strong dislike to him?'

'I wouldn't say it was a strong dislike exactly.'

Jill would have said it was exactly that.

They were out of the main street, heading towards the church. Here, because the snow hadn't been cleared from the pavement, walking side by side was difficult.

'You must have got on well with Bradley,' Jill mused.

'Me? What makes you say that?'

'Wasn't he going to help you with your campaign?'

'Oh, that. Yes, he was.' She shoved her mittened hands deep in the pockets of her coat. 'I expect the publicity would have helped him, too.'

'Ah, yes. Of course.'

'A dreadful thing to happen,' Hannah went on, trotting out the well-worn phrase. 'I do feel for his poor wife. It's just awful to think of something like that happening here in Kelton.'

'It is,' Jill agreed. 'I never really knew him, but I do like Phoebe.'

'Yes.'

'I suppose you went to their legendary parties?'

'No.'

Jill was surprised.

'We did have invites, of course,' Hannah went on, 'but we could never make it for some reason or another.'

'You didn't see Bradley and Phoebe socially?'

'No. Why would I?'

Because Bradley liked to meet local celebrities and Hannah was just that. Lately, her face hadn't been out of the *Rossendale Free Press*.

'No reason, I suppose.' The pavement narrowed and Jill stepped into the road.

'I don't know how many friends Phoebe

168

has,' she went on when she was able to walk beside Hannah again, 'but she needs every one of them right now. It will get easier for her once the killer has been caught. It will give her closure. Until then, she won't be able to get on with her life.'

'I suppose so.'

'The trouble is,' Jill went on, 'that people don't talk. Either they feel they're betraying a confidence or it's just natural for them to keep gossip to themselves. It would be so much easier, and so much better for poor Phoebe, if people talked.'

'I suppose it would.'

Jill was hoping to shame her into saying something, but Hannah remained tight-lipped.

'Your grandfather often walks in Black's Wood, doesn't he?'

'I don't know about often. He sometimes does, yes. Why do you ask?'

'Do you think he'd tell us if he'd seen something or heard something?'

'Of course he would. Why wouldn't he?' As well as defensive, she sounded angry.

'Yes, I'm sure you're right.'

They had passed the church and were only a couple of hundred yards from Hannah's house.

'If you hear anything, anything at all, will you let me know, Hannah?'

'Oh, yes, of course I will. It's just awful to

169

have this hanging over Kelton. No one can relax, can they?' It seemed to Jill that Hannah was relieved to have the conversation almost over. 'Although I doubt if people will talk to me. Besides, who would know anything about it? I'm sure no one local is responsible.'

Jill wasn't sure of any such thing.

'Perhaps you're right,' she said. 'Well, it's good to see you, Hannah. Give Gordon my regards, won't you?'

'Of course, I will. Thanks, Jill. Good to see you, too.'

She marched off quickly, hunting in her pocket for her house keys as she went. Jill stood watching until she dived inside her house and closed the door on the world.

Chapter Fourteen

Max was getting seriously annoyed. No one was talking. They exchanged their knowing glances, they spoke in riddles, but no one said anything of value. No one claimed to have seen anything.

Except Ella, of course. She'd seen Bradley Johnson on that fateful afternoon.

No one else had, though.

In Kelton Bridge, where it was impossible to sneeze without the whole damn village

170

taking bets on an early death from pneumonia, someone must have seen something.

'Can I get you a drink, Chief Inspector?'

Max dragged his attention back to Phoebe Johnson. 'A coffee would be welcome. Thanks.'

She left him in the sitting room and he could hear her clattering around in the kitchen.

Max sat, then stood up again with his back to the fire. He was restless. Until someone gave him something to go on, he couldn't get his teeth into this investigation.

When Phoebe returned, carrying a tray on which sat two coffees and a plate of mint chocolates, it struck him again how composed she was. Too composed for a woman whose husband had been murdered?

How could one tell? Relationships came in all shapes and sizes, and people dealt with grief in countless ways.

'Thank you.' He picked up his coffee, sat in a chair by the fire, and waited for her to sit opposite. 'You said your sons hadn't been in Kelton for six weeks,' he began. 'Are you sure they didn't pay a visit more recently? Perhaps a brief flying visit?'

The question startled her. 'A flying visit?' She took a sip of her coffee. 'Oh, yes, that's right. They popped in a fortnight ago, the Saturday before...' Her voice trailed away. 'Sorry, that slipped my mind.'

Just as it had slipped Keiran's mind. And Tyler's.

'That's OK. We've been talking to their friends at the universities and–'

'Why?'

Because they're a pair of lying so-and-sos. Because, as Max's dad would say, they both needed a bloody good hiding.

'It's routine. We're trying to build up a picture of your husband's movements during his last days. Why did they visit?'

'No reason. I gather they were at a loose end and decided to call in.'

According to a friend and fellow student of Keiran's, the lad had been 'summoned' to the manor.

'You'd have to ask them,' she added lamely.

'Where are they today?'

'I've no idea.' She smiled at that. 'It's been a long time since I've expected to know where they are and who they're with, Chief Inspector.'

Outwardly, she was polite and helpful. But inwardly? Or perhaps she really had forgotten her sons' visit to the manor, and perhaps she was clueless as to their current whereabouts.

'Would you ask them to give me a ring when they return?'

'Of course. If you think it's necessary.'

Max did.

'I'm still curious about how your husband came to meet Thomas McQueen,' he said.

'Can you think back and try to remember exactly what your husband said about him?'

'I don't think he ever said anything. He gave me a list of people he wanted at that last party and Mr McQueen was on it. I've no idea how they met.'

'McQueen is a bit of a dubious character.' He decided to settle for the understatement. 'He has a somewhat colourful past. Did your husband know about that?'

'I've no idea. I've told you, Chief Inspector, he never mentioned the man to me.'

'Someone suggested your husband had dabbled in blackmail,' he said quietly, and she let out a shocked gasp.

'I'm sorry,' Max said, 'but we need to examine every possibility.'

She nodded her acceptance.

'I don't suppose you knew anything about blackmail?'

'Of course not. And I don't believe it for a moment. It's yet another horrid rumour, that's all. People were jealous of him. Of us. Of our lifestyle. People spread malicious lies.'

Before Max could comment on that, Tyler's car was heard pulling up outside.

'That'll be Tyler and Keiran,' she said. 'I'll tell them you'd like a word.'

Max timed it. Almost three and a half minutes to tell them he'd like a word?

When they arrived, it was Tyler who, once again, dominated the room. Yet, according to

173

students at Lancaster, Keiran was the party animal. He was the one who, allegedly, went on drinking binges and was often too 'out of it' to get to lectures.

'Chief Inspector,' Tyler greeted him. 'I gather you want to ask us yet more questions?'

Tyler was cocky and arrogant.

'I just wondered why neither of you mentioned coming to the manor a fortnight ago,' Max said pleasantly.

'There was nothing worth mentioning,' Tyler assured him. 'We were only here for an hour.'

'That's right,' Keiran agreed. 'We were out for a drive and called in for a quick coffee with the folks.'

'And your father was here?'

'Yes.'

Keiran looked scared to death. Or hungover. Perhaps both.

'You say you were out for a drive? Why was that? Where did you go?'

'Until a month ago,' Tyler explained patiently, 'we were both driving around in old wrecks of cars. Keiran still is. I was given some money for my twenty-first and last month I decided to get a new one. We fancied going out and putting it through its paces.'

'Ah, I see. And where did you go to put it through its paces?'

'We drove down the M6 from Lancaster,

and were planning to go into Manchester for a wander round the shops. Because we stopped off here for a coffee, though, we decided to go straight back to Lancaster.'

'Your visit was unannounced?'

'Yes. A spur of the moment thing,' Tyler insisted.

Max didn't believe him.

'And you saw your father? He wasn't working?'

'We saw him – a quick hello and goodbye,' Keiran explained.

'And how did he seem?'

'How do you mean?'

'Was he pleased to see you? Was he busy? Was he about to go out? Was he having a relaxing day at home?'

'He was fine. As Keiran said, we only stopped for a quick coffee.'

'And your car?' Max asked. 'Did it perform well?'

'Very well,' Tyler said, and Max recognized the satisfaction of a young person pleased with his car.

'You've got the Mini One convertible, yes? 1.6?'

'That's right.'

'About fifteen grand on the road?'

'Give or take, yes.'

'That's a lot of money for a student to fork out,' Max remarked.

'As I said, I had some money for my

twenty-first. And Dad helped me out with a loan. He said I could pay him back as soon as I was working and had a decent income.'

'More coffee, Chief Inspector?' Phoebe asked.

'Not for me, thanks.' Max waved a dismissive hand. 'Someone at your university Keiran, was under the impression that you visited the manor at your father's request. Summoned was the word used, I believe.'

'For God's sake.' Tyler always answered for his younger brother. 'Whatever gave them that idea? Well, Chief Inspector, it's nonsense. It was a spur of the moment, social call. Nothing more and nothing less.'

Max was wasting his time. Whatever these three people knew, and he was sure that Phoebe knew more than she was saying, he wasn't going to uncover it here.

'Right, I'll be off then,' he said. 'Thanks for your time. When I have any news, I'll be in touch.'

He could sense the relief they felt at his imminent departure.

Max decided that the team needed to spend more time questioning students at Lancaster and Sheffield Universities. If Keiran had complained to a friend about being 'summoned' by his father to Kelton Bridge, he could well have complained about other things.

It would be useful to find out how Tyler

176

bought that car, too.

As Max walked back to Jill's cottage, he thought about his relationship with his own brother. They were close, yet they hadn't spent every minute together. They'd had their own friends and only got together for special occasions. When Dave had been at university, he'd hung out with his own friends. Max had never been near the place. Yet Keiran and Tyler didn't seem to move without the other by their side.

This case, he decided irritably, was one of those that brought more questions than answers.

Chapter Fifteen

Jill was back at Styal on Monday morning and she was shocked by Claire's appearance. She looked ill. Her skin was dull and grey, and dark circles surrounded her eyes.

'Have you had trouble sleeping lately?' she asked her.

'No more than usual.'

'You look tired.'

Claire grinned at that. 'I've got plenty of time to sleep.' That was true enough. If you could stand the noise, you could sleep all day if you chose.

'I don't think I'll be able to come again,' Jill told her.

Claire looked horrified, just as Jill had suspected – and hoped – she would. She was enjoying these visits. They broke up the monotony of her days, and provided mental stimulation. Claire could tell her what she chose. She could whet her appetite, make her think she was about to reveal the where-abouts of her daughter's body. In short, she could play games for as long as she chose.

'Why?'

'Funding,' Jill explained. 'It's obvious you're not going to tell me, or anyone else for that matter, what you did with Daisy's body. It's a waste of taxpayers' time and money. A waste of my time and yours, too.'

'Who says I'm not going to?' Her lips twisted sulkily. 'I said I might. And I might.'

'Might? That's no good. The taxpayers don't like paying for might.' Jill shrugged. 'It's no big deal. No one can make you talk.'

'They can't.' Claire looked at Jill. 'So what will you do instead?'

'Me?' Jill chuckled at that. 'I've got masses of work to do. I'll be glad to be sitting in the office able to get on with it.'

That much at least was true. She had staff assessments to deal with. She was behind with them.

Added to that, she had a book to finish. Her deadline was the end of January and she knew from experience how Christmas and New Year celebrations interfered with deadlines. She'd finished chapter four which dealt, admirably she thought, with releasing mental trivia to de-stress, but there was still a long way to go.

Harry and Ben were due home this afternoon so at least her evenings would be free for writing now. She'd grown used to having Max around, or used to having his clutter around, she supposed. It was difficult to get used to having him about the place because they'd seen so little of each other.

'Will they send someone else to talk to me?' Claire asked sulkily.

'No. They'll write it off as a lost cause.'

'So they don't care?'

'They care,' Jill answered, 'but they know you won't talk. So,' she went on brightly, 'what shall we talk about today? Tell you what, let's talk about Thomas McQueen.'

'Never heard of him.' Claire began rubbing at her arm. A big red scab was healing, but it would soon be raw again.

'OK. Let me refresh your memory. He's the man you rented a flat from. Shortly before Peter walked out, when he was working on the farm, you lived in flat number four, Rose House, Jubilee Avenue. Remember? That belongs to McQueen.'

Claire gave a sulky shrug. 'Does it?'

'He was the chap on the television the

night you hurled a chair at the set.'

'Was he?'

'Yes. He's a short, fat thug of a bloke who wears his hair in a ponytail. An arrogant bastard. A crook through and through.'

'Really?'

'Really. If there were any justice in this world, he'd be locked up. Like you.'

'What for?'

'Drug dealing possibly.'

'Is that all?' she scoffed. 'Bloody hell, he's guilty of a lot more than that.'

'Ah, so you do remember him.'

'I remember hearing stories about him,' Claire admitted.

Jill leaned back in the flimsy plastic chair. 'Tell me what you know about him. Everything you can think of.'

'Like what?'

'Anything at all. How did you come to rent the flat?'

'We'd been kicked out of the one on Burnley Road,' Claire explained, 'and a punter told me about one that was empty.'

'What was the punter's name?'

Claire shrugged. 'No idea. I never asked their names.'

'Was he a regular?'

'I went with him half a dozen times. Anyway, it was him who gave me a phone number for the flat. Peter phoned and we moved in. We were only there a few weeks.'

'And you didn't know it belonged to Mc-
Queen?' Jill asked doubtfully.

'No. A bloke called round on Fridays to
collect the rent.'

'What was his name?'

'I never asked.'

Claire had scratched so hard at the patch
on her arm that blood was dripping from it.
Her hands were shaking, too.

'I think you're lying, Claire. You know Mc-
Queen. I bet you got heroin from him? He
sells it, doesn't he?'

'I don't want to talk about him,' Claire
replied. 'You'd be wise to forget him, too.
People around McQueen have a nasty habit
of ending up dead.'

'Like who?'

Claire's mind seemed to be a lifetime away.

'There were a lad who supposedly worked
for McQueen.' She licked cracked, dry lips.
'He's dead now. I saw it on the telly.'

'Oh? Who was that?'

Clare shrugged.

'Muhammed Khalil?' Jill ventured, and
Claire visibly jumped.

'Just a hunch,' Jill explained. 'Do you
think McQueen had anything to do with his
death?'

'If he did, he'll get away with it.' Claire was
scratching her arm even more vigorously.
'All his money, his flash house, his cars, his
bodyguards – he's got the lot, hasn't he? No

one will touch people like him. They're all too far up his arse.'

'No one's immune from the law, Claire.'

'McQueen is.'

She stopped scratching her arm and began nibbling on fingernails that were already down to the quick.

'What do you know about Muhammed Khalil?' Jill asked. 'Did you know any of his friends?'

'Course not. It were his girlfriend who reckoned he worked for McQueen. Chammy. She sometimes worked on Dale Street with us.'

'Chammy who?'

'I only ever knew her as Chammy. You can't miss her, though. Six feet tall, dark hair. Asian. She were always busy.' Claire flicked a hand through her own, now greying hair. 'Lovely dark hair she has.'

Jill wouldn't get too hopeful. Claire's memories were a couple of years old and girls like her and Chammy moved around a lot.

'What about McQueen, Claire? What do you know about him?'

Claire was silent for a long time.

'I'm tired now,' she said at last.

'Tell me about McQueen,' Jill urged her.

'I don't know nothing about him.' She pushed back her chair and stood up. 'I don't want to talk no more.'

Damn it.

Chapter Sixteen

Max couldn't believe the state of his office. At some point during the night, the paper fairy must have visited and deposited mountains of crap. It was everywhere. His office alone must account for the devastation of half a rain forest.

Or perhaps his office had been broken into and ransacked during the night. How the hell could you tell?

He picked up three memos, saw they were related to budgets, and threw them in an already overflowing wastepaper bin.

He checked the incident log on his computer and, although it had been a busy night, there was nothing that looked as if it had anything to do with his case.

Harry and Ben had arrived home on Monday full of talk of their trip to France. Now, though, they were getting excited about Christmas. At this rate, unless they had a major breakthrough, Max would be lucky to see them at Christmas.

And how the hell had that sneaked up on him again? In three weeks, Christmas would have been and gone.

His own office was free of decorations but

he only had to open his door to see that the odd length of tinsel had appeared. That was DS Warne's fault. As soon as December arrived, she turned into someone with the mental age of a five-year-old.

Max hated Christmas. It was a complete waste of time and money. All it did was get in the way of life.

He knew he must sort through that paper-work in case there was anything important lurking there but, before he had a chance, DS Warne herself burst into his office.

'You're gonna love this, guv.'

Christmas fervour aside, Grace was a damn good sergeant. Because she still had enthusiasm for the job, and still had ideals, her excitement was infectious.

'I hope so. What have you got?'

'Firstly, I found Claire Lawrence's Chammy.' Grace was breathless with excite-ment. 'She'd been living with some bloke in Manchester, but she's back in Harrington now. She's still working the streets. I man-aged to have a quick chat with her. It was quick, too. According to her, Muhammed Khalil dumped her and then took up with another girl – another prostitute. English girl.' Grace looked at the notepad in her hand. 'Tessa Bailey. Tessa hasn't been seen for a couple of weeks, but I've put the word out.'

Max was impressed. It was only three days

since Jill's chat with Claire Lawrence.

'It's not much,' Grace admitted, 'but Chammy, when pushed, said Muhammed claimed he did work for Tom McQueen.'

She was right; it wasn't much.

'But that's not all. Your friend and mine, Tom McQueen, was having dinner at the Royal in Harrington the night after that party Bradley Johnson gave.' She grinned at Max. 'I'm surprised you didn't have the next table, guv.'

'Me harass a friend of the Chief Constable's? Perish the thought. And what's so interesting about that?'

'McQueen paid,' she said. 'Which probably means that his guest was there at his invitation, don't you think?'

'Probably,' Max agreed. 'Who was his guest?'

'None other than the late Bradley Johnson.'

'Well, well, well. Strange that McQueen can remember the party – just about – and forget that he had dinner with the bloke the next night.'

'Exactly what I thought, guv.'

'Strange that Phoebe Johnson didn't remember, too.'

'Do you want me to go and have a word with him?' Grace asked eagerly.

Max raised dark eyebrows at that. 'You can come with me, but McQueen's mine.' He stood up and pulled his jacket from the back of his chair. 'Let's see if we can find him. God, I'm getting pissed off with this bloke.'

'Be great to nick him, wouldn't it?' Grace agreed wistfully.

'It would but, so far, we have nothing more than obstruction...'

When Grace stopped the car outside the metal gates that kept intruders out of Thomas McQueen's home, Mrs McQueen was taking shopping bags from the boot of a silver Mercedes. She looked up and must have recognized Max because she walked over to the gates and entered the appropriate code.

'Very gracious of her,' Grace murmured, as she drove through.

Barbara McQueen was standing by the front door, shopping bags hanging from both arms, as they got out of the car.

'Are you here to see Tommy again?' she asked.

'We'd like a word,' Max told her. 'Is he here?'

'He was. You'd better come in. Mind,' she added as she headed for the front door, 'you won't be welcome. He's got his accountant with him today. Mention the amount of income tax he pays, and Tommy always gets stressed. Reckons he's paying single-handed to keep all these illegal immigrants in

186

luxury.' She laughed at that.

Max guessed that Tom's tax bill was a lot less than it should be. If it wasn't, his accountant would have been sacked long ago. Or bludgeoned to death.

'Damn it!' Finding the door locked, she hammered on it, received no response and had to put down her bags to hunt through her handbag for her key. 'Perhaps you're out of luck, Chief Inspector. Looks like no one's in after all.'

Unfortunately, the dogs were in. Overweight or not, that Rottweiler wasn't to be trusted. It was looking longingly at Max and slavering, while the Westie leapt around Barbara McQueen's legs.

'Come in,' Barbara said, 'and I'll give Tommy a shout.'

A shout was something of an understatement. If McQueen had been within a ten-mile radius of the house, he would have heard his wife yelling for him.

'I'll phone him for you,' Barbara said, dropping bags on the carpet in the hall to hunt through her cavernous handbag once again, this time for her mobile phone.

'Thanks.'

'You can't accuse me of not being helpful to the police,' she said smoothly.

Max didn't comment on that. Like Grace, he was too busy keeping his limbs out of reach of the Rottweiler.

She hit a number on her mobile, and while she waited for her call to be answered, Max tried to remember any previous meeting with her. He couldn't, yet every time he saw her, he had a sense of déjà vu.

'Tommy, darling,' she said at last, 'the coppers are here to see you again... Well, I don't know, do I...? How long are you going to be then...? OK... Right... Yes, yes... Bye, darling.'

She ended the call, opened her mouth to speak and then broke off.

'Can we see Mr McQueen?' Grace broke in impatiently.

'Yes.' Barbara's gaze remained on Max as she answered. 'He's on his way home. He'll be here in about ten minutes.'

'We'll wait,' Grace told her.

And still Barbara continued to stare at Max.

'I knew it!' She suddenly laughed. 'I knew I recognized you.'

'I think you have the advantage.' Damn it, he never forgot a face. He hadn't forgotten hers, technically, he supposed, but he'd forgotten where and when they had met.

'I can even tell you the date,' she said like a child with a secret. 'It was years ago, I wouldn't care to think how many, but it was the fourteenth of May. You'd been to a funeral in London.'

Max felt his world shift as the memories

raced back to him.

He'd travelled to London the previous day, spent the night there and then attended the funeral of Bill Darby, his first boss when he joined the force. It had to be eight years ago now.

'That was you?' he said, and he could have kicked himself. Of course it was.

He could remember the journey and he could remember their conversation, but he wouldn't have been able to say if his companion on the London to Manchester train that night had been brunette or blonde, tall or short.

'We got drunk together,' she explained, more for Grace's benefit than his.

'It was your birthday,' Max recalled.

'Yeah, and I'd been dumped by Mark Yates.' She smiled. 'I thought it was the end of the world.'

Max could remember thinking that Mark Yates must have been mad. She'd been attractive, full of life and fun. He supposed she still was. Dim, but fun-loving.

He'd bought her a drink to console her. And then another.

Bill's death, at the age of forty-three, had been a stark reminder both of Max's own mortality and of his general dissatisfaction with life. He'd been heading home to his wife and kids. Going home to a dull, stale marriage.

189

So they'd had another drink.

'What happened to you?' Barbara asked. 'Your marriage? Did you work it out?'

'Linda died.'

'God, I'm sorry.'

'Thanks,' he said awkwardly. 'She was ill at the time,' he explained, 'but we didn't know. I thought she was–'

'Depressed,' Barbara answered for him. 'That's what you said. Depressed.'

She was being kind because Linda was dead. Max might have mentioned the word depressed but, with a few drinks inside him, he'd uttered far more damning words than that. He'd dreaded going home to Linda. Only the thought of his kids had stopped him suggesting that he and Barbara continued to drown their respective sorrows in a bar in Manchester.

'Two boys you had, is that right?'

'Yes. Harry and Ben. They're fine.'

He hadn't forgotten that train journey. For Max, it had been a turning point. Pouring out his troubles to an attractive stranger had shown him exactly how much he hated his marriage and how he longed to be free. Two strangers complaining about the problems in their lives, and he hadn't even asked her name. Or if he had, he hadn't bothered to remember it.

Two weeks after that train journey, he'd met Jill.

'What about you?' he asked her, ignoring Grace's impatient sigh.

'If you remember, I was coming to Harrington to visit my aunt,' she said. 'It was on that visit that I met my Tommy.' She gave him a broad smile. 'Who'd have thought it, eh? We were both as miserable as sin that night, and here we are, as happy as Larry.' She coloured. 'Well, I am. I'm sorry about your wife. Really sorry.'

'Thanks.'

Grace sighed again, and Barbara brushed off all thoughts of that train journey. 'Do you want a coffee or something while you wait for Tommy?'

'Coffee would be good. Thanks,' Max said.

'Same for me, please,' Grace said grudgingly.

How had that young woman with whom he'd shared a three-hour train journey come to marry a man like Tom McQueen? OK, so she wasn't very bright, but even so, she was a kind, thoughtful person. A fun person. Did she have any idea how her husband filled his spare time?

Perhaps she didn't. After all, Tom McQueen had dinner with the Chief Constable no less.

Snippets of that long-ago conversation came back to Max. 'Stuff love,' a drunken Barbara had said. 'I'm going for money next time...' Maybe she had been serious. Perhaps a healthy bank account was Tom McQueen's only attraction.

She'd been heartbroken about her break-up with Mark Yates, or had appeared so. Yet only days later she'd met Tom and been swept off her feet. No, he couldn't believe that. If he were a betting man, he'd stake a lot on her marrying for money.

They stood around in her kitchen drinking their coffee and spoke of everything from the weather to the new wine bar in Bacup. Yet Max couldn't shake off thoughts of that train journey. The forced trip down Memory Lane had unsettled him.

In fact, when Tom McQueen finally arrived, he'd completely forgotten what they had called for.

'The party you attended at Kelton Manor, Mr McQueen?' Grace asked. 'Did you see Bradley Johnson after that?'

Thankfully, Grace was eager to get her questions answered and Max dragged his mind back to the present.

'No. I've already told you lot that,' McQueen answered.

'You didn't have dinner with him at the Royal in Harrington the following night?' Max asked him. 'You want to get your memory checked out, Tom. It could be early onset Alzheimer's or anything. I'll have to help you out here. You paid on your Visa card. You ordered – what was it, DS Warne?'

She consulted her notebook. 'Grilled asparagus followed by duck breast in orange and cointreau sauce.'

'Ring any bells?' Max asked.

'You're right,' McQueen said. 'Yes, I remember now. Babs was away, weren't you, poppet?'

'Yes, that's right.'

'Where?' Max asked, suspecting she was lying.

'Visiting my aunt,' she replied, smiling sweetly at him. 'She'll verify it. Do you want me to phone her now?'

'No need for that.' Max turned his attention back to Tom McQueen. 'You were saying?'

'As Babs was away, I planned to eat out. I always do. I was on my way to the Royal when I bumped into Bradley Johnson. I asked if he cared to join me. After all, I'd enjoyed his hospitality the previous night. So we had dinner together.' He gave Max a sly look. 'That's not a crime, is it?'

'No.'

'And as you've been so thorough, Chief Inspector, you'll know that, after Johnson called a taxi to take him home, I stayed there for another couple of drinks.'

'So we believe,' Grace said. 'What did you talk about during your dinner?'

'This and that. Nothing of any importance.'

'I don't suppose you can remember that, either,' she said, sarcasm dripping from her voice.

'Not really, no. Oh, I remember he went on about his sons and how well they're both doing. He'd helped one of them buy a car, I seem to recall. A typical parent,' McQueen added. 'One of those who can't help boring people to death by raving about their kids. Blimey, and he thought I was missing out. The thought of kids bores me rigid. And you, eh, Babs?'

'We've never wanted children,' Barbara McQueen explained.

She was lying. On that train journey, she'd told him how lucky he was to have children. *I couldn't bear to die without leaving something behind, my own flesh and blood. It would make life so pointless, wouldn't it?*

'That's convenient,' Max murmured. 'Both of you not wanting children, I mean. If one partner wants children and the other doesn't, it can cause a lot of problems.'

'We're very lucky,' Barbara murmured. 'There was a time when I thought – well, I suppose most women do, don't they? But then my cousins had children and I realized it wasn't for me. I'm far too selfish for that.'

So she'd changed her mind? It was feasible, Max supposed.

'What did Johnson say about the car he'd bought his son?' he asked McQueen.

'God knows. I'd lost the will to live by then. It was a top of the range something or other.'

'A Mini?'

'Yes, that was it. He was very proud of the one son, but the other was giving him problems, I gather. And no, he didn't go into details so I don't know what sort of problems. He didn't say, and I didn't ask. I was more interested in my – what was it? – oh yes, duck in orange and cointreau.'

'Tommy likes his food,' Barbara put in.

'So I see,' Max murmured. 'And this meeting with Johnson was pure coincidence, Tom? Are you sure about that?'

'I am. I would have mentioned it earlier, but I'd forgotten all about it. Just a boring meal, Chief Inspector. Nothing more and nothing less.'

'I hope so,' Max told him. 'If I find there was more to it, you'll be up on a charge of obstruction.'

McQueen seemed to find that amusing. Sod him.

They left soon afterwards and Grace drove them back to Harrington.

'That sounds like quite a train ride,' she said drily. 'You made an impression there, guv.'

'I'd forgotten all about it.' That was almost true. He hadn't forgotten the journey, but he had forgotten the woman.

'It was like a mutual admiration society back there.'

'Just leave it, Grace!'

Chapter Seventeen

Snow had fallen. It was crisp and crunchy underfoot and the sun, almost set now, had shone all day. Not that Max had seen much of it. He'd spent most of the day at his desk, going over everything again and again.

He'd called on Jill more out of a sense of duty than anything else. He felt bad because he hadn't seen much of her since the boys had returned from France. Come to that, he hadn't seen much of Harry and Ben, either.

He walked with his hands in his pockets. Jill, beside him, had hers encased in black gloves. He was well aware of the foot of space that separated them.

'You OK?' she asked.

'Me? Fine?'

'Right,' she said in a way that made it clear she didn't believe him but, if he couldn't be bothered to tell her, she couldn't be bothered to ask.

Max wasn't fine. Hadn't been fine since his chat with Barbara McQueen, in fact.

With one look, one reminder, she'd

brought back memories that Max had chosen to forget. Painful memories.

Back then, his marriage, along with several others he'd known about, had been hell. He hadn't understood the reasons for it, either. Most of the time, he'd accepted that it was his own fault for working long, erratic hours and drinking too much. Linda had hated that. But surely, there had been more to it than that. All he had known was that, given the choice, he would never be part of a relationship again.

Obviously, he would have given all he had for the doctors to find a miracle cure. Linda had been the mother of his boys and, if strength of will could have saved her, she would still be his wife, and still be loving his sons. As it turned out, strength of will had been as ineffective as medical treatment.

Since her death, he'd forgotten the hell that was their marriage and only remembered the sense of guilt and loss her death had left him with.

How effortlessly Barbara McQueen had reminded him of the man he had been then.

Would he have left Linda if she'd lived? Would she have walked out on him? It was impossible to know. Yet Max had known he couldn't have taken much more of it.

What madness, he wondered, was pushing him into a relationship with Jill?

He was happy with his lot. Why change it?

People said that kids were a tie. His weren't. They never complained about the limited time they had with him. Instead, they enjoyed what little there was to the full. Linda, he recalled, had wasted many a free evening complaining about how few there were...

Thank God he had his work. With so many other things demanding his attention, he didn't have to think about the future.

'That was a big sigh for someone who's fine,' Jill said drily.

'Sorry, I was miles away.' Or years away. 'I was just wondering if you'd had any more thoughts on Bradley Johnson's killer?'

'I'm not on the case,' she reminded him, 'so I only know what you've told me. But from the photos...' She paused. 'There was no remorse shown. And there was no attempt made to hide the body. It was someone who didn't care if they were caught or not. His watch was still on his wrist and that would have been a temptation, as would the cash in his wallet. But not to your killer. Your killer held Bradley Johnson in contempt.' She looked at him and gave him a rueful smile. 'In a word, no. There's nothing I haven't already told you.'

'Someone who held him in contempt?' Max grimaced. 'That narrows it down one hell of a lot. Practically everyone in the village falls into that category.'

Max couldn't say he had any sympathy for

the man. To his way of thinking, people who resorted to blackmail deserved all they got.

They walked on into Black's Wood and both stopped at the spot where Bradley Johnson had met his Maker. Before meeting Him, though, he'd met someone else. Who?

'I still think he was planning to meet someone at the pub,' Max said. 'Whoever killed him hit him from behind. Probably hid behind this tree.' He ran his hand down the trunk of the sturdy chestnut.

'I'm not so sure.' Jill looked at the path, well-used by dog walkers, that stretched ahead. 'If it was blackmail, and I bet he'd planned on filling that money belt he was wearing, the Weaver's would be too public. This is an ideal spot for doing the dirty deed. I think he was expecting some poor unfortunate – our killer – to meet him here and hand over the cash. Neither would want to be seen. The pub would be too crowded.'

'But would they expect it to be crowded on a Wednesday afternoon?' Max was doubtful. On that particular Wednesday, the Weaver's Retreat had been busy, but only because a crowd had turned up unexpectedly after a funeral. 'It was busy that day, but Johnson would have expected it to be quiet.'

'True.'

'There was nothing found to suggest that anyone had been here waiting,' Max went on. 'Impatient feet hadn't trampled the ground.

No cigarettes or chewing gum had been discarded.'

'Of course, we don't know that it was blackmail,' she pointed out. 'Maybe he'd been to the bank and deposited the contents of his money belt.'

'No. We checked.'

Max realized they weren't alone in the wood.

'I've never been here without bumping into him,' he muttered beneath his breath as he spotted the other person in Black's Wood. 'He spends all his time here.'

Jack Taylor was heading straight for them with not one but two collies. His back stiffened when he spotted them and Max half expected him to do an about turn. He didn't.

'Hello, Jill,' he said pleasantly.

'Is Archie all right?' she asked, nodding at the two dogs.

'Yes, he's fine. Well, as fine as he's likely to be. He has good days and bad days. Some days, you'd never believe there were owt wrong with him. Others, like today, well, I said I'd give Jess a good walk for him.'

He nodded curtly at Max. 'How's it going, Sherlock?'

'Badly,' Max said truthfully. 'It would help, of course,' he added sarcastically, 'if people could remember where they were on the day in question.'

Jack seemed to find that amusing. 'Ah, it's

a bugger when your memory goes.'

'It is,' Max agreed, knowing Jack's memory was as sharp as an unused razor blade.

'I don't suppose you've remembered, have you, Jack?' Jill asked him. 'It would be a great help if the police could eliminate a few more people.'

'Me? Oh, yes. I was in Rochdale that day.'

'Then why the hell didn't you say so?' Max exploded.

'You didn't ask, lad.'

'What? I've asked you countless times.'

'Ah, but I didn't remember until last night and you haven't asked me today.'

'Right,' Max said, teeth gritted. 'As you've remembered you were in Rochdale, perhaps you'll be able to give me the names of any witnesses who might be able to corroborate your story.'

'Story?' He chuckled at that. 'It's no story. I'd gone to get a battery for my watch.' He pulled back the sleeve of his overcoat to reveal a watch that was older than Moses. It had been made long before they ran on batteries. 'Not for this one,' Jack added, noting Max's disbelief, 'but for my spare. I expect I've still got the receipt. The date might be on that.'

'I'll have a look at it.'

Jack nodded slowly. 'I'll have to see if I can find it.'

'Either you find it, or I'll have you on a

charge of obstruction,' Max informed him.

'Oh, dear. We wouldn't want that, would we, Sal?' he murmured to his dog.

'We wouldn't.' Max could cheerfully throttle the bloke. He'd often wondered what drove people to commit murder. The answer was standing in front of him. 'So when will you be at home?'

Jack looked at his watch again. 'I'm taking Jess back to Archie's, then stopping off at the butcher's. About sixish, I reckon.'

Max needed to be in the incident room for a briefing at six. 'I'll see you at about seven thirty,' he told him. He should be finished by then.

'Let's hope Jess hasn't eaten it. She's a devil, this un.' He nodded at Archie's dog as she raced around nearby trees at a break-neck pace.

'It takes one to know one,' Max muttered.

'So it does,' Jack agreed. 'Now, is there anything else I can help you with?'

'Not for the moment,' Max replied.

'Right.' Jack called the dogs. His own collie raced to his side, but Archie's dog was still running around the trees in a demented fashion. 'See what I mean?' Jack said. 'Come here, Jess. Jess!'

Reluctantly, Jess heeded the call and Jack Taylor carried on his way with both dogs trotting beside him.

Max expelled a frustrated sigh as he

watched them. 'Why does he enjoy pissing me off so much?'

'I've no idea, Max,' Jill replied with amusement.

They walked on and Max tried to picture Jack Taylor as a killer. It simply didn't seem feasible. It even seemed unlikely that he had anything to hide. So why did he enjoy pissing him off?

'Do you think he does know something?' she asked curiously.

'I don't know. Yes, I do. Instinct says yes.'

'If it's blackmail we're talking, and I suppose we assume it is, his granddaughter would be an ideal candidate.'

Max had considered that. So far, though, it looked as if Hannah Brooks had never so much as parked illegally.

'Let's face it,' Jill went on, 'parliamentary candidates can have their futures ruined over nothing. Sleeping with the wrong person. Smoking a joint at uni. Making innocuous remarks about Africans, Asians, the young, the old–'

'True.'

'On the other hand, would her grandfather know about it? She idolizes him. I'm not sure she'd want him knowing something of which he might disapprove.'

'I still think Tom McQueen's involved somewhere. Just why did he have dinner with Bradley Johnson?'

'You don't believe McQueen's story that it was a coincidence then?'

'If that bloke told me my name was Max Trentham I'd have to hunt out my birth certificate to check.'

It was almost eight o'clock when Max knocked on Jack Taylor's door. A light was shining in the hall so Max assumed he was in. No dog barked, though, so that wasn't encouraging.

He knocked again, harder this time, and was about to give up when he heard a muttering from the other side. The door was finally opened.

'Ah, Sherlock, I thought it might be you.' Jack looked out. 'Another blustery night.' He considered things for a moment. 'You'd better come inside before you catch your death. What you need, lad, is a good, thick overcoat.'

'It's at home,' Max told him, adding a muttered, 'along with the deerstalker.'

Jack smiled at that and finally stood aside to let Max enjoy the warmth of his home.

They went into the kitchen where Jack had been polishing brass fire irons. An old newspaper was spread across the table and a couple of blackened cloths, old pillowcases by the look of it, sat on that.

Would a man worried about an imminent visit from a copper sit and polish brass? Max didn't think so.

He'd never thought of Jack as worried, though. Stubborn, tight-lipped and highly principled, but not worried. All the same, if he did know something, he'd take that knowledge to the grave with him if he so chose.

'Would you like a brew?' he asked Max.

'I'd love one,' Max said, surprised by the offer. 'Thanks, Mr Taylor.'

'The name's Jack.'

Awkward, stubborn, determined to waste Max's time – yet Max couldn't help liking the old sod.

Max sat at the kitchen table and gazed at his distorted reflection in a brass coal shovel.

'You've done a good job,' he remarked.

'I like brass.' Jack's hand rested on the huge teapot. 'You need to clean it regularly, and do a thorough job, but it's worth the effort. It's a rich, warm metal. Not like silver.'

Max had never thought of it like that, but he knew exactly what he meant. He was about to say so when he saw Jack reach up into a cupboard and bring out a bottle of Famous Grouse.

He poured a generous measure into both mugs, then looked to see if Max was watching him.

'I often have something about now,' he explained. 'You need it this weather. It keeps out the cold.'

'A medicinal dram?'

'If you'd rather not...'

'No,' Max said quickly, having visions of his drink going down the old ceramic sink. 'You're right, it'll keep out the cold. Besides, I'm not on duty.'

'Is that a fact?' Jack chuckled. 'I bet there's something somewhere that says you can't question me if you're off duty. You coppers have gone soft,' he added, sitting opposite Max and putting their mugs in front of them. 'The other day, outside the bank, there were a couple of young lads, no more than fourteen, mouthing off at two coppers. The coppers treated them like bloody royalty. Why the hell didn't they belt 'em one?'

'Because they'd have been on an assault charge before you could say "hello, hello, hello",' Max informed him.

'Pah. Gone soft, they have.'

'It's not us coppers,' Max argued. 'It's society as a whole. Everyone has rights, these days, even scum.'

'Rights,' Jack scoffed. 'If you cause a disturbance, do damage, pinch something – well, you should lose all rights. It stands to reason.'

Max couldn't agree more.

'It's the same in schools,' Jack went on. 'In my day, you spoke when you were spoken to and not before. Step out of line and a few lashes meant you couldn't sit down for a week. These days, kids are abusive to teachers. Violent even.' He broke off to shake his head in bewilderment. 'We're in a sorry state. If there were a war tomorrow, I shudder to think what would happen. A bloody disaster, that's what.'

'Oh, I don't know. There's a lot that's wrong with the country admittedly, but there's a lot of good around, too.'

'Hm.' Jack wasn't convinced.

Max took a swig of his tea and was surprised to find that it tasted good. He'd never laced tea with whisky. Coffee, yes, but not tea.

'You make a good cup of tea, Jack.'

'I thought you'd appreciate it, lad.'

'Are you trying to grovel your way into my good books?' he asked suspiciously, and Jack laughed.

'No. I'm trying to get you drunk so that I can bash you over the head and drag your body into Black's Wood. I reckon I'd make a good killer. What do you think, Sal?' he asked, fondling the dog's ears.

'Talking of murder,' Max began, 'I don't suppose you've managed to find–'

Before he could finish, Jack left the room and returned with a tiny scrap of paper that he handed to Max.

It was a receipt for a watch battery costing three pounds ninety-nine pence. The time shown on it was 4.45 p.m., which, if it belonged to Jack, put him in the clear.

'You could have found this anywhere,' Max pointed out.

'I could,' Jack agreed nonchalantly, 'but I didn't.'

'How do I know that?'

'You'll just have to take my word for it, won't you?'

'Come on, Jack, if I took everyone at their word, I'd never make an arrest.'

'You mean people lie to you? Tut tut. Whatever next?' He put down his mug and leaned, elbows on the table, towards Max. 'I'm not lying to you,' he said seriously. 'I swear on my life, on my dog's life even, that I was in Rochdale getting that battery.'

Max believed him.

'You know something, though, don't you?'

'Like what?' Jack demanded.

'Ah, if I knew that, I'd be as wise as you.'

'I know nothing that'll make any difference to anything,' the old man vowed.

Which meant he did know something.

The collie had moved nearer to Max's feet and he leaned down to stroke her.

'Tell me about your granddaughter, Jack,' he suggested, straightening.

'What the hell does my Hannah have to do with anything?' Jack's good mood was slipping.

'I'd like to know if Bradley Johnson ever attempted to blackmail her.'

208

'Why would he do that? What's she ever done?'

'I don't know,' Max replied, 'but we know he wasn't above a spot of blackmail.'

Jack shrugged as if the subject was of no interest to him whatsoever.

'I'm sure we've all done things we wouldn't want the world to know about,' Max pushed on, 'and someone in Hannah's position would make a prime target for blackmail. Personally, I don't care who our politicians sleep with, or if they're drunken drug-takers, so long as they do the job we're paying them to do.'

'I quite agree with you.'

'But other people do care. If Hannah experimented with drugs at university or had an affair with a married man – well, it could jeopardize her future.'

'I expect it could,' Jack agreed.

'So, as far as you know, Johnson didn't attempt to blackmail her?'

'Why the bloody hell should he?' he demanded again.

'I don't know. I was hoping you'd tell me.'

'Bloody nonsense. And don't you go pestering Hannah,' he added darkly. 'She's just lost a baby, you know.'

'Yes, and I'm truly sorry about that.'

'Have you got kids?' Jack asked.

'Two boys. Harry and Ben.'

'Then you'll understand that she's had a

rough time of it.'

'Yes.'

Had Hannah Brooks done something to attract Johnson's attention? And like what? As far as they could tell, she'd never so much as thought twice about anything that might smear her spotless character.

'Another cup of tea before you go?' Jack asked, and Max nodded.

'Thanks. Easy on the tea though, Jack, eh?'

Chapter Eighteen

Tessa Bailey, Muhammed Khalil's alleged girlfriend, had proved elusive. She was well known by the other girls working the streets, but no one had known where she was. That wasn't surprising, Max supposed. Once word got out that people were looking for her, she would have done a runner. Extensive inquiries into Muhammed Khalil's murder hadn't brought up her name and she hadn't come forward. That wasn't surprising, either. People like Tessa didn't come forward.

However, unluckily for her, she'd been found in Blackburn. She was still working as a prostitute and after what, judging by the dark circles around her eyes, was a profitable night, she'd been seen going to Asda for a pack of cigarettes early this morning.

She sat facing Max now in interview room three. It was cold in there and Max didn't begrudge the mug of tea that was currently warming her hands.

'Right,' he began, 'what do you know about Tom McQueen?'

Her face, pale and grubby, registered shock. 'Eh? What the–? Now you look here, I don't know who you're talking about.'

Whatever she'd been expecting to be questioned about, it wasn't that.

'Liar.'

'I don't. Why the 'ell should I?'

'Because your ex-boyfriend knew him.'

'Which ex-boyfriend?'

'Muhammed Khalil.'

'Who says he were my–?'

'Don't play games, Tessa. We know you lived with him.' Max didn't want to alienate her. That would get him nowhere. 'McQueen won't know you've spoken to us, I promise.'

'Says who?'

'Says me.'

'Oh, yeah?'

'Yeah.'

She sat back in her chair, and Max watched some of her natural confidence return. In her early twenties, she probably scrubbed up well. When she bothered. Her dark hair was long and lank, her teeth were yellow, and there were still traces of yesterday's make-up round her eyes, but her figure was good and her skin was clear.

'What am I here for?' she demanded. 'You're supposed to get me a lawyer. I know my rights.'

'You can have a lawyer if you want one,' Max replied easily. 'As to why you're here, that's up to you. You can either tell me what you know about McQueen, or you can be charged. We'll start with soliciting or benefit fraud, something like that.' He shrugged in a friendly manner. 'The choice is yours.'

She chewed on bitten fingernails while she considered her options.

'I've never spoken to McQueen,' she said at last.

'You haven't missed much. He owned the flat you shared with Muhammed Khalil, yes?'

She nodded. 'Yeah.'

'Right. Now, McQueen claimed that Khalil paid four hundred pounds a month for the privilege. Is that right?'

'If he says so.'

'He does. He even produced a rent book showing the amounts paid.'

She shrugged at that.

'The thing is,' Max pushed on, 'I don't believe Khalil handed over that sort of cash every month. How could he? Most of the time he was out of work and, for some reason, he never got round to claiming benefit either.'

'That were his business.'

'And now I'm making it yours, Tessa. Did Muhammed pay rent?'

'Sort of.'

'Sort of? What the hell does that mean?'

'It means–' She stopped, probably to consider a benefit fraud charge, before continuing reluctantly. 'He did pay for the flat. It's just that – well, he did a few odd jobs for McQueen. It got took out of that.'

Now they were getting somewhere.

'So he was on McQueen's payroll?'

'Nah.' She looked at Max as if he were insane. 'Muhammed got the flat cheap. Then, when he didn't have the rent money, and McQueen put that up every month, McQueen said he could do a job for him.'

'What sort of job?'

'Dunno. He was doing odd jobs for him before I lived with him.'

'So was he fetching and carrying? Selling? Something like that?'

She nodded and looked on the verge of tears now. 'Is that a yes?' Max asked.

'Yeah.'

'Drugs?' Max asked.

'I dunno about that.'

Perhaps she didn't. She'd have a damn good idea though.

'And Muhammed was happy with this arrangement, was he?'

She reached into the pocket of her denim jacket and pulled out a tissue that looked as if it had cleaned roads in a previous incarnation.

'Here.' Max took a white handkerchief from his own pocket and handed it over. 'There will be less germs on that.'

'Ta.'

She blew her nose and dabbed at eyes that swam in moisture.

'No. He weren't happy,' she said finally. 'He wanted to see McQueen and tell him he wanted paying properly. The trouble were, he couldn't get near the bloke.'

'I see. So what did he do?'

'Nowt. Well, as far as I know. He did talk of breaking into McQueen's house, but it meant nowt. That way, he said, the bloke'd have to listen to him. He wouldn't, though. Blokes like him don't listen to no one.'

'Are you sure he didn't try something like that?'

'Course I am. McQueen's got a bloody great guard dog for one thing.'

'But he might have tried something else? Or he might have tried getting past the dog?'

She thought long and hard. 'He decided he'd get money another way. There were some stuff he had to deliver and–'

'What sort of stuff?'

'Dunno.'

'Tessa!'

'Crack,' she whispered finally.

So McQueen was dealing crack now. Why not? There was a growing market for it. Many addicts were using it alongside heroin.

'Right. Carry on.'

She took a deep breath. 'Muhammed decided he'd sell it on and then tell McQueen he were robbed. He got a mate to beat him up so it looked real.'

Max winced. That was a very foolish, not to say dangerous thing to do.

'How did McQueen take that?'

'Badly. He didn't believe him. Muhammed thought the best thing to do were to pack up and clear off, just in case McQueen sent someone for him.'

'And?'

She shook her head.

'And then Muhammed was dead,' Max guessed. 'Right?'

'Yeah.' She blew her nose again.

'There's something else, isn't there? Come on, Tessa. Out with it.'

'After – after that, McQueen asked for me. He knew my spot on the street, and he asked the other girls if I were about.'

'And? Did he find you?'

'About a month later, yeah. He'd been with a couple of the other girls by then.'

'Tom McQueen goes with prostitutes? Are you sure?'

'Of course I'm sure. Bleeding hell. We

215

didn't play Scrabble.'

'He went with you?'

'Yeah. And it scared me to death, I can tell you. I thought it was cos of Muhammed, you see. It couldn't have been, though. Well, he never mentioned it and I didn't.'

Max was still trying to accept that Tom McQueen paid for sex. Why the hell hadn't they discovered that particular gem?

He wanted every working girl questioned.

'So what do you think, Tessa? Do you think McQueen killed Muhammed?'

'Nah,' she scoffed. 'He'd have got one of his thugs to do it, wouldn't he?'

He would. But McQueen would have issued the order and that was good enough for Max.

'Who else was working for him, Tessa?'

'Dunno.' She spotted his doubtful expression. 'I don't. Honest. Muhammed never knew, neither. When McQueen wanted a job doing, he'd have a newspaper delivered to the flat. Muhammed knew then that he had to go to the phone box and call him. Even then, he never spoke to the man himself. It were a mobile he used to call and someone else answered it.'

'I need names,' Max urged her.

'You won't get any from me. I swear, I never knew. Muhammed didn't, either.'

Max believed her. If McQueen was good at anything, it was covering his tracks.

216

'Muhammed reckoned it were someone at Reno's who answered it,' she said, 'but he weren't sure. A couple of times, he could hear music and stuff. Reminded him of Reno's.'

Reno's was Harrington's trendy nightclub and Max had thought a law-abiding management ran it. He'd get it checked.

'Thanks for that. Now, does the name Bradley Johnson mean anything to you?' he asked her.

'The bloke who were killed? No. I don't know him. I saw it in the paper, but I never knew him.'

'McQueen did.'

'Yeah, well, we ain't on each other's Christmas card list.'

'That's not a bad thing.' He nodded at her untouched tea. 'That'll be cold.'

She took a sip and grinned at him. 'No wonder you're a detective.'

Max couldn't help smiling. 'Would you like another?'

'No, ta.' Cold or not, she drank it all. 'McQueen won't get to know I've talked to you, will he?'

'Not from me he won't.'

'And me benefits–?'

'Not my department, Tessa.'

'Ta.' She looked at him for a moment. 'I'll tell you summat else about McQueen. It's only a rumour, and probably complete bollocks, but I've heard a couple of people say that he likes kids. Young kids, not teenagers, like them pedro–'

'Paedophiles?' Max asked in astonishment.

'So folk reckon, yeah. He's married,' she added quickly, 'well, you'd know that, and she's supposed to be a looker. But people reckon it's all for show.' She pulled a face. 'As I said, it's probably just talk.'

'Probably,' Max agreed, thinking of the Barbara who had once longed for children and since changed her mind. 'I don't suppose you can give me the names of the people you heard that from, either?'

'Sorry. I would if I could, but I don't know them. It's just talk.'

'OK.'

'So can I go now?' she asked eagerly.

'You can.'

'Ta.'

Max returned to his office in the knowledge that they might, just might, be getting something on McQueen. He'd known, suspected at least, for some time that he was dealing. He simply couldn't get hard evidence. And when McQueen was arrested, he wanted to make sure that all charges would stick. No mistakes could be made.

He thought of Barbara McQueen and wondered just how happily married she was. On that London to Manchester train journey, she'd been his for the taking. Or so he'd liked to believe at the time. Had he lost his touch? Or would his irresistible charm get him an invite to her home? McQueen was away a lot so perhaps she got lonely.

Max decided that if he couldn't get into McQueen's home by fair means, he would have to resort to foul.

Chapter Nineteen

Jill and Ella were warming themselves on the radiator in Jill's kitchen. Ella had called in with sprigs of holly from her garden and was chilled. Jill, who'd been trying for over an hour to coax her boiler into life, thought she'd never be warm again. At the moment, the radiators were humming with warmth, but her cottage still felt cold.

'You used to have a holly tree in your garden,' Ella remarked, 'but it was ripped out to make way for the shed. A shame.'

Jill looked out at her frozen garden. The shed must have been there for twenty years.

'I'm going back a bit,' Ella admitted, and Jill laughed.

Ella was often 'going back a bit'. There was little she didn't know about Kelton Bridge's past.

'Perhaps I'll plant a new one.' But Jill's gardening skills were on a par with her culinary expertise. 'Or perhaps I'll leave well alone. I can pull up the odd weed and mow the lawn, but anything more technical is beyond me.'

'There's nothing technical about a holly tree,' Ella pointed out. 'Which reminds me, I've decided to get a computer.'

'Never!'

'Yes. You'll have to give me lessons. I've signed up for a course at the college – six sessions especially for Luddites like me – so I'll see how that goes.'

In the past, whenever Jill had told her how useful a computer would be, Ella had scoffed at the very idea.

'You'll be getting a mobile phone next, Ella.'

'Not on your life. Let's see if I can work this computer first.'

She gazed at Jill for a few moments. 'I suppose you're finding it quiet now that Max has gone home.'

'It's good to have my own space.'

Ella rolled her eyes at that. 'You're a hopeless liar.'

'No. Really. It is.'

'Perhaps it is,' Ella allowed, 'but you'd give all you had to have him back. I'm not blind, my girl.'

Jill was enjoying her own space. If things had been OK between them, she might have wanted him back at her cottage. But things weren't OK. Max was having one of his distant phases. It wasn't the first, not by a long way, but it was damned annoying. All Jill wanted was a normal, healthy relationship and that was practically impossible with Max. He came close enough for her to think that they had a future, and then he stepped right back.

She was about to say so, or words to that effect, when her doorbell rang.

'Saved by the bell,' Ella said drily.

Jill assumed it was the postman, but Jack Taylor and his dog were standing on her doorstep.

'Is Ella here by any chance, Jill?'

'She is, yes. Come in.'

'No, I won't do that. I've got the dog,' he added unnecessarily. The dog was currently sniffing Jill's hand in the hope that biscuits were hidden there.

'That doesn't matter. Come on in out of the wind. We're in the kitchen.'

He hesitated long enough to let the last of that hard-won heat out of the cottage and then stepped inside.

'I saw you walking this way,' he greeted Ella, 'so I guessed you'd be here. Gossiping,' he added with a wry smile.

'Gossiping? Now look here, Jack–'

'Ella Thorpe, you've–'

'Ella Thorpe? By, it's been a long time since I've been Thorpe.'

'Born a Thorpe and born a talker. That's you.'

'There's a world of difference between talking and gossiping.'

'Yes,' he allowed, 'so there is.'

He handed over the carrier bag he'd been holding. 'I've brought those leeks I promised you. Or would you rather I took them to your place to save you carrying them? I can leave them on the step.'

'No, I'll take them. Knowing you, you'll forget.'

'Of course I won't forget, woman. Streuth, I'm not senile yet.'

'Yet,' Ella teased. 'I'll take them. And thanks, Jack.'

Once again, the easy banter between the two surprised Jill. They'd both been born and brought up in the village, but even so, there was a closeness that, unless she was mistaken, went deeper than that.

'Would you like a cup of tea or a coffee?' she asked Jack.

'Thanks, Jill, but no. I can't stop. Thanks, though.'

With that, he was gone, letting another icy blast of air into the cottage.

'Do you want some leeks?' Ella asked.

'And what would I do with them?' she answered with an amused shake of her head. 'I'm sure Jack's an expert grower, but unless they come with a label stating the minutes

222

and the power level required for a micro-wave, forget it.'

'For heaven's sake, Jill, surely you can cook a leek.'

'Um, I don't know. Never tried.'

'Tell you what,' Ella said, 'you can give me computer lessons and I'll teach you how to cook.'

'It's a lost cause. Truly.'

'We'll see.' Ella nodded at Jill's floor. 'You'll need to clean that now. Jack won't go anywhere without that dog of his.'

'It's company for him.'

'It is,' Ella said softly, 'and he'll need as much of that as he can get when Archie's gone.'

'They're close, aren't they?'

'Yes. They were the same at school. Had to do everything together. Archie,' she added smiling at the memory, 'was my first boy-friend.' She laughed at Jill's astonishment. 'I was ten and he was twenty-one, but I had a dreadful crush on him. His friends teased him about me, but he didn't mind. He was always kind to me. A lovely man. Jack's the same.' She picked up the carrier bag. 'Any-way, enough of this gossiping. I'd better be going, Jill.'

Jill needed to get moving, too, and when Ella left, she set off for headquarters. There were a dozen jobs that had to be done before she could leave for Styal.

The place was heaving. At first, Jill thought something important had happened, but no, it was merely the usual organized chaos. People were shouting, phones were ringing and a couple of uniforms were playing football with a crumpled ball of paper.

Jill had wanted a word with DS Warne, but there was no sign of her. She had to be the only person not in the building.

'Fletch, have you seen Grace?'

Unlike Grace, DS Fletcher was at his desk. He was doodling on a pad while he ate a Mars bar.

'She's out at Kelton interviewing the Johnson boys.'

'Oh? Anything new?'

'Diddley squat,' he said between mouthfuls. 'Which means the boss is in a foul temper.'

'Ah.'

'It's all very well, but we can't invent evidence, can we? And we must have interviewed everyone within a ten-mile radius of Kelton.'

'Something will turn up.' God alone knew what, but something would. 'It always does.'

He nodded at that, but didn't look convinced.

'Where is Max anyway?' she asked.

'He's gone to see the lovely Mrs McQueen. The charming Tommy is away, by all accounts, so the boss has gone to see – Babs.'

'That sounds cosy,' she said lightly, alerted by something in his tone.

'Very. According to Grace, they were all over each other last time they met. I gather they have a history.'

'Max and Tom McQueen's wife?' Surely not. There hadn't been so much as a whisper of a past when Jill had accompanied Max to the McQueens' house.

'Yup. It was years ago, when Linda was still alive. Seems like Max wants to renew the, er, acquaintance.'

'Really?' Jill was amazed that Fletch couldn't hear her heart pounding. 'I wouldn't bet much on his chances. I bet McQueen's wife aims a lot higher than a copper with two kids, three dogs and a mother-in-law.'

'Probably,' Fletch agreed, laughing. 'Still, so long as it keeps him out of my hair, I'm not losing sleep about it.' He looked at her. 'You must think you had a lucky escape. Rumours of marriage were being bandied around when you two were together.'

'That was a long time ago, Fletch. Right, I'm off to Styal. See you.'

'See you, Jill.'

Fletch returned to his doodling and Jill left the building with her heart still hammering wildly.

The bastard.

God, he was a lot of things – moody, arrogant and downright stubborn among them – but she'd always thought he was honest. What the hell had given her that idea? Honest men don't spend the night with another woman when they're supposed to be working late.

Shock had turned to blind fury as she rammed her car into gear, the wrong gear, and juddered out of the car park. No wonder he'd been distant lately. Why couldn't he just say he'd had a better offer? Why did he have to humiliate her by throwing her a few crumbs now and again?

Barbara McQueen of all people, too. If Tommy found out about it, Max would be at the bottom of the canal sporting the latest design in concrete boots. And that, Jill decided, as she almost drove into the back of a red BMW, was the best place for him.

Bastard!

She arrived at Styal without incident and was soon sitting opposite Claire. And feeling just as depressed as her companion looked.

On closer inspection, however, she decided she was wrong. Claire, still on suicide watch, looked worse than Jill had ever seen her. Her face was empty, like a house where the lights are on but there's no one home. As if she'd vacated her body.

'Christmas is a lonely time, isn't it?' Jill murmured. 'It's OK if you have children but, otherwise, it all seems a bit pointless.'

'It's just another day here.'

'I bet you get turkey for dinner.'

'Yeah.'

They spoke of the mundane. At least, Jill spoke, and Claire, if she was feeling generous, contributed one of her monosyllabic replies.

'I thought you weren't coming here again,' she sneered.

'I managed to persuade them,' Jill replied easily. 'I said you were going to tell me all about Thomas McQueen.'

'No way. I'm not talking about him.'

'Why not? You don't like him so it's no skin off your nose, is it?'

Claire thought about that, then shook her head. 'I don't spose he talks about me, so I won't talk about him.' She looked at Jill, her eyes filled with despair. 'I need to get out of here.'

'Then you know what you have to do,' Jill said reasonably. 'Tell me where Daisy's body is and–'

'And what?' she scoffed.

'If you showed some remorse and let the police find Daisy's body, a judge might be inclined to look sympathetically at your case.'

'Big deal.'

'It could be, yes.'

'You don't understand. I need to get out of here now. This minute.'

'Then cooperate, Claire.'

The sudden smile was smug, and Jill felt a

great urge to hit her.

'And make your job easier? Why the hell should I?'

'No reason. My job's easy enough. It's no big deal driving here, chatting to you, and driving home again. The pay's good, too. Your daughter doesn't matter to me. Why should she? I never knew her. To me, she's just the same as any other kid.'

Claire always became agitated and more talkative when Jill reduced her daughter to an object.

'There are dozens of kids just like yours,' she went on. 'Some make good, others don't. I don't suppose yours would have done much with her life. A druggie working the streets, just like her mother.'

'My Daisy's clever!' she burst out.

On the rare occasions she spoke of her daughter, Claire always used the present tense as if Daisy was sitting at home waiting for her.

'So you say. Mothers always say that, don't they? And who can prove you wrong? Let's face it, according to you, she doesn't even deserve a decent burial place or a headstone with her name on so that people know she existed. No, I don't believe she was clever.'

'You should see her school reports. They all say how clever she is.'

'Teachers always write stuff like that. It's supposed to encourage them. The standard phrases will have been trotted out on every pupil's report.'

'She could read before she went to school. I taught her myself.'

'So she was clever, so what? She wasn't that great or you wouldn't have dumped her in some piece of ground where no one can see her or know she existed.'

'You don't know what you're talking about. You're just like all the rest.'

'I walked through the cemetery in Stacksteads the other day and there was a grave there covered in toys, messages, flowers. That child was only seven when he died. Now he was a clever kid. He must have been. Everyone wants to tell the world how wonderful he was.'

'You haven't got a clue!' Claire cried.

'I haven't,' Jill replied truthfully. 'The police have to knuckle down and do their best to find Daisy's body. With the best will in the world, though, they don't have the time or the funding. And why should they care? They're supposed to prevent crime. It's all a bit pointless after the event. So in the case of some kid—'

'Her name is Daisy!' This came through gritted teeth.

'In the case of some kid who didn't matter—'

'She matters! I can't tell you where she is. I can't!'

'Can't?' Jill said. 'Why not?'

'I've told you, I need to get out of this place.'

'Then tell me where you buried Daisy.'

'I need to get out of this place. That's all. I need to get out!'

This was the first time Claire had seemed remotely bothered about spending her days in Styal. She had never once mentioned wanting to get out.

'Has something happened?' Jill asked curiously. 'You're not being bullied, are you? If you are–'

'What the hell could you do about it?' Claire scoffed.

Jill ignored that. 'Has something happened?'

'No.' Again, Claire looked defeated by life.

'So why–?'

Jill could have kicked herself.

Right from the start, she had failed to get her teeth into this case. She'd known something didn't fit but, until now, she hadn't had a clue what was wrong. Like a fool, she'd believed all she'd read in police and psychiatric reports. Instead of meeting Claire with an open mind, she'd come here assuming that all she had to do was persuade Claire to tell her where Daisy was buried.

'You didn't kill Daisy, did you, Claire?'

Every last drop of blood drained from Claire's already pale face. She couldn't have

230

looked more terrified if Jill had been holding a gun to her head.

'She's still alive, isn't she?'

Blood began to ooze from an almost healed scab on Claire's arm as she scratched at it.

'You're mad, you are,' she said wildly, pushing back her chair and heading for the door. 'Fucking mad. I don't want to see you again.'

Claire had gone, leaving Jill with her own confused thoughts.

Chapter Twenty

On Thursday afternoon, Max was in Mill Street, Harrington, heading for the coffee bar. He'd had one of those days where he'd chased himself around in circles and got nowhere. Lately, he'd had a lot of those. Since leaving home at seven that morning, he hadn't even found time for a coffee.

He rounded the corner into Bridge Street and collided with a heady mixture of perfume, shopping bags and yelping female.

'Sorry. My fault.' His arms went out instinctively to steady the unfortunate woman. 'Oh, Mrs McQueen – Babs. Sorry.'

'What are you doing here? God, you almost gave me a heart attack.' She gathered herself. 'You almost knocked me off my feet.'

'Sorry,' Max said again.

'So what *are* you doing here?' she asked again, still looking shaken.

'I was on my way to Starbucks,' he explained, nodding up the street. At this rate, he'd never get his coffee. 'How are you?'

'Fine. Well, tired out. I've been out all day. Busy. You?'

'Fine. And I'm sorry about – I wasn't looking where I was going.' She seemed to be waiting for him to say something, and he wasn't sure what. 'Would you like a coffee?'

'Well, I – oh, go on then. Yes, why not?'

Conversation was impossible as they battled their way through a crowd of shoppers laden with carrier bags that hung heavy with gifts and wrapping paper.

Starbucks was busy and noisy. The music was far too loud, but no one seemed to care. Perhaps customers were too grateful for a break from Christmas shopping to notice.

Max needed to think seriously about Christmas. Presents needed buying and, although he could do that on Christmas Eve if necessary, he ought to put a few cards in the post. It was a damn nuisance.

They managed to find a table by the window and Max got their coffees.

'So how have you been spending your day?' she asked him when he put them on the table.

232

'Chasing myself silly.'

'Oh dear. And was Tommy able to help you yesterday?'

'He did his best, but no, not really.'

It was Barbara McQueen that Max had really wanted to see, but Tommy had returned early from Amsterdam and scuppered that. Max had resorted to asking him, yet again, about the dinner he'd shared with Bradley Johnson.

'How is Tommy anyway?' he asked. Yesterday, he'd been in a foul mood and making noises about police harassment again. Max had been forced to grovel.

'Busy,' she replied. 'He's always busy. I expect he told you that he came back from Amsterdam so he could go to an auction this morning?'

Max nodded.

'It's for some run-down terrace house that's up for sale,' she told him. 'If he buys it, he'll turn it into flats – probably student accommodation.'

'Where is it?'

'Burnley Road. You wouldn't catch me living there but students aren't fussy, are they?'

'They can't afford to be,' Max pointed out.

'I suppose.' She sipped at her coffee. 'It's a good job Tommy's a decent landlord. Nothing's too much trouble for him. They only have to mention a dripping tap, and the plumber's there the next day. And he's not like some who put the rent up every week.'

St Thomas? No, Max couldn't believe that.

'Someone said something about that,' Max said, pretending to search his memory. 'Oh, yes, it was someone who knew Muhammed Khalil. You remember Muhammed Khalil? The lad who was murdered in Harrington?'

'No.' She looked as if she'd never heard the name.

'Yet another unsolved murder case,' Max said lightly. 'But yes, he rented a flat from Tom. He used to say the rent went up quite frequently.'

'Honestly, some people are never satisfied, are they?'

'Apparently not. Don't you remember the case? It was headlines on the local news for weeks.'

'Vaguely,' she said. 'I just couldn't remember his name.'

'He used to do some work for Tom, didn't he?'

'Oh, I wouldn't know about that. Tommy's business is just that, Tommy's business. I'm not interested in it. So long as it pays the bills, eh?'

'Quite.'

Max drank his coffee and, all the while, he could see Barbara's brain ticking over.

'What sort of work?' she asked eventually.

'No idea,' Max replied easily. 'Maybe he did some plumbing or something like that.'

'Ah, yes, that's possible.'

She thought a while longer.

'It's expensive keeping property maintained,' she said at last. 'He has to put rents up to survive, doesn't he?'

'Of course. Property isn't the best business to be in at the moment,' Max sympathized. 'Still, Tom knows what he's doing. I'm sure he'll be OK.'

He put down his cup.

'I wonder what Mrs Johnson will do with Kelton Manor,' he mused, changing the subject. 'I don't know what they bought the place for,' he lied, 'but they've had a lot of work done on it. If she sells, she'll probably find herself out of pocket.'

'A hateful house,' Barbara said. 'Old, dark and creepy.'

Max thought it a beautiful house. Perhaps it didn't have enough urinating boys for Barbara's taste.

'Do you think so?' he said, surprised.

'Yes, I couldn't stand it. Mind you, I wouldn't want to be stuck out at Kelton Bridge. It's a dead hole.'

He wouldn't argue with that.

'Bradley and Phoebe Johnson must have liked it,' he pointed out. 'Well, one of them must have. I wonder if it was Bradley or Phoebe's choice.'

'My guess would be on Phoebe,' she said easily. 'She had the money, didn't she? At

235

least, I think she did. Bradley must have made some, of course, but her family were stinking rich, weren't they? That's what Tommy told me, anyway.'

'Pretty well off, I gather, yes.'

'Knowing Bradley, that's the only reason he stuck with her. Well, let's face it, she doesn't have much else going for her, does she?'

Phoebe Johnson was an attractive woman. Pleasant, too. Max hadn't ruled her out as a murder suspect, but he'd always found her fairly easy to deal with given the circum-stances.

The 'circumstances', as far as Max could tell, were that she and her husband had en-joyed a volatile relationship, possibly because she could be possessive and was prone to bouts of jealousy. As Bradley Johnson had had several affairs during their marriage, Max supposed that was understandable.

Tyler and Keiran were as close as two brothers could be, but Tyler was the one who had been expected to follow his father into the business. It was Keiran, whose last exam results had been poor and who spent more time at parties than at lectures, who had a difficult time with his father. Neither son had been particularly close to their father.

It was possible that all they wanted to hide from him was the fact that they were as dysfunctional as the majority of families.

They finished their coffees and Barbara

decided she must call for a taxi.

'I never bother bringing the car when I'm going to be out all day,' she explained. 'It's a nightmare trying to park and far easier to use taxis.'

She took a pink mobile phone from her handbag, tapped in a number, then changed her mind and hit a number that she had on speed dial.

'Engaged,' she explained, hitting the redial button. Four times she tried, and four times she shook her head. 'I expect the girl in the office is chatting to her boyfriend.'

'I'll give you a lift.' Max needed to be back at headquarters for the six-thirty briefing, and he didn't really have time for sitting in Harrington's traffic. But there was always the possibility he might learn something of interest from Barbara McQueen.

'Are you sure?'

'Of course.' Maybe Tom McQueen would still be at his auction and Barbara would invite him inside. He couldn't go poking around in Tom's office, unfortunately, but, in more relaxed surroundings, Barbara might be more chatty. Yet she didn't seem particularly chatty today.

Traffic was beginning to build up in readiness for the rush hour, but it wasn't as bad as Max had feared. They talked about this and that, and all the while Max wondered if Barbara was as innocent as she claimed.

Surely she knew she was married to the biggest crook in Harrington?

'Oh, damn!' she said suddenly. 'I was supposed to stop off and collect a couple of cases of wine. Hell, Tommy will go mad if I forget. Max–'Her tone was suddenly flirty, and very feminine. 'I don't suppose you'd stop at Taylor's, would you? It'll take me five minutes tops. Promise.'

'Fine,' he said. Whether Tom McQueen was home or not, he'd have to drop her off and head straight back for the briefing.

He stopped the car outside Taylor's Wine Merchants and she dashed inside. In less than five minutes, the young assistant, laughing at something Barbara had said, was carrying two cases of red wine to Max's car. Once they were stowed in the boot, they continued on their way.

It was raining now. Heavily.

When Max pulled up in front of those huge gates, McQueen's car was nowhere to be seen. That meant nothing, though. Yesterday, it had been in the garage. Presumably, Barbara's Mercedes was in the garage, too.

'Would you mind bringing the car through the gates?' Babs asked. 'I'll get soaked otherwise.'

'Of course.'

'Tommy will help me carry the wine,' she went on. 'At least, I'm assuming he's home.

238

He said he wasn't going anywhere this afternoon.'

Max edged the car forward.

'One-nine-four-seven,' she said, giving him the code to unlock the gates.

Max would remember that. There was no knowing when it might come in useful.

He stopped the car about a yard from the front door and was amazed to see her take an umbrella from her bag. She unfurled it before she was out of the car.

'I'll give Tommy a shout to help me with the wine,' she said.

'No need.' Max was out of the car and grabbing one of those wine cases. He didn't want to see Tommy again, for the second day running, and risk accusations of harassment getting back to his boss.

'Thanks, Max.' The house keys dangled from her fingers. 'You're a star.'

She opened the door – and began to scream.

Max hurried to catch her up and then he had exactly the same view.

'Holy shit!'

Barbara had been right about one thing: Tom McQueen wouldn't be going anywhere this afternoon. Anywhere except the morgue, that is.

Chapter Twenty-One

The atmosphere in Phil Meredith's office was extremely uncomfortable and Jill wished she could be anywhere else. Even Styal had a more relaxed air than this.

Meredith was in a foul mood, not only with Max, but with the world in general. Jill could understand his feelings of helplessness, but there was no need to vent his anger on her.

'What I can't understand,' he snapped at Max, 'is what the hell you were doing at the scene in the first bloody place. Christ, how many times had you been warned to keep away from McQueen?'

On first walking into the office, Jill had thought it cool. Cold even. Perhaps Meredith's anger was responsible for the rise in temperature. She felt like dropping on to one of the leather chairs, but neither she nor Max had been invited to sit so she stood alongside Max.

'I bumped into Mrs McQueen in town,' Max explained patiently. 'I was heading to Starbucks for my first coffee of the day, and invited her along.'

'Why?' Meredith demanded in amazement.

'They have a past,' Jill informed him. 'They met years ago apparently. I'm surprised you didn't know, Phil. It's the talk of the nick.'

Jill was struggling to walk five yards without hearing about the boss and his new 'piece of skirt'.

'We don't have a past,' Max argued, staring at her in astonishment. 'Christ! Who said that? We met once, years ago, and spent a couple of hours in each other's company.'

Met once? So why was it the talk of the nick? Speculation was that Max and Barbara McQueen were having an affair.

'So having bought her this bloody coffee?' Meredith demanded.

'It was raining,' Max explained as if he were talking to a pair of morons. 'She tried phoning for a taxi, unsuccessfully, so I felt obliged to offer her a lift. On the way back, she wanted to stop and pick up a couple of cases of wine. When we got to the house, I took the wine from the car and she opened the front door.'

'Very cosy. And then?'

'Then we walked through the front door and found Tom McQueen lying in a pool of blood with six bullets in him.'

Jill shuddered at that. She hadn't liked Tom McQueen, or Barbara for that matter, but she wouldn't have wished such a thing on anyone.

Meredith, who'd been sitting behind his desk, stood up and paced across to the window and back.

'So why in hell's name is she screaming police brutality?' he demanded of Max.

Why indeed? Jill wondered. That wasn't Max's style, far from it. And if office gossip was to be believed, the pair of them were far too intimate for that.

'It wasn't brutality,' Max scoffed. 'It was trying to protect a crime scene. She was all over him – insisting he was still alive, insisting that if she removed a bullet he'd be OK. She was hysterical. More importantly, she was destroying evidence. There was more blood on her than him so I had to manhandle her a bit.'

'You're like a bull at a bloody gate.'

Meredith, shaking his head in furious bewilderment, returned to his seat. 'So what have we got?'

'There are – were – two closed circuit cameras guarding the house,' Max explained, 'but they'd both been put out of action. They weren't concealed so we can't necessarily assume it was someone who knew the property well. It seems as if someone broke in through the kitchen window. We're checking every inch of the garden, so something might turn up, but there's nothing so far.'

'Bloody hell!'

'His minder, John Barry, has done a

runner,' Max added.

'Then find him!'

'We're on to it,' Max assured him. 'We're still waiting for forensics to come up with something, but we do know it wasn't the same gun that was used on Khalil. We're searching the area for the murder weapon.'

Meredith looked at his watch and absently smoothed his thinning hair. 'I need to make a statement to the media,' he said. 'I want you both back here, in this office, in one hour's time. And I want you to have some answers for me. Right?'

'Right,' Jill agreed, too relieved to escape to wonder what sort of answers they might give him or to venture to ask if she was now supposed to be working on the case.

Max didn't even deign to answer. He had the door open before Meredith changed his mind.

As Max strode towards his office, cursing as he went, and shouting to Grace and then Fletch to forget what they were doing and follow him, Jill wondered if she should suggest a coffee. She decided against it.

'Right,' Max said, when the four of them were in his office, 'what have we got? Grace?'

'Not a lot, guv.'

'Fletch?' Max demanded.

'Um, about the same, Max. Not a lot.'

'OK,' Max said, throwing himself down his chair. 'Let's recap. We'll start in January.

Muhammed Khalil, tenant and, let's say employee, of Tom McQueen, is shot dead. Ten months later, Bradley Johnson, a friend of McQueen's, is bludgeoned to death. Following that, our chief suspect – *my* chief suspect–' he corrected himself, 'turns up looking like a sieve.'

'You're assuming the cases are connected,' Jill pointed out. As Grace and Fletch had pulled up chairs, she did the same. 'Khalil was murdered almost a year ago, and then nothing.'

'Nothing? His landlord is shot. I wouldn't call that nothing.'

'I meant nothing until now. We don't know that it's connected.'

'It's connected,' Max snapped. 'Khalil, Johnson and McQueen. All connected.'

'Someone believes we're getting close to the truth,' Fletch decided.

'Then he's a bloody sight more confident than I am,' Max retorted.

'I really don't see how they're linked,' Jill said.

'Of course they are,' Max said, dismissive. 'Khalil was McQueen's tenant – one who did the dirty on him – and Johnson was close to McQueen.'

'They had dinner together, and McQueen was invited to a party at the manor. That's all,' Jill argued. 'It's hardly conclusive, is it?'

'That's all we managed to drag out of Mc-

Queen,' Grace pointed out.

'Quite,' Max agreed. 'Right, you two,' he said, addressing Grace and Fletch, 'we need to know everything there is to know about Bradley Johnson. We want his every move from the moment he arrived in England all those years ago.'

'OK,' Fletch said slowly.

'We've already found out as much as we can, guv,' Grace argued.

'Then find more. The reason we're stumbling about like idiots,' Max told them, 'is because we haven't found the connection. As soon as we know how Johnson and McQueen are linked, we'll have the answer to this mess.'

Jill wished she felt as confident.

'Get to it,' Max urged them. 'And let me know as soon as you have anything, no matter how insignificant.'

Grace and Fletch went off to do his bidding. Jill stayed where she was.

'I really don't think Bradley Johnson is connected,' she said again. 'Khalil was shot dead. And as you said yourself at the time, whoever killed him was a damn good shot. That person wouldn't have gone into a wood in Kelton Bridge to bash someone over the head a couple of times.'

'That doesn't mean he's not connected.'

'Bradley Johnson was hit over the head three times. His killing had a very amateurish feel to it. If it were the same person, they would have shot him. They wouldn't have risked someone coming along and stumbling across them in Black's Wood.'

Max thought for a moment, then shook his head. 'No, you're wrong, Jill. I understand what you're saying, but there has to be a connection between Johnson and McQueen. Something deeper than the two becoming acquaintances when Johnson moved to Kelton Bridge. And what the hell brought Johnson to Kelton in the first place? Why did he choose that particular village? Hm?'

'Why not? You fancy escaping London and moving to the country so you go on the internet and see what properties are available. If he'd found a similar property in Cheshire or Lincolnshire, perhaps he would have gone there.'

'And perhaps he wouldn't. Maybe something attracted him to this particular corner of Lancashire. Maybe *someone* attracted him. Maybe that someone was Tom McQueen.'

Jill wasn't convinced. Hell, she wasn't even on the case so what was she supposed to know? All she'd had were snippets of information from Max.

Or was she on the case? Meredith seemed to think she was, but it would be nice to be asked. Or even told.

'What's Meredith expecting from me?' she asked Max.

'The same as he's expecting from me. That's the name, address and contact numbers for our killer – or killers – by early afternoon at the latest.' He smiled briefly. 'Simple, kiddo.'

The easy familiarity infuriated her. Either he was having an affair with McQueen's wife or he wasn't. If he was, there was no need for him to creep around her.

'All the same,' he went on seriously, 'I thought I could nail McQueen. Who the hell is higher up the food chain than him?'

'It could be anyone. He was a crook and everyone hated him. Keep pushing people about and, eventually, what goes around will come around.'

'Hm. And where the hell has John Barry disappeared to?'

'Who exactly is John Barry?' she asked, having heard the name mentioned a couple of times.

'McQueen's minder. Or driver. Depending on your viewpoint.'

Jill glanced at her watch and Max, seeing that, rose to his feet.

'Time to see Meredith,' he said reluctantly.

'And tell him what?'

'God knows.'

They were almost at Meredith's office when Grace caught up with them.

'We've found Peter Lawrence,' she told them breathlessly. 'Well, we've almost found

247

him. He's returned to Rochdale, right on our doorstep. We know where he's living but he was blind drunk on Tuesday night and hasn't been seen since.'

'He's probably on one of his binges,' Jill said, excited. 'I want to know the minute he's found.'

'Count on it,' Grace said.

They walked on to Meredith's office.

'When are you at Styal next?' Max asked.

'Monday morning.'

It would be wonderful if she could tell Claire that they had found Peter. That might wake her up a bit.

Chapter Twenty-Two

Jill had it all planned out. She knew exactly what she intended to say to Claire. Word for word.

Yet when she arrived at HMP Styal and saw Claire, she knew it was going to be one of those days when Claire was impossible to deal with. Something had happened – and she still thought the staff needed to check that Claire wasn't being bullied – because Claire was fidgety and unsettled. Physically, she was in the same room as Jill. Mentally, she was in a world of her own.

'What's the news from Styal then?' Jill asked lightly. 'Has anything been happening here?'

'Nothing ever happens here.'

'You look – upset,' Jill pointed out.

'Do I?'

'How do you get on with the other women?' Jill asked. 'Are they OK?'

'I keep away from them,' Claire said.

'Why's that?'

'Half of 'em are mad and the other half are as high as kites.'

'Drugs, you mean?'

'Yeah.' Claire's hands were visibly shaking. 'I'm clean,' she reminded Jill, as she often did. 'Have been for almost a year now.'

'I know. That's great, isn't it? Daisy will be proud of you.'

Her use of the present tense had Claire focusing on her. For the first time since coming to this room, she gave Jill her full attention. Yet she didn't comment.

'What's been happening in the outside world?' she asked instead.

'Not a lot,' Jill replied.

'I saw on the telly that McQueen, the bloke you were asking me about, had been killed.'

'Yes, that's right.'

'He won't be dead. He'll be faking it.'

'He's dead all right,' Jill assured her. 'Two people found him and one of them was DCI Trentham of Harrington CID.'

'I don't believe it,' Claire said.

'Believe it or not, it's true.'

'Nah.' Claire wasn't convinced. 'They said someone shot him.'

'That's right.' Jill nodded. 'He was found in his house with six bullets inside him.'

'It won't have been him.'

'Of course it was him,' Jill insisted, wondering why Claire was so difficult to convince. 'His wife and DCI Trentham found him. Believe me, Claire, he's as dead as it's possible to be.'

'You'll see.'

Claire was scratching at that scab on her arm again. Soon, it would be bleeding. Her hands, still shaking, refused to be still. If she wasn't scratching her arm, she was winding a strand of hair round her finger or chewing on her bottom lip.

'I'll be talking to Peter later today,' Jill said casually. 'Any messages for him?'

'Peter?'

'Yes. He was arrested in Rochdale last night – drunk and disorderly. Assuming he's sobered up enough, I'm going to have a little chat with him.'

Claire was breathing heavily, her emotions all over the place.

'He'll be delighted to know his daughter isn't dead after all,' Jill said quietly.

'What do you mean?'

'You didn't kill Daisy.'

'I did. Who says I didn't, eh? McQueen? He's a liar. Daisy is dead. She's gone. No one can touch her now. I killed her. That's why I'm here.'

McQueen again. What the hell did he have to do with anything?

'I don't believe you,' Jill said.

'She's dead.'

'No. She isn't. Perhaps Peter will know where she is. He's sure to come up with a few ideas. He idolized her, didn't he?'

'He buggered off and left us!'

'Yes, but he still idolized Daisy.'

'She's dead. Gone.'

'Nope, I still don't believe you. Of course,' Jill added, 'if you told me what you'd done with her body, I'd have to believe you, wouldn't I?'

'I can't.'

'Of course you can't. You can't tell me because there isn't a body. Daisy is alive. All we need to do now is find her. And we will.'

'Go to hell!' Claire pushed back her chair and staggered to her feet. 'You can go to hell. And don't come back. I'll refuse to speak to you. They can't make me. I'll kill myself before I speak to you again!'

It was almost two o'clock that afternoon when Jill arrived at headquarters. Shortly after that, she and Grace went to interview room two to see a sober Peter Lawrence.

251

He looked nothing like the photographs Jill had been shown, but she supposed that was because he was sporting long, greasy hair and an untidy beard now. He had also put on a lot of weight, not only around his girth but in his face, too.

If she'd had to guess his age, she would have gone for late forties or even early fifties. She knew for a fact that he was thirty-three.

His clothes – black jeans, grey T-shirt and blue anorak – were filthy.

'Why am I being kept here?' he demanded sulkily.

'We want to ask you some questions,' Grace told him.

Grace was tall and reed-thin, and she stood no nonsense from anyone. Even the most hardened criminals didn't knock her from her stride.

'Where have you been for the past six months?' she asked him.

'What's it to you?'

'I'm curious,' she told him.

'Here and there,' he answered with a cocky smile.

'Could you be more precise?' Jill asked him.

'I had a spell in Liverpool – lorry driving,' he said, jeans-clad legs stretched out under the table. 'And I've been up north. Scotland.'

'Why?'

'Why not?'

'Have you made any attempts to see your

wife since you came back to the area?' she asked him.

'That bitch? She can rot in hell for all I care.'

'What about Daisy?' she asked quietly.

'What about her?'

'Where do you think she might be?'

'How should I know what that lunatic did with her?'

Jill took a breath and hoped to God she was right. If she was wrong, and Daisy *was* dead, she was going to cause a lot of heartache.

'I think she may be alive, Peter.'

The cockiness left him and every emotion flitted across his face. His eyes filled with moisture and his bottom lip trembled.

'Alive?' His voice was a hoarse, frightened whisper.

It had crossed Jill's mind that, maybe, Peter was involved with Daisy's disappearance. She could see now that he firmly believed his daughter to be dead. The possibility that she might be alive was almost more than he dared to think about.

'I don't know for sure,' Jill told him, 'but I think it's possible. I've spoken to Claire, but she's frightened for some reason. Do you know why that might be?'

'She's a lunatic. Totally insane.'

'But why would she be frightened?' Jill asked again.

'Dunno. A bad trip or summat, maybe.'

'She's clean, Peter. She's no longer using.'

'So she says. I've heard that before.'

'She's been tested in prison and she's clean.' Even Claire couldn't fake that.

A thousand questions hovered on his lips, but he was too frightened to ask a single one. Too frightened to believe that his daughter might be alive.

'Why did you leave Claire and Daisy?' Jill asked him.

'Because I couldn't stand her,' he said simply. 'Claire, that is. She was a lunatic. She used to beat me around. I know how that sounds, her being a woman and all that, but it's the truth. She had one hell of a temper.'

They knew that.

'And you used to drink a lot,' Jill said.

'You would have, too, if you'd had to put up with her.'

'But why did you abandon Daisy?' she asked him.

'I had no choice, did I? I couldn't live with Claire. Even Daisy used to stay out of the house as much as she could, poor kid. You want to try living with a lunatic.'

He pulled his fingers through greasy, tangled hair.

'What makes you think Daisy's alive?' he asked at last. 'Is that what Claire's told you?'

'No,' Jill told him. 'Claire is adamant that Daisy is dead. I just have a feeling that she's alive. I believe – and I could be wrong–' she warned him, 'that Claire was frightened. Still is frightened. Frightened for herself and for Daisy, I imagine.'

'What of?'

Jill hadn't the remotest idea. 'That's what I was hoping you would tell me.'

But where did they begin? Claire refused to see Peter and no one could force her. Besides, even if they could, she wouldn't speak to him. Added to that, Peter had abandoned his family almost a year before Claire walked into that police station claiming she had murdered her own daughter. Anything could have happened to Claire in the interim.

'When you were together,' Jill began, 'how was she?'

'I've told you, she was a lunatic.'

'That's not much help,' she pointed out. 'How was she with you? With Daisy?'

'I dunno.' He thought for a moment. 'She was OK at first,' he said at last. 'She had one hell of a temper and when I went out drinking with me mates, she'd think nothing of belting me. Hit me with a saucepan once.'

Jill could believe that.

'You said at first,' she reminded him. 'What was she like before you left?'

'Crazy. She was off her head a lot of the time so—'

'Heroin?' Grace put in.

'Yeah. Drink's one thing. I mean, most

255

people like a drink. Some people, me included, like a lot of drinks. There's no harm
in that, is there? "Have a drink," I'd tell
Claire, "it's a lot cheaper." We hadn't got no
money for heroin. But she wouldn't.'

'Where did she get her heroin?' Jill asked
him.

'Anywhere she could.'

'Tell me about Thomas McQueen?' Jill
suggested.

'*The* Thomas McQueen. Him who was
shot?'

'The very same.'

'I don't know anything about him. Why
the hell should I?'

'Claire knows – knew him. She becomes
quite agitated when his name is mentioned.
She can't believe he's dead. She's convinced
herself that it's just a story put about by
someone.'

He pulled a face at that. 'If she knows him,
he'll be someone who pays for sex. That's
the only people Claire ever knew. That was
summat else she told me she'd given up. She
never did, though. She'd go with anyone for
money.'

'We're not sure that Tom McQueen went
with prostitutes,' Jill said.

Only Tessa Bailey had claimed he did.
None of the other girls on the street had
admitted to going with him.

'If Claire knows him, he must have.'

'Flat four, Rose House, Jubilee Avenue,' she said, refreshing his memory. 'You lived there for a couple of months, remember? That belonged to McQueen.'

'I'm not friggin' stupid,' he said. 'I know that.'

'So Claire could easily have met him?'

Peter laughed at that. 'Oh, yeah, like he'd come calling. Christ, woman, he owns half of Harrington. Most folk have lived in his flats or houses at some time or other.'

That was a valid point.

'He didn't call round to see if we were pinching the silver,' he added scathingly.

'But it's possible Claire could have met him?'

'No, of course it's not. Bloody hell. Are you crazy or what? She never knew him.'

'When I suggested to her that Daisy was still alive,' Jill told him quietly, 'she demanded to know who had said such a thing. She thought Thomas McQueen might have told me. Now, why do you think she would have thought that?'

That shook him.

'I dunno,' he said, not quite as confident. But then he shrugged it off. 'I tell you, Claire's as mad as they come. She's one crazy woman. You can't believe a word she says.'

Chapter Twenty-Three

The following evening, as Max was driving into Kelton Bridge, he saw that the whole village was in darkness. A blizzard was blowing and he guessed one of the power lines had been brought down.

Driving was hazardous with visibility so poor.

His headlights picked out a shadowy figure. It was Jack Taylor and his ever-present dog. Jack, his head bent into the wind, was walking quickly, a big bag in his hand.

He was heading towards Black's Wood.

Why the hell was he going there at this time of night and in such appalling conditions? No one in their right mind would take a dog for a walk in this weather.

Sometimes, Max wished he'd been born with a less inquiring mind. He wished he could simply think that Jack Taylor had gone mad, carry on his way without giving the matter a second thought, walk into the warmth of Jill's cottage and pour himself a stiff drink. Sadly, he couldn't. His curiosity was aroused.

He drove on for a few yards, then parked his car.

As luck would have it, his overcoat was on the back seat. He checked the boot and realized that the gods really were smiling on him. He had a torch, a working torch at that.

He pulled on his coat and buttoned it. It was a pity he didn't have walking boots in the back. Still, no point hoping for miracles.

Not wanting to alert Jack to his presence, he didn't switch on the torch. The snow provided a light of sorts and that would have to suffice.

All he could see was the shape of a man and an animal. It was enough; it could only be Jack and the dog. The shapes entered Black's Wood. Still wishing he'd never laid eyes on the bloke, Max followed.

He couldn't see anyone now, but he could hear footsteps crunching on the snow.

Snow had drifted and it engulfed Max's shoes. Twice he stumbled over a branch. Fortunately, he managed to keep all expletives to himself. All the same, he'd be black, blue and bleeding at the end of this escapade.

Only a man who knew every square inch of this wood would venture here in these conditions.

Jill had said they were looking for someone who knew the wood well and he'd stake his life on no one knowing it better than Jack Taylor.

But that was madness. No way could Jack be involved in something this big. That, of course, was assuming the deaths of Khalil, McQueen and Bradley were linked.

They had to be.

A branch caught Max in the face, almost taking his right eye with it. The wind had eased a little, although it still howled through the trees, but the snow gave an illusion of light. The trees were huge dark shadows and the path nowhere to be seen.

At last, Max was out of the wood. There was no sign of Jack Taylor or his dog. Max took a moment to get his bearings. He'd never walked this way before. In the past, he'd taken the track through the wood from Ryan Walk until it came out almost opposite the pub.

Now, he was nowhere near the pub. He was – he was right at the side of Archie Weston's cottage.

Instead of heading north to south in that wood, he'd obviously veered off to the west. No wonder the track hadn't been visible.

With Jack out of sight, he switched on his torch. His light was the only one to be seen. Kelton Bridge, or at least the row of houses where Archie lived, was in total darkness.

He hesitated briefly, then walked up the path and knocked on the front door.

Archie was quick to answer and looked at Max in complete amazement.

'You'd better come in, lad.'

'Thanks.'

He walked into the sitting room, where Jack Taylor stood warming himself in front of the fire. The two dogs were leaping all over each other and ignored Max totally.

'Well?' Jack greeted him.

'I was passing,' Max said, 'and thought I'd call and see if Archie was all right – with the power cut, I mean.'

Jack looked Max up and down, from the windswept hair to the sodden shoes and trousers.

'Just passing?' he repeated. 'My, you must think I'm senile. If I'd known you were following me, I'd have kept to the road. You don't want to be wandering through the wood at this time of night, Sherlock. You never know who might leap out and hit you over the head. Besides,' he added drily, 'it'll be better for your shoes.'

'What's that?' Archie asked, coming into the room, having bolted the front door.

'I was telling Sherlock here to keep away from the wood at this time of night. Look at the state of his shoes.'

'Ah.' Archie laughed at that, a dry, rasping, painful sound. 'I expect,' he said to Jack, 'that he spotted you and thought you were up to no good.'

'No bloody doubt,' Jack said with a scowl. 'I came here,' he explained to Max, 'because I didn't know if Archie had enough candles or enough food in. Now that he can't get out much, we have to look after him.'

'Indeed,' Max agreed. 'And are you all right for everything, Archie? I can easily nip to the shop.'

'I'm not a bloody invalid,' Archie assured them both in a sharp tone. 'I'm no worse now than before they made their diagnosis. Christ, if I hadn't been to the blasted doctor's, people'd still think I'd just got a bad cough.'

Jack grunted at that and Max kept quiet.

The room was surprisingly well lit given that there were only half a dozen candles and the glow from the coal fire.

'Well, this is quite a party,' Archie said, his tone more cheerful. 'Would anyone like a dram?'

'May as well, now we're here,' Jack agreed.

'That would be very welcome, Archie. Thanks.' If Max was going to be humiliated by Jack Taylor, he'd far rather suffer it with a drink in his hand.

'I'll get 'em.' Jack was halfway to the kitchen.

'Sit by the fire,' Archie told Max. 'You'll dry off. Mind you, I expect your shoes will be ruined.'

'Never mind,' Max murmured, taking the old, upright armchair next to the fire.

'I wonder how long the power will be off,' Archie mused, sitting opposite him. 'I don't suppose the workmen will want to go out in this weather. On the other hand, the over-time payments will be nice, especially if they can hang it out till after midnight.'

'Let's hope it's soon fixed, Archie.'

'Yes. You get used to electricity, don't you? I'm not so bad, but these people without a coal fire, or without any means of making a hot drink, must find it hard. Then there are those who can't go five minutes without their televisions.' He shook his head at such stupidity.

Jack came back carrying a tray on which sat three large glasses of whisky, the whisky bottle and a jug of water. Elderly they might be, but they knew how to live.

'This is very civilized,' Max said.

'Oh, yes. You need something in this weather,' Archie said.

'So how's it going, Sherlock?' Jack pulled an old wooden chair closer to the fire and sat on that. 'It seems to me that you've got dead bodies turning up left, right and centre. First Johnson, and now that bloke from Harrington.'

'Thomas McQueen, yes. Did you know him?'

'No,' Jack scoffed. 'What would a bloke like that want with the likes of us?'

'Another wealthy man,' Archie pointed out. 'They say that the love of money is the root of all evil.'

'They do,' Max agreed, 'and they're right.'

'You should visit the pub,' Archie suggested. 'They've all got their theories there, haven't they, Jack?'

'They have.' Jack chuckled at that.

'And what might those theories be?' Max asked.

'Some are a bit colourful,' Archie warned him. 'Someone reckoned you were looking for a gang from London.'

'Really?'

The two collies had worn themselves out with their antics and made their way to the fire, managing, without being noticed, to grab the dark brown rug to themselves. 'You're not then, do we take it?' Archie asked.

'No. I think it's more local than that.'

'Someone else reckoned those lads of Johnson's might be guilty,' Jack informed him. 'Mind you, they reckoned the boys would inherit his money. They won't, will they? Well, not unless they kill the mother, too.' He grinned at Max. 'You'd better keep a close watch on her or you'll have another corpse on your hands.'

'It wasn't only that,' Archie reminded Jack. 'They reckoned the boys were dubious characters. Capable of murder. Mind, one theory was that the wife, Phoebe, did it. Now she would inherit the lot.'

'Does she have an alibi, Sherlock?' Jack asked.

'Not a very good one,' Max said. 'Who

thought she might have killed her husband?'

'Can't remember,' Jack said, looking to Archie.

'I can't either. She might be your culprit though,' Archie said.

The whisky was warming, as was the fire. In fact, with the shadows from the candles dancing on the walls, it was extremely cosy.

'You said it was blackmail,' Jack reminded Max.

'It's one theory, yes. We know Johnson had blackmailed someone in the village – someone else who doesn't have a decent alibi–' he added, 'and blackmail is a very dangerous occupation. Some people pay up, some have the good sense to contact the police, but others–'

'Take the law into their own hands,' Jack finished for him. 'Ay, well, I'd fall into the latter camp. I certainly wouldn't pay up, and it'd be a waste of time expecting you lot to sort it out. I reckon I'd have to take the law into my own hands.'

'And there's you without a decent alibi, Jack,' Max said with mock disapproval.

He believed Jack's story of being in Rochdale at the time of the murder. At least, he wanted to. He supposed he must keep an open mind.

'Blackmail's a nasty, deceitful occupation,' Archie said grimly. 'Folk like that deserve all they get. Not,' he added, almost wistfully, 'that anyone would have anything on me. My life has been a very quiet, simple one.'

'An honest one,' Jack corrected him. 'Like mine.' He turned and looked at Max. 'Our generation – we were more content with our lot. We left school, took jobs – usually in the pit – we married and we brought up kids. We didn't change jobs at the drop of a hat, abandon our kids or flit from one wife to the next like your generation does.'

'And that's all very commendable,' Max said.

'It's how we live,' Jack said simply.

'It were whatshername,' Archie remembered, wriggling sock-covered feet on his dog's back. 'That young lass – what were her name, Jack? Fred and Martha's granddaughter?'

'Melanie,' Jack said. 'Melanie Bishop.'

'Ah, that's it. It were her who reckoned the wife had done it. She worked at the manor, cleaning and helping them unpack. I don't know much about it, but she didn't like the job and she didn't like her employers.'

'Oh?' The name Melanie Bishop meant nothing to Max.

'She's living in Rochdale now,' Jack put in. 'Twenty she is, and living with some lad in Rochdale. She works in one of those shops there. Wilkinson's probably. Somewhere like that anyway.'

Max made a mental note to send someone

to find her. She might, although it was doubt-ful, be able to tell them something of interest.

'She reckoned they were all crazy,' Archie said with amusement.

'Why was that?' Max asked.

'I don't know really,' Archie admitted. 'She reckoned they were always shouting at each other. Said they both had violent tempers. The wife, Phoebe, threw a vase at her husband once. Well, so she said. But you know what these kids are like. You can't get any sense out of them.'

Archie refilled their glasses and Max made another mental note. He must buy the old boys a bottle of Scotch each.

They liked to play games with him, and they found him a great source of amuse-ment, but he did like them. Both of them. He just hoped the whisky loosened their tongues a little and they gave him some-thing of use.

But talk moved on to cop shows on TV.

'When we first had a telly,' Jack was say-ing, 'we used to watch *Dixon of Dock Green*. Now he were a good copper. Could catch anyone, he could.'

Max smiled at that. He'd watched repeats of the programme. In black and white.

'Then came *Z-Cars*,' Archie said. 'I always used to watch that. That were OK, although in one episode, the dog got shot. Shame that. I hate to see animals hurt on the telly.

Oh, I know it's not real or anything, but all the same.'

Max wasn't surprised by that. Archie was a gentle old soul.

The two men reminisced about old TV programmes, and Max knew he was wasting his time. He'd get someone to talk to Melanie Bishop but, other than that, they weren't going to be of any help whatsoever.

All the same, he'd keep well in with them. They heard things in the village, and they saw things. It could be that they'd hear something of use. And that's what he desperately needed. He'd had enough lectures from his boss about the lack of progress in this case.

Chapter Twenty-Four

With her deadline upon her, Jill was hoping to finish a chapter of her book, but her computer's battery ran down and put paid to that. She had plenty of candles and, thankfully, her gas fire was working well, so she was warm. She would have been warmer still if she could have moved closer to the fire, but three cats were sprawled in front of it and Sam, in particular, never took kindly to being evicted from a prime spot.

She was minutes away from going to bed

when Max turned up. No phone call, no warning, no nothing.

She had to work with him, and she was professional enough to do that. What she didn't have to do was put up with him treating her home like his own. That was yet another problem with their relationship: they were too familiar with each other.

She hadn't seen him since Friday, when they'd both been too shocked by McQueen's murder and too busy trying to pacify Phil Meredith to worry about anything else. But his relationship with Barbara McQueen was still the most interesting piece of gossip at the nick.

'Streuth,' he said, pulling a face, 'it smells like a brothel in here.'

'You'd know that better than me.'

'I'll get us a drink, shall I?' He dumped several files on her sofa and shrugged out of his jacket.

While Jill watched, admiring his nerve if nothing else, he went to the kitchen, filled two glasses with whisky, added a generous amount of water to hers and returned to the sitting room.

He stopped then and looked at her. 'Is something wrong?'

'What could possibly be wrong?'

Even the cats, detecting her change of mood perhaps, had given up their places by the fire and wandered off.

Max handed her a glass of whisky. 'Come on then. Out with it. What have I done now?'

'You? Why should you have done anything? God, my life doesn't revolve around you, you know.'

'So if I've done nothing wrong, how come I'm taking the flak?' he asked drily.

'Flak? I haven't said a word.'

'No,' he agreed slowly, and Jill could almost hear his brain ticking over. 'I bet a shag's out of the question, though.'

'With me? Good grief, I am honoured. I thought you had other fish to fry these days.'

His eyes widened at that, before dark eyebrows crinkled into a frown. 'What?'

'I suppose I should admire your bravery,' she said, sitting down and taking a big swallow of whisky. 'Not many men would have been brave enough, or insane enough, to mess with Tom McQueen's wife.'

'Ah,' he said, understanding finally dawning. 'So we're back to that.'

A slow smile broke out and Jill wanted to hit him. Bloody hard.

'It's still the talk of the nick,' she pointed out. 'The DCI's love-life is always a matter for speculation and when he's having an affair with–'

'Hey, steady on. Having an affair?'

'So rumour has it.' She nodded.

'Is that what they're saying? Me and Barbara McQueen?'

270

'They are. And why not? She shared a bed with Tom,' Jill pointed out, 'so she's obviously not fussy.'

Another infuriating smile at that.

'Ah, but a copper's pay wouldn't keep Babs in visits to beauty salons. Not,' he added quickly, 'that I have any interest in her.'

'Really? So what exactly is this past you had?'

'Oh, for Christ's sake! This crackpot rumour started with Grace. She was with me when we realized we'd met.'

'It must have been a memorable meeting.'

'Yes, it was actually,' he replied, nodding. 'We were on a train coming back from London. I'd been to a funeral, and she'd been dumped by her boyfriend of the moment. I was going back to Linda, she was going to stay with an aunt. We both needed our spirits lifting.' He raised his glass. 'So we had a couple of drinks on the train.'

'And then what?'

'And then nothing. She took a taxi to her aunt's and I drove home to Linda and the boys.'

She didn't know whether to believe him or not. The fact was, she did believe him. So why was everyone making such a big thing of it? And how come, if nothing happened, he could still remember it? Why did he agree that it had been memorable?

'You want to get out more, Max, if you call

271

'that memorable.' She was striving to be calm and reasonable, but it was difficult.

'It was memorable because it made me realize how much I hated my marriage. Barbara was fun. Not that much fun,' he added hastily. 'But fun. I was going home to Linda and I was dreading it. If it hadn't been for the kids, I'd have done a runner that night.'

'Was this before or after you knew me?' She had to know.

'Before. About two weeks before.'

Terrific. So, having decided his marriage was in ruins, he would have been on the lookout for anyone available and Jill had been available.

If she kept at this conversation, she'd make herself angrier and more depressed than she already was. She had to forget it for the time being. But–

'How come you're so keen to renew the acquaintance?' she asked, wishing she could, just for once, keep her mouth shut.

'I'm not,' he replied easily. 'What I wanted was to get closer to McQueen. Inside his house–'

'What? Are you mad? You were almost suspended before Bradley Johnson was killed. If Meredith had found out–'

'There was no reason why he should. Anyway, it's irrelevant now that Tom's dead. I have all the access I need.'

'What is it with you?' she asked curiously.

'Why do you refuse to do anything by the book?'

'Because it doesn't get results, Jill. You know that as well as I do. Look round the nick and what do you see? Disillusioned officers. Well, except Grace maybe. If we go by the book, there's no way we'll get a conviction.'

'So you decided to take the law into your own hands,' she said. 'Great.'

'And now you sound like Meredith.'

Jill didn't really want to think about it. Just how far would he go to secure a conviction?

Sod him.

'You haven't asked me how Styal was,' she said, changing the subject, 'or how my chat with Peter Lawrence went.'

'No need to. Grace told me all about it.'

'And did she tell you that I'm beginning to think that Daisy is still alive?'

'She did.' The expression on his face told her what he thought about that idea. 'No way,' he said confidently.

'I think so.'

'Oh, come on, Jill. No one, not even someone as mad as Claire Lawrence, would volunteer to get themselves locked up in Styal.'

'Claire's as sane as you or me,' she said calmly.

'So why would she do such a thing? Why would she claim to murder her own daughter?'

'I don't know. Maybe she's scared of some-one. I don't know, Max, but I think Daisy's still alive. And let's face it, without Daisy's body, there's not a lot of evidence.'

'Claire walked into the nick clutching a pillow and an empty bottle,' Max reminded her. 'There were traces of Daisy's saliva, and hair, on the pillow.'

'So? That doesn't mean she's dead.'

'We searched every inch of Harrington,' he pointed out. 'It was the biggest search I've ever been involved in.'

'I know. I still think Daisy is alive.' She wasn't one hundred per cent sure, though. 'That's the theory I'm working on anyway.'

'No way.'

'So?' she asked, nodding at the pile of files he'd dropped. 'What are those for?'

He looked tempted to continue their conversation, but changed his mind.

'Bradley Johnson,' he said. 'We don't have a clue. Not a bloody clue. I want you to look through those and see if you can come up with anything.'

'Oh, great. Working by candlelight.'

At the mention of candles, he wrinkled his nose. 'They really do smell awful.'

He nodded at the files. 'I've told you most of it, I think,' he said, sitting beside her. 'And you've seen the photos. Any ideas?'

'None that I haven't told you,' she said. 'My opinion? Bradley was blackmailing

someone. He was expecting to meet someone in the wood–'

'The wood or the pub?'

'The wood,' she said. 'It would be away
from prying eyes. The victim – and by that I
mean the person he was blackmailing –
would have suggested the wood so it will be
someone who knows it well. It will have
been premeditated.'

'What about suspects?' Max asked. 'What
about his wife, Phoebe?'

'She'd have motive perhaps,' Jill said. 'I
don't think their marriage was all it's
cracked up to be. And the affairs, she won't
have been thrilled about those.' But she
didn't want to think of handsome, charming, two-timing bastards. Not, she reminded
herself grimly, that Max could be described
as handsome. Attractive in a weathered,
world-weary sort of way perhaps, but not
handsome. Two-timing bastard, yes.

'But if she was going to kill him, she'd do
it at home,' she went on, concentrating on
the job in hand. 'It would be easy enough to
hide a few valuables, trash a few things and
claim he'd disturbed a burglar. And I doubt
she's been in the wood more than once in
her life.'

'Maybe. How about the sons then?' Max
asked.

'They weren't anywhere near, were they?'

'Not as far as we know,' he agreed reluctantly. 'Joan Murphy then?'

Jill had considered Joan, dismissed her, then considered her again.

'Since when has she been a suspect?'

'Since she closed her shop on the day Johnson was murdered.'

That was news to Jill.

'She claims she needed two days, the Wednesday and her usual Thursday, to change the window display and check on her stock.'

'Then it's possible, I suppose,' she said. 'He humiliated her in the worst possible way. She thought it was love whereas, in reality, he was just laughing at her and conning her out of her money. Worse, he was conning her out of the money that her much-loved father had worked hard for. Yes, she's a possible.'

Jill had learned from bitter experience that she couldn't allow personal feelings to colour her judgement. Just because she'd found Joan friendly didn't mean she wasn't a killer. Jill hadn't known Joan was having an affair or being blackmailed by Johnson, or that she'd been abandoned by her own husband, so she couldn't be expected to know if she was a killer or not. All the same, the idea didn't sit comfortably.

'Hannah Brooks?' Max suggested.

'Hannah? No.' She was firm on that. 'She's too clever and too ambitious for that. She has her sights set high, Number 10, I shouldn't wonder. The last thing she'd do is murder someone.'

'Surely, that depends if he had something really damning on her that would put an end to her dreams. And she was out walking on the afternoon that he was killed,' Max reminded her. 'Then she was rushed into hospital the following day. Doesn't that strike you as one hell of a coincidence?'

'Yes, but I don't think she's your killer.'

'How about Tom McQueen or one of his henchmen?' Max asked. 'If he killed Khalil and Johnson found out – maybe Johnson's plans to blackmail him backfired.'

She expelled her breath on a sigh. 'I don't think Johnson's murder was professional enough for McQueen. This was premeditated, yes, but your man – or woman – is someone who didn't give a damn if they were caught or not.'

'So who else do we have?' Max murmured. 'People with dogs – yes, I know, but all the same. Olive Prendergast has an alibi, Archie Weston has one and so does Jack Taylor. Well, Jack possibly has one. He showed me a receipt to prove that he was in Rochdale at the time in question, but he could have found that anywhere. I'm supposed to take his word for it,' he finished drily.

They were still discussing the case at one thirty that morning when the electricity was finally restored.

Max was on his feet, blowing out candles.

'Look at the time,' he said in amazement.

She was well aware of the time. Just as she was well aware that he'd been drinking and shouldn't drive home. She guessed what was coming.

'What time are you coming over to our place next week?' he asked, taking her completely by surprise.

'Next week?'

'Christmas Day,' he clarified that. 'Do you want me to collect you or will you get a taxi?'

She didn't believe she was hearing this.

'I'm spending Christmas Day with my parents,' she told him with a calmness she wasn't feeling. How dare he assume she was waiting for him to click his fingers all the damn time?

'What? But you always spend it with us.'

'Then it must be time for a change.'

'But I've told Harry and Ben you'll be there.'

'Perhaps you should have asked – sorry, told – me first.'

'Oh, come on, Jill. How the hell will you spend a whole day with your parents? It's miles to drive so you won't be able to have a drink, and you'll have to endure your mum cooing over Prue's kids while she goes on about her poor unmarried daughter. You'll go mad.'

The infuriating thing was that he was right.

'I'm sure I'll cope,' she replied airily.

'But I've told the boys,' he said again. 'They'll be so disappointed.' He put on his little-boy-lost expression. 'Come to us,' he coaxed. 'Please.'

She really shouldn't fall for it. On the other hand, she always enjoyed Christmas with Max and the boys. They had fun.

'I'll think about it,' she promised, somewhat reluctantly.

'Thanks.'

'And now,' she said, 'it's late and I'm off to bed. What are you going to do? Call a taxi? Or will you drive home drunk? You forget all the other rules, you may as well disregard that one as well.'

'Firstly, I'm not drunk,' he pointed out. 'Secondly...'

'Secondly?' she prompted, knowing damn well what he was angling for.

'I suppose I've been relegated to the spare room,' he guessed.

'No, Max. You've been relegated to other premises. Any other premises.'

'What? Oh, for Christ's sake, Jill. Is this because of Barbara McQueen? I told you, that was work, pure and simple.' He leaned forward, all sincere. 'Come on, Jill, be reasonable.'

'Why?'

He stared back at her.

'Why should I be reasonable?' she asked again. 'If being reasonable means jumping when you say jump, why the hell should I? One minute you're all over me, the next I can barely get two words from you.'

For some reason, that seemed to shake him.

'Me and you,' he said at last, 'we're both scared. We've got a lot in common, kiddo. A lot of emotional baggage. We've both had bad marriages and all that involves. We've both lost spouses – in different ways, admittedly – but we both have the guilt that goes with that.'

'Guilt? Speak for yourself.'

'OK then, I'll speak for myself. I get scared, Jill. Scared to death of ending up in another hell of a marriage.'

'Well–'

'Just as you're scared that, as soon as you relax, I'll be off shagging Miss Sex on Legs.'

Jill couldn't decide how to respond to that. He was right; she was frightened of getting hurt again. She hadn't realized that he felt the same, though, and the knowledge, as well as the fact that he was man enough to admit it, threw her momentarily.

'Or perhaps I'm wrong,' he said with a shrug. 'You're the psychologist, not me.'

And still she didn't know what to say. It was easy enough to believe he had a point. However, she also knew just how easily he could charm his way out of anything.

'I'll bring you coffee in bed,' he murmured

coaxingly. 'I'll fire up the boiler. And get rid of dead mice and birds.'

A smile was trying to get through, but she fought it back.

'Cater to your every sexual need,' he added, and a splutter of laughter bubbled up inside.

'You're the bane of my bloody existence, Trentham!'

Chapter Twenty-Five

Christmas Day had dawned bright and frosty, but the temperature had risen slightly and clouds had gathered. Jill peered out at the sky, but no snowflakes were forthcoming.

'I suppose you had a bet on there being a white Christmas,' Kate guessed knowingly.

'I thought it was a dead cert.'

'I bet it will snow,' Ben said.

Jill gave the boy a squeeze. 'I bet it will, too.'

They had exchanged presents, eaten a huge lunch, all cooked by Kate, and everyone, even Harry and Ben, was too lazy to move now. The dogs were equally lethargic – or suffering ill effects from all the sprouts Ben had slipped them.

Jill was glad she'd decided to spend the day with Max and the boys, and with his mother-in-law, too. Kate was a good friend.

It was Kate who finally roused herself. 'I'm going to load up the dishwasher.'

'I'll help,' Jill offered immediately. 'I might not be able to cook, but I'm great at throwing stuff in a dishwasher.'

People like Kate, people who could cook and master the domestic side of life, were a marvel to Jill. Kate had not only managed to cook Christmas lunch for the five of them, she had also managed to keep the kitchen tidy.

'So how much did you bet on it being a white Christmas, Jill?'

'Only a hundred quid. And what's that between friends? Not that the bookie's my friend at the moment.'

Kate laughed at that. 'Too many losers?'

'Far too many.' Jill was disgusted with herself. 'If there's an old nag destined for dog meat running, you can bet your life I have money resting on the thing. In my defence, though, I haven't had much time to study form lately.'

'Tell me about it,' Kate said, rolling her eyes. 'Max is a stranger at the moment.'

Jill was all too aware of that. He was running himself ragged, they all were. The frustrating thing was that there was no progress. There seemed no answer to any of it.

'I remember one year,' Kate remarked, breaking into her thoughts, 'it began to snow just before midnight so there's plenty of time yet. Mind you,' she added with a chuckle, 'that was years ago, when Harry was a toddler and Linda was pregnant with Ben.'

Although they rarely mentioned Linda, Jill knew this would be a bitter-sweet time for Kate.

'Christmas must be difficult for you, Kate.'

'Linda was my daughter and I miss her every day,' she replied quietly. 'And yes, I suppose Christmas is more difficult. I so wish she could be here with the boys. She loved them so much. They were her life.'

Jill nodded her understanding, but couldn't help thinking that, if she had lived, Linda would have lost her marriage because of her devotion to her children. The way Max saw it, as soon as the boys were born, Linda became obsessed with them...

'On the other hand,' Kate went on briskly, 'we have to accept what life throws at us, don't we? At least I know that Harry and Ben are happy and healthy. That's all Linda would have cared about.'

What about Max? Jill wanted to ask. Wouldn't she have cared about his happiness, too?

Kate filled a bowl with hot soapy water.

'And I won't get maudlin at Christmas,' she went on, plunging crystal glasses into the suds. 'We're all happy. We're together.'

283

'Yes.'

'And,' Kate added with a half-smile, 'I'm bright enough to realize that Max is far happier with you than ever he was with Linda.'

Jill cringed inwardly at that. Kate *was* a good friend, but it must be so hard for her to see Jill doing the things that Linda should be doing.

'He's not exactly with me, Kate.'

'As good as. And it makes me happy. You're good for Max, Jill, and, therefore, good for the boys.'

But they weren't an item. They worked together, they even slept together on occasions, but they couldn't manage the whole 'couple' thing. Perhaps they were incapable of making a relationship work.

'So tell me the latest on your mum's plans for the wedding anniversary party,' Kate suggested.

Jill was relieved to be on easier ground.

'Don't ask. I think there will be a couple of hundred of us at the Royal Hotel. No, make that a hundred and ninety-nine because Dad's refusing to go.'

'Oh, dear.' Kate laughed at that.

'I foresee disaster.'

'I can see your mum's point, though,' Kate said seriously. 'It's a long time. An achievement. It should be celebrated in style.'

Jill agreed, up to a point.

'Even Dad agrees with that. But he wants

to celebrate in style with his mates at the working men's club. As Mum said,' she added, grinning, 'it could all end in divorce yet.'

By the time the kitchen was tidy, the dishwasher switched on and the coffee made, Max and the boys were outside kicking a football around.

'It looks like the dogs are winning,' Jill remarked.

'I don't care who wins. It's just good to see Max spending time with them.'

'He's busy right now,' Jill replied, 'but you know what it's like. Things will soon quieten down. Once this case – cases – are sorted, life will return to normal.'

'I hope so.'

So did Jill.

It was almost four o'clock when Max got the call.

Jill saw his expression change as he listened. She saw a fury in his eyes and a familiar setting to his stubborn jaw-line.

'Who was the first officer at the scene?' he demanded of the caller.

Jill's heart sank. Now what had happened?

He finally slammed his phone shut.

'I've got to go,' he said, adding more gently for Harry and Ben's benefit, 'but I'll be back as soon as I can.'

Knowing he wouldn't say too much in front of the boys, Jill followed him outside

285

to his car.

'Tessa Bailey,' he said, fury in every breath, 'has been found at the back of Burnley Road. A stabbing.'

'Is she alive?'

'Just.'

'God, Max.'

'Yeah. I'll see you later, OK?'

'Yes.' She knew she would stay until he got back, no matter how late that was.

The rest of the day dragged. Jill and Kate had fun amusing the boys, but Jill's mind was wandering.

What *was* the answer to all this?

First, McQueen's double-crossing tenant, Muhammed Khalil, is murdered, then Bradley Johnson, then McQueen himself. And now Khalil's girlfriend had been attacked. What the hell was going on?

Max was home just after nine o'clock and his first job was to pour himself a large drink. Jill had been knocking back wine so she didn't have anything else. She needed a clear head.

He didn't say much and Jill could understand that. Stabbings weren't the most popular of subjects for Christmas Day conversation with his mother-in-law and his sons.

But Kate soon returned to her flat and then, very reluctantly, Harry and Ben, who were almost asleep on their feet, went to bed.

Max poured himself another generous drink.

'How's Tessa?' Jill asked him.

'She's in intensive care. Apparently, the next twenty-four hours are crucial.' She could tell he was still furiously angry. 'What do you think, Jill? Who's responsible?'

Jill stared at him in amazement. That was the thing about criminal profiling, she thought grimly. People either thought it was mumbo-jumbo or they assumed that all they had to do was give you the victim's name and you could pluck the killer from the air.

'Max, I know nothing about it,' she pointed out, appalled that he, of all people, should expect so much. 'How the hell would I know? Someone who doesn't celebrate Christmas, I imagine.'

His glass stilled halfway to his mouth.

'Like a Muslim,' he said softly.

'Well, yes, could be,' she agreed. 'Then again, it could be anyone. Tell me what happened.'

Jill sat in the armchair next to the beautifully decorated tree. All Kate's work, of course.

Max stood with his back to the fireplace.

'Tessa and a girl called Mags share a flat in Burnley Road,' he explained, 'and they had a few friends round for the day. They'd been doing what everyone does today – eating, drinking, watching TV. They were smoking

287

some dope, I gather, but nothing worse than that. There were nine of them there.'

He took a slug of whisky.

'They ran out of cigarettes,' he continued, 'and Tessa said she'd run down to see if the corner shop was open. It wasn't,' he added as an aside. 'Closed at four, apparently. Anyway, when Tessa hadn't returned after an hour, they set off to look for her.'

'And it was these friends who found her?' Jill asked.

'Yes. She'd been stabbed several times and left for dead.'

Max reached into his pocket for his own cigarettes. Once he had one lit, he said, 'Why try and kill her? What did she know that she didn't tell me?'

Jill had no idea.

'McQueen's murder has thrown me,' she admitted. 'If he was still alive, I'd assume he'd had Khalil killed because the lad double-crossed him, and then had Tessa killed, or almost killed, in case she knew something.'

Max paced around taking long pulls on his cigarette.

'We're right back at square bloody one,' he said grimly.

Chapter Twenty-Six

On 27th December, Jill was in her office at headquarters going through every piece of paper this inquiry had generated. A lot.

So much for Christmas, she thought with a sigh. Christmas Day and Boxing day had passed in a blur, no snow had fallen so she'd lost her bet, and now it was back to normal.

The building was quiet for a change. Almost every officer was on the streets, asking questions and handing out photographs of both Muhammed Khalil and Tessa Bailey.

Jill was concentrating on anything relating to Bradley Johnson because, try as she might, she couldn't find the link between him and Tom McQueen. Admittedly, they had met socially a couple of times, but that was weak to say the least. There seemed to be no connection at all between Bradley and either Khalil or poor Tessa.

When Max sought her out later, she was sitting back in her chair, hands linked behind her head, eyes closed.

'Busy?' he asked drily.

She smiled. 'Just thinking.'

'About what?'

'Claire Lawrence.' She rubbed her hands

over her face and tried to gather her jumbled thoughts into some semblance of order. 'She once said something like "he won't touch her again", meaning Daisy. I assumed she was talking about her husband, Peter. Maybe she wasn't.'

'I'm with you so far,' Max said as she paused.

'She's also very uneasy about Tom McQueen. She can't, or won't, believe he's dead.'

'And?'

'Tessa, when you spoke to her, said there were rumours about McQueen liking young kids.'

Max perched himself on the edge of her desk.

'What if McQueen *was* abusing children?' she went on. 'What if he abused Daisy? Claire might pull a stunt like this to protect her daughter.'

'Tessa's the only one to have mentioned anything of the sort,' Max said doubtfully. 'There's been nothing else to suggest a hint of it. Still,' he added, 'it's a theory and we've precious few of those. We need to talk to Claire Lawrence. I'll organize it.'

He was on his way out of her office.

'Any news on Tessa?' she called after him.

'She's still holding her own.'

That was something, Jill supposed.

Max stopped the car outside HMP Styal the following morning and Jill's spirits took their usual plummet.

Max killed the engine. 'Ready?'

'Yes,' she replied. 'Let's go and bash our heads against a wall for a while.'

This morning, because Max's presence demanded it, Jill supposed, they were shown to a different room, one that was smaller but light and airy.

'DCI Trentham, Harrington CID,' Max introduced himself to Claire.

He was in one of his moods when he'd stand for no nonsense whatsoever and Jill guessed that Claire would enjoy every second of this. She loved to pit her wits against authority.

'I am honoured,' she said, voice dripping with scorn.

'You are,' Max agreed, 'and I haven't come here to be pissed about. I want some answers from you. You can start by telling me everything, and I mean everything, you know about Thomas McQueen.'

Claire looked to Jill and grinned. 'Is this the good cop, bad cop routine?'

'I'm not a cop,' Jill pointed out.

'OK. Good shrink, bad cop,' she corrected herself sarcastically.

'You once said you wouldn't let McQueen touch Daisy again,' Jill lied.

'I said no such thing!' Claire cried.

'Did he touch her?' Jill asked.

'She's just a kid. Why would he touch her?'

Once again, Claire used the present tense when talking of her daughter. There was no doubt, well, very little doubt in Jill's mind that Daisy was still alive.

But where could she be?

'We've heard,' Max said, 'that McQueen liked young children.'

'You're right there,' she said immediately.

'Did he touch Daisy?' Jill asked again.

Claire shrugged. 'I don't want to talk about him.'

'But I do,' Max told her, 'so you have no choice in the matter. How do you know Mc-Queen liked young children?'

'I don't.'

'You just said he did.' Already Max was losing patience.

'McQueen is dead,' Jill reminded Claire. 'You can say what you like about him. He's dead, Claire.'

'So you say,' Claire retorted.

'Six bullets in him,' Max told her. 'Two in his chest, one that narrowly missed his heart, one in his neck, two in his head – one of which was at point blank range. I was there when his wife found him. I saw him.'

Claire hung on Max's every word, fascinated. But still a part of her refused to believe it.

'He's dead, Claire,' Jill insisted. 'He can't

hurt you, Daisy or anyone else now.'

Claire began rubbing at the almost healed patch on her arm. Jill had seen her do that so many times before that she longed to cuff her hands behind her back.

'Did McQueen touch Daisy?' Max asked again.

'He wasn't into sex with kids if that's what you're thinking,' Claire scoffed.

'But you said he liked young children,' Max reminded her on a frustrated sigh.

'He did, but he didn't want sex with them.'

Then what the–

'Crack,' Max said, realization dawning.

'Who killed him?' Claire asked.

'I've no idea – yet,' Max said. 'Was he giving crack to children?'

Claire nodded, lips clenched tightly shut, gaze resting on the spot of blood oozing from her arm.

Not for the first time, Jill wondered how lowlife like McQueen got away with such acts for so long. How did they keep their victims quiet? The answer, she supposed, was sitting opposite her. Fear. McQueen terrified people into silence.

But outwardly, McQueen had been a pillar of respectability. He had even made friends with the Chief Constable no less.

'What did you do,' she asked Claire, 'when you realized he was getting to Daisy?'

'I didn't say he was,' Claire pointed out.

'OK, so what would you have done if he had?'

Claire smiled at that, but didn't answer.

'I'm tired now,' she said instead.

'Tough!' Max snapped back at her.

'You wanted to protect Daisy, didn't you?' Jill pressed on. 'You wanted to shield her from heroin – or crack. You were determined that Daisy wouldn't end up an addict, selling her body to feed a habit, like her mother. You wanted a better life for her, didn't you?'

Claire didn't answer.

'But how can you fight a man like Mc-Queen?' Jill went on. 'You can't, can you? Men like him, men with all that wealth, power and influence, consider themselves above the law, don't they? They trample over everyone who gets in their way. They make threats, don't they, Claire? And they don't hesitate to carry out those threats, do they?'

Claire, hands trembling violently, nodded.

'How did he threaten you, Claire?' Max demanded. 'And don't say he didn't because we know damn well he did.'

'How do I know he's dead?' she asked, her voice thin and rasping.

'You can take my word for it,' Max told her.

'Mine too,' Jill added.

Jill could see that, finally, Claire was allowing herself to believe that McQueen could be dead.

'He threatened to kill Daisy.'

Max was about to speak, but Jill nudged his thigh to silence him.

'He started paying me for sex,' Claire said, her eyes dull. 'He was just another punter, you see. Then he gave Daisy crack. How could he, eh? How could he do that? He came to the flat one day and I pulled a knife on him. I warned him that, if he went near Daisy again, I'd kill him. Fucking hell, me threatening McQueen. Later that night, someone – someone he'd sent – came to beat me up. He wanted Daisy, but she wasn't there. He said he'd be back for her.'

Claire, having given what was possibly the longest speech of her life, fell silent. Her arms were wrapped tightly around herself, hugging her fear to her.

'So you walked into the nick clutching a pillow and an empty medicine bottle,' Jill guessed.

'Yeah.'

'Claire, where's Daisy?' she asked quietly.

The weariness left her for a moment. 'She's dead. I killed her.'

Never in a million years. Daisy was in hiding. But where? Somewhere near a canal? On a narrowboat?

'The man McQueen sent to beat you up,' Max said. 'Who was he?'

'Dunno.'

'What did he look like?' Max persisted.

'A brick shithouse.'

'Big arms and shoulders? A massive, bullish head sitting on those shoulders? Look like an ex-boxer, did he?'

Claire visibly started at what had to be an accurate description. 'He might have.'

When the interview was over, Jill had one more thing to say to Claire.

'You remember you said you'd like to live on a narrowboat, Claire?'

'No.'

'Oh, I'm sure you do,' Jill said pleasantly. 'Well, that's what I'm going to do. Not live on one, but look round a few. In fact, I'm going to look at every boat in the country if I have to.'

She joined Max at the door.

'See you again, Claire.'

They were almost at the car when Max said, 'OK, I give up. What the hell was that about narrowboats?'

'Daisy's living on one,' Jill replied confidently.

'Really?'

'Yes, really.'

'And, um, do you have any idea in which particular county this narrowboat might be?'

'Well, no. Not yet. I intend to work on that.'

Chapter Twenty-Seven

It was New Year's Eve, and Jill and Grace were walking along sterile hospital corridors that stretched on seemingly for ever. Visitors wandered around looking lost and depressed. Doctors strode about as if they hadn't yet mastered the art of being in the right place at the right time.

'What are you doing tonight, Jill?' Grace was totally unaffected by her surroundings.

'I'm at the village hall in Kelton – a few drinks, fireworks. It's a fundraising thing. You?'

'Just a few friends round. We'll let off some fireworks at midnight, but we're both working tomorrow. Worse luck.'

Grace hit a button for the lift. 'Let's see if this thing works,' she grumbled. 'The last time I used it, it refused to stop at level three. In the end, having sailed up and down half a dozen times, I had to get out at level four and walk.'

Today, however, the lift deposited them at level three and they walked along yet more sterile corridors to Ward 33 where Tessa Bailey was in a side room.

'You'll find her very groggy still,' the ward

sister warned them. 'And try not to tire her out. She's been through a lot.'

'Don't worry, we won't,' Grace assured her.

Tessa was as white as the pillows against which she reclined. Two different substances were being given intravenously and she clasped a mask, possibly for oxygen, in her hands.

Several cards sat on her bedside locker and two balloons had been tied to her bed.

'How are you feeling, Tessa?' Jill asked her as soon as the introductions were out of the way.

'Dog rough,' she replied, but then she added a more considered, 'I suppose I'm OK really, and it's cheap board and lodging.'

'Room service, too,' Jill agreed. 'It could be worse.'

It could be much worse. Tessa was lucky to be alive.

'Yeah.'

'What can you remember about the attack?' Grace asked, keen to get down to business.

'Nothing really.'

'Try, Tessa,' Grace urged her.

'I left the flat and walked down the alley to go to the shop,' she explained slowly. 'I got almost to the end. In fact, I think I did get to the end. Then I don't know what hit me. I just don't know.'

'Think carefully,' Jill suggested. 'I know it's painful to remember that day, but we need all the help you can give us. What could you see?'

'Nothing. It were dark. Well, almost dark.' She thought for a moment. 'I could see lights on in the Indian takeaway across the road from the alley. I don't know if it were open or not, but I remember thinking I'd call in and see if they sold fags if the shop were closed.'

'Good,' Grace said. 'Then what?'

'I were cold,' Tessa remembered. 'Me teeth were chattering.'

'What could you hear?' Jill prompted.

'Nothing. It were quiet. Eerily quiet, like you don't often hear. There's nothing and no one about on Christmas Day.'

'What about the smell?' Jill asked. 'What could you smell?'

'Fresh, cold air,' she answered. 'Do you know what I mean?'

'Yes.'

Jill loved that smell, loved the way her cats smelled when they came inside from the frosty air.

'Then there were summat else,' Tessa said, frowning. 'I could smell smoke. Pipe smoke or summat like that. It weren't normal fag smoke, and it weren't a joint. It were a pipe or a cigar, that sort of smell.'

'You're doing really well,' Jill encouraged her.

'Oh, yeah, there were summat nice. One of

them expensive perfumes.' She sighed. 'But that's it. I don't remember nothing else. Here,' she said suddenly, 'you don't think he were waiting for me, do you?' The thought had struck her for the first time and she looked terrified. 'Were he waiting for me?'

'We don't know for sure,' Grace told her. 'It might have been a mugging or something, and he was disturbed. We think, though, that he was waiting for you, yes.'

'It's too much of a coincidence, Tessa,' Jill explained. 'First your boyfriend is murdered and we know he tried to pull a fast one on Thomas McQueen. Then McQueen's shot.'

'God Almighty!'

Tessa really hadn't connected the killings with the attempt on her own life. She had truly believed that she'd been in the wrong place at the wrong time.

Which meant she didn't know who might want her dead.

'We believe,' Grace said, 'that you know too much. At least, someone believes you do. Have you any idea who killed Muhammed?'

'No.' She was terrified.

'What about Tom McQueen?' Grace asked. 'He's killed and then, less than two weeks later, you're attacked.'

'God Almighty!' she said again.

She pulled the mask on to her face and breathed deeply for a few moments.

'I always assumed McQueen killed

Muhammed. Well, one of his thugs,' she said, her breathing still laboured. 'McQueen's dead, though. It couldn't have been him, could it?'

'We don't know,' Jill said, adding a confident, 'but we will find out.'

'Your attacker,' Grace said. 'Did they make any sounds at all? Could you detect an accent? English? Asian? Local?'

Tessa shook her head. 'I didn't hear nothing. One minute I were walking down the alley, the next I were lying here. God knows what happened in the days in between.'

Nurses came to record Tessa's vital signs and, after assuring Tessa she was safe, and that a policeman was stationed outside her door, Jill and Grace set off down those sterile corridors once more.

'That was a big help,' Grace said, frustration showing. 'Who's going to tell the boss we're looking for a pipe-smoking transvestite? You or me?'

'Toss you for it?' Jill suggested.

'We'll both do it. There's safety in numbers.'

It was a beautiful clear night as Jill walked the short distance to the village hall.

Outside the building, the bonfire was piled high and excited children clutched paper hats decorated with rockets and Catherine wheels ready for the competition. Speakers

301

had been rigged up for music and, presumably, so that everyone could hear the sound of Big Ben ringing in the New Year.

The smell was delicious. Hot-dogs and burgers were being cooked and potatoes baked. It was the treacle toffee that appealed to Jill, though. She'd had toast for breakfast, but her hospital visit had robbed her of her appetite until now.

'Go inside and spend a lot of money, Jill.' Ella was in charge of the baked potatoes. 'Don't worry, I'll save you some food.'

'I'm going nowhere until I have treacle toffee,' Jill assured her.

'Is Max coming?'

'Who knows? He said he'd try to be here. I expect he will because he half promised Harry and Ben.'

With a bag of toffee in her pocket, and a chunk in her mouth, Jill went inside.

Various stalls lined the walls and they were already busy. Villagers were buying books, trying their luck at the tombola or guessing the number of sweets in the jar. The bar in the adjoining room was doing a good trade too, she noticed.

The Reverend Harrison took to the stage and grabbed the microphone. He welcomed everyone, thanked them for coming, urged people to dig deep into their pockets, and then invited Hannah Brooks on to the stage to announce the results of the children's

New Year hat competition.

'I've had the most difficult task of the evening,' Hannah told them.

She looked incredibly smart, dressed more for dinner than a fireworks party. Smiling and confident, she soon had her audience laughing.

'The hats are wonderful and every child deserves a prize,' she said. 'However, there has to be a winner so here's the moment you've all been waiting for. In third place is Chloe Duckworth. Well done, Chloe. In second place, Jeremy Webb. An excellent job, Jeremy. And the winner is – could I have a drum roll, please?'

A taped drum roll sounded.

'The winner is Sophie Jones.'

There was much applause as the children took to the stage to collect their prizes.

Jill walked over to inspect the hats. Hannah was right; it was almost impossible to judge them. Jill wondered if she'd had such patience as a child. No, of course she hadn't. It would have been left to her parents to make hats in the shape of Big Ben or giant fireworks.

Between chunks of toffee, Jill chatted with Hannah and Gordon, then with Jack Taylor and Archie Weston.

She spent money, grabbed herself a large glass of mulled wine and ventured outside.

Hannah, Kelton Bridge's very own celebrity, was soon escorted outside for the ceremonial lighting of the bonfire. Closely watched by members of the local fire crew, she lit the fire in four places and stepped back to admire the flames as they leapt skyward.

Jill was on her second bag of toffee, and feeling slightly sick, when Max and the boys arrived.

'Who wants toffee?' she asked, offering the bag.

'No, thanks. I want a hot-dog,' Ben told her.

'And I'm having a burger,' Harry said.

'Max?'

'No, thanks. You could always save it till tomorrow.'

'Ah, but that's the problem. I can't.'

When Harry and Ben dashed off to spend Max's money, they wandered over for a chat with Ella. She soon thrust baked potatoes that oozed melted cheese into their hands.

When they were out of Ella's sight, Jill handed hers to Max.

'I can't eat another thing.'

Max had no such problems.

'I don't suppose you've spotted any pipe-smoking transvestites hanging around, have you?' he asked, sarcasm evident in the lift of dark eyebrows.

She had to smile. 'No, but there's plenty of time yet. Nothing would surprise me any more.'

Flames leapt higher from the bonfire. If they weren't careful, it would have burnt itself out before midnight.

It was good to see the residents of Kelton Bridge enjoying themselves. Good to see everyone preparing to welcome a brand new year.

There were a few absentees, of course. No one from Kelton Manor had turned up. Jill wouldn't have expected them to. Joan Murphy, having spent her first Christmas and New Year without her husband, wasn't there either. But most people were.

Activity increased around the bonfire. The music coming from the speakers faded. People fell silent. Then someone began a countdown. When that ended, everyone held their breath until, finally, Big Ben chimed in the New Year.

A huge cheer went up and people hugged their neighbours.

Jill lifted her face for her kiss from Max. She hadn't expected much, just a perfunctory peck on the cheek perhaps, but–

'The perfume that Phoebe Johnson wears,' he said. 'If you were Tessa Bailey, would you describe it as expensive?'

Jill rolled her eyes. 'Happy New Year to you too, Max.'

'What?'

'Never mind. Phoebe's perfume? Yes, I probably would.'

Chapter Twenty-Eight

'Aw, come on,' Fletch complained, 'you're eating me out of Mars bars.'

Jill and Grace had both helped themselves from Fletch's desk.

'I'll go and stock up in a minute,' Jill promised. 'I need a coffee anyway.'

The three of them were at Fletch's desk going through yet more details of Bradley Johnson's life.

'It's OK, it's lunchtime,' Fletch said. 'I'll get us a sandwich or something.' He held out his hand for donations.

'I've got no change,' Grace told him.

Jill hunted in her pockets. 'Me neither.'

'I don't want change,' he said, hand still outstretched, 'I want crisp, clean notes. Still, it's no skin off my nose. You can both starve for all I care.'

They gave him notes and he went off for food.

Jill, ignoring her grumbling stomach, carried on looking at statements from students at both Sheffield and Lancaster Universities.

She found it odd that so many students from each university knew both brothers.

Tyler and Keiran, it seemed, stuck together and, if you were a friend of Tyler's, you were automatically a friend of Keiran's. But brotherly love wasn't a crime. It might be unusual, but it wasn't against the law.

Max was probably right. The Johnsons were merely trying to cover up the fact that all hadn't been well in the family. People assumed that other families were 'normal', that children excelled at everything, that spouses never exchanged a cross word...

It was a good idea sending Fletch for food because he never failed to return with enough to feed the entire force.

'The lemon meringue is mine,' he warned them.

That suited Jill who had her eye on the chocolate muffin.

'So what do we know about the family?' she said, grabbing a beef sandwich. 'According to Melanie Bishop, the young girl they employed to clean, Bradley and Phoebe had a volatile relationship. Also, we know that the sons, despite their claims to the contrary, both had a difficult relationship with their father. He pushed them hard, he constantly reminded them of the sacrifices he was making by putting them through uni. In short, he put them under a lot of pressure.'

'He was a right bastard really, wasn't he?' Grace said.

'Financially he was OK,' Fletch put in

between mouthfuls of sandwich. 'But we know he lived on cash. The fifteen grand that Joan Murphy paid him, for example, never found its way to any bank that we know of. Caterers for that party, car servicing – all paid in cash.'

'He handed over a cheque for Tyler's car,' Grace pointed out.

They concentrated on eating for a few minutes.

When Fletch had finished the slice of lemon meringue and had a cup of tea in his hand, he spoke with resignation. 'None of this brings us any closer to discovering his connection to Tom McQueen.'

'That's true,' Grace agreed. 'As far as we know, he met McQueen at a dinner in Harrington back in October. McQueen was invited to that party at Kelton Manor and then they had dinner together – which may or may not have been pre-planned.'

'Maybe there isn't a connection,' Jill said.

She knew exactly what Fletch and Grace thought of that theory. As far as they were concerned, there was one killer. That man, they believed, had shot Muhammed Khalil, bludgeoned Bradley Johnson, put six bullets into Tom McQueen and then stabbed Tessa Bailey.

Jill wasn't so sure.

Max, who had been in meetings all morning, came over to them at that point.

'Well?'

No one had good news for him. In fact, no one had any news at all.

'We're still looking for a link between Bradley Johnson and McQueen,' Jill told him, 'and I'm not convinced there is one.'

'Of course there is.'

'Then why didn't our killer shoot Bradley Johnson? He's got a gun, the one he used on Muhammed Khalil, so why bash Bradley Johnson over the head? Surely, if you're happy firing a gun once, you're happy doing it twice. And not only did he have one gun, he apparently had two.'

'Khalil was shot in a busy, noisy town,' Max pointed out. 'Bradley Johnson met his end in a quiet wood in Kelton Bridge. The sound of gunfire would have carried for miles.'

'OK,' she agreed, unable to argue with that logic, 'but the person who shot Khalil is not the same person who put an end to Tom McQueen. Whoever shot McQueen was more emotionally involved. They weren't confident handling a gun, either. A single shot killed Khalil yet our killer fired six times at McQueen.'

'Hm,' Max murmured.

Fletch hit his keyboard and his computer sprang into life.

'We've gathered as much info as we can on Johnson's movements over the last year,' he said. 'And we've done the same for Mc-

Queen. They really didn't move in the same circles, Max.'

Jill looked at the screen as Fletch scrolled through a long list of dates.

'Whoa!' Jill pointed at the screen. 'Go back a bit, Fletch. OK, stop there. June the thirtieth. What was Bradley Johnson doing at Warwick University?'

Fletch frowned. 'It was an awards dinner.'

'What's significant about that?' Max asked her.

'What's Bradley's connection with the university?' Jill asked Fletch, ignoring Max for the moment.

'I don't know.'

'Find out,' Jill suggested.

'What's so interesting about Warwick?' Max asked again.

'Hannah and Gordon Brooks got their degrees there. At least, I'm fairly sure they did. I was chatting to Gordon one day and he said that he and Hannah met there.'

Fletch picked up his phone, tried to speak to someone at the university and, understandably, got nowhere. 'Holidays,' he explained.

'Bloody hell.' Max wanted answers now. 'Call Phoebe Johnson, Fletch, and see what she knows about it.'

Fletch looked up the number for Kelton Manor while Max tapped his foot impatiently.

'Mrs Johnson,' Fletch said when he was connected, 'your husband attended a dinner at Warwick University on the thirtieth of June this year. Can you tell me what that was all about?'

Judging by Fletch's silence and the scribbling he was doing as he listened, Phoebe was giving him every detail of the menu.

'And when was that?' he asked her. 'I see … yes … and how long did it last?'

Fletch finally ended the call.

'Well?' Max asked.

'About twelve years ago, she couldn't be sure, Johnson's company was developing a piece of computer software and they were running trials at the university. Apparently, Johnson spent a couple of months there and is – or was – very highly regarded.'

'I thought he was living in the States twelve years ago,' Max said, frowning.

'That's right. According to Phoebe, he used to fly over here for a couple of weeks at a time.'

'Hannah Brooks is thirty-two,' Jill said. 'Twelve years ago, she and Gordon would have been at Warwick.'

'Bring them both in,' Max ordered.

'Is that wise?' Jill ventured. 'The press are camped on the doorstep and if news gets out that we're questioning the local Tory candidate, they'll really go to town.'

He considered that for a moment.

311

'And,' Jill went on, 'Hannah will be aware of that. She's more likely to be cooperative away from the nick and, more importantly, the press.'

'OK.' Car keys jangled from Max's fingers.

'I expect they'll be back at work today,' Jill pointed out.

Max sighed impatiently. 'Right, we'll be there at six o'clock. And if there's a whiff of scandal, I'm hauling her – both of them, in fact – down here. Sod her career!'

Jill put the last bite of a Mars bar, one she'd stolen from Fletch, into her mouth at five minutes to six, at the precise moment that Max stopped the car outside Gordon and Hannah Brooks' house. He applied the brakes so forcefully that she almost swallowed it.

'It could be nothing more than coincidence,' she reminded him when she'd recovered sufficiently.

'Ooh, will you look at that? A pink farmyard animal just flew over the bonnet.' He killed the engine. 'I've had more coincidences than I can take lately. I was convinced that blasted grandfather of hers knew something, too.'

'Let's tread carefully, shall we?'

'Softly, softly,' he vowed.

As soon as they were inside and had been ushered by Gordon into the lounge, Max got straight to the point.

'Against my better judgement,' he told the couple, 'I've agreed to question you both here. But if I hear any more lies, you'll both be taken straight to the nick and the sodding press can make what they will of it.'

So much for softly, softly, Jill thought.

But perhaps Max had taken the right approach. The couple didn't have time to play games, and Hannah – Jill was watching her closely – had visibly paled.

'What on earth's going on?' Gordon asked.

Two nights ago, at the village bonfire, Hannah had been glowing with confidence. Now she was shaken and she looked frightened.

'Will you sit down?' she offered.

Jill sat, but Max didn't. At the best of times, he found it difficult to sit still, and Jill knew these weren't the best of times.

'I'm going to ask you both again,' Max said. 'When did you first meet Bradley Johnson?'

Hannah and Gordon sat together on the sofa. Jill was sitting opposite them, her view obscured every time Max walked in front of her. He couldn't even stand still, never mind sit.

'Well,' Hannah said, 'it was about a week after they moved into the manor. Isn't that right, Gordon?'

'I can't remember the precise details,' he said, 'but yes, it wouldn't have been much longer than a week.'

'Let me jog your memory.' Max was having none of it. 'Warwick University. Twelve years ago. Ring any bells, does it?'

Gordon finally broke the silence.

'Twelve years ago, we were both at university in Warwick. That's where we met.'

'So I believe.' Max walked in front of Jill again. 'And that is where you first met Bradley Johnson, yes?'

'No.' Gordon couldn't seem to grasp what Max was getting at. 'No, of course not.'

'Hannah?' Jill prompted. 'It's where *you* met him, isn't it?'

Hannah's shoulders slumped. The air seemed to leave her body in a long shudder.

'Yes,' she admitted at last.

Max had his usual rant about obstructing the police, perverting the course of justice and a whole load of other stuff. It had Hannah looking terrified and Gordon more confused than ever.

'I don't understand,' he said.

'I met Bradley at university.' Hannah's voice was flat with resignation. 'It was before I knew you, Gordon.'

'But why? I mean, you never mentioned it. I didn't think – oh, no!' he said suddenly. 'Don't tell me he was the American. He was, wasn't he?'

'Yes.'

'But he's – was – years older than you.' Gordon stood up as if such close proximity

314

to his wife would cause him physical harm. 'Twenty years, Hannah!'

'For God's sake, Gordon, I know that.'

'It seems you have some explaining to do, Mrs Brooks,' Max said impatiently. 'Perhaps you'd be so good as to do it to me first.'

She nodded.

'From the beginning, Hannah,' Jill prompted. 'Tell us how you met Bradley.'

Jill couldn't decide if her sympathies lay with Gordon or his wife.

'I was young,' Hannah began, 'and it was the first time I'd left the village. Going to university was a real eye-opener for me. I made friends with the other girls, but I can't say I had much in common with them. They were only interested in boys and experimenting with drugs. But I wanted friendship so I tagged along with them.'

Jill could identify with that scenario. She, too, had been amazed to find that, when she had been busy studying, her fellow students had found time for a full and varied social life.

'One evening, we all gatecrashed a party,' Hannah continued. 'I was the odd one out as usual, and while the others enjoyed themselves, I ended up talking to Bradley. He was over from the States. His company was involved in a research programme at the university.'

'Good God!' Gordon crossed the room to

a chair there and dropped into it.

'We had an affair,' Hannah said quietly.

'Did you know him, Gordon?' Jill asked curiously.

'Me? Hell, no. I knew she'd had an affair with a Yank,' he said bitterly, 'but I had no idea who it was, or that he was old enough to be her father. I was just the mug who happened along to pick up the pieces when it was all over.'

'It wasn't like that.' Tears swam in Hannah's eyes, but Jill guessed she wasn't about to let them fall.

'And you've kept in touch all these years?' Jill wanted to know.

'No.' Hannah looked at them both. 'Do you want the truth?'

'We wanted the truth weeks ago!' Max was furious.

'We were together – it was off and on because Bradley stayed for a fortnight and then spent a week or two at home in America – but we were together for a couple of months,' Hannah explained. 'For the time he was at Warwick, in fact. I suppose he liked the idea of a young student chasing him, and I enjoyed being in the company of a clever, sophisticated man. I knew it was over when he left, of course. We'd agreed, you see, right from the start that there would be no strings. He had a wife and I needed to study for my degree. I was heartbroken, though.'

She paused long enough to take a tissue from the pocket in her skirt and blow her nose. Her gaze darted everywhere but it studiously avoided Gordon who was looking more and more shocked with every word.

'Six weeks after he left,' she continued, 'I realized I was pregnant.'

'What?' Gordon sprang out of his chair and looked as if he would have physically shaken Hannah if Max hadn't intervened.

'Calm down, Mr Brooks!'

'Pregnant?' Gordon cried, ignoring Max. 'And you never said a word?'

Still Hannah couldn't look at Gordon.

'I was on the pill,' she said, 'but I'd had a touch of food poisoning so...' She left the sentence hanging in the air.

'I contacted Bradley easily enough through his business,' she went on, 'and we met up on his next trip to London.' She took a breath. 'We agreed I should have an abortion. Well, I say we agreed, but I'd already decided that I had little choice. I thought Bradley had a right to know, that was all.'

'Jesus!' Gordon's face was twisted with disgust.

Jill sympathized. Gordon was still trying to come to terms with the loss of his unborn child and now he was hearing that Hannah had aborted another child. Bradley Johnson's child.

317

'I had the abortion and never heard from Bradley again,' Hannah said. 'During the following year, I met Gordon and we fell in love.'

'Love?' Gordon screamed at her. 'You don't know the meaning of the word.'

He turned to Jill and spoke with difficulty. 'I'm sorry, but I need to get out of the house. I can't listen to any more of this and I can't bear to look at her.'

'You're going nowhere,' Max informed him. 'I still haven't decided whether to take you both down to headquarters and carry on there.'

Gordon returned to his chair on the edge of the room.

'So, Hannah,' Jill said, 'you claim you had no contact with Bradley until he came here?'

'That's probably a lie, too,' Gordon muttered.

'It's the truth,' Hannah said.

Jill didn't believe her. 'Are you sure? If we find out that you're not telling us the truth, Hannah, you'll be in serious trouble.'

'Did you have any contact with Johnson before he moved to Kelton Bridge?' Max demanded. 'Yes or no.'

'Three phone calls,' she admitted at last. 'The first was a year or so before he came to the village.'

'He called you?' Max asked.

'Yes. He was quite chatty at first and then

he told me how he'd seen a news item on the internet about me. I'd been discussing my views on abortion. He wanted to know if my prospective voters knew I had personal experience.'

So he'd blackmailed her.

'And of course they don't.' Gordon snapped. 'You two-faced bitch!'

Hannah flinched as if he'd hit her.

'What was the second call about?' Max asked. 'He called you again?'

'Yes. He was taunting me. Said he was going to leave London and move somewhere he could keep an eye on me and my career.'

'And the third?'

'Very short and sweet,' she replied bitterly. 'He simply said he hoped I'd give the new owners of Kelton Manor a warm welcome.'

Jill had no sympathy for Bradley Johnson whatsoever. To her certain knowledge, he'd used Hannah and Joan Murphy. Hannah had been a young, innocent and unworldly student. Joan had been equally naive. Johnson had acted like the school bully who picked on those least able to fight back. With Hannah looking forward to a life in politics, he must have thought he'd been made for life.

'What happened when he moved to the village?' Jill asked her. 'How often did you see him?'

'I didn't,' she replied. 'Well, only if I was with Gordon, or in the company of others.

We had invites to his parties, but I always had excuses at the ready.' She twisted a tissue in her fingers. 'I did see him in the street once. That was about eight weeks before he was killed. He'd just heard I was pregnant and he asked if I was planning to let this one live.'

Jill felt her stomach clench. Even without allowing for Hannah's miscarriage, that was cruel beyond words.

'He said I wasn't to worry about him letting the cat out of the bag, as he put it. He told me he would keep quiet.'

'At a price?' Max guessed.

'Yes.'

'How much?'

'Ten grand.'

'Did you pay him?' Max asked.

'No. I kept stalling him. I'd arrange to meet him and not turn up. Once, I told him I was trying to get the money together.'

'And he accepted that?' Max was doubtful.

'He knew I was scared and that must have been enough for him.' She paused, briefly. 'Then he began sending notes. He pushed them through the letterbox. Two, sometimes three a week.'

She looked straight at Max. 'As I appear to have little else to lose, I'll tell you something else. The day he was killed? I saw him. We passed each other on Ryan Walk. He must have been in a hurry because all he said was, "Well, well, if it's not my Pregnant Hannah." I told him – I told him to fuck off, if you must know. He carried on his way and – do you know what he did? He laughed.'

The colour had returned to Hannah's face. Shock and fear had been replaced by fury.

'That man was all set to take everything from me,' she rushed on, 'and he had the audacity to laugh at me.'

'What did you do?' Jill guessed Hannah hadn't taken kindly to that.

'I didn't kill him if that's what you're thinking. I could have – cheerfully – but I didn't. I ran after him, all set to give him a piece of my mind, to tell him that if he exposed me, I'd tell the world what *he* was.'

That tissue was in shreds now. Tiny pieces were scattered across her skirt like snow-flakes.

'Before I caught up with him,' she continued, 'Ella Gardner came out of the wood and stopped to talk to him. I turned around and came home.'

She buried her face in her hands. Jill thought she was going to break down, but, no, her emotions were still firmly in check.

'The notes he sent you,' Max asked, 'what did they say?'

'Stuff like, "When's Hannah going to hand over the money?" Another said, "Abortion is murder, Pregnant Hannah." They were all short.'

Jill shuddered. Bradley Johnson had played

with Hannah in the same way that her cats sometimes played with mice.

'I don't suppose you still have those notes?' Max asked.

'No. I destroyed them.'

'Who else knew about this?' Jill asked her.

'No one.'

'Your grandfather knows,' Max said. 'As sure as night follows day, Jack Taylor knows.'

She sighed. 'Yes, he does. I told him. But no one else knows.'

Hannah stood up and brushed specks of tissue from her skirt.

'So Chief Inspector, Jill, that's it. If all this comes out, I'll have lost everything. I've already lost my baby–'

'And your marriage!' Gordon was clearly past caring about Max's threats. He stormed from the room and out of the house, slamming the front door after him.

Max quickly brought things to a close and, within a couple of minutes, they were back in the car.

'I want to get to Jack Taylor's before Gordon gets there,' he explained.

'You think he's going there?' Jill didn't. She thought Gordon would be licking his wounds alone. They were extremely deep wounds that would take a long time to heal.

'I don't know.' Max fired the engine. 'But I'm damned if I'm giving them time to get their stories straight.'

Chapter Twenty-Nine

Jill was exhausted by Hannah's story. Saddened, too. She sometimes wished she'd chosen any career in the world other than one that brought her into contact with murderers and their victims. She heard stories that were too terrible, saw things that time could never erase. It must be bliss, she thought, to arrive at Asda at eight o'clock, and sit on the check-out all day talking of nothing deeper than the weather and the price of milk.

Max said nothing as he drove them to Jack Taylor's house. Perhaps he, too, was wishing he had a job sweeping the streets or cutting grass.

He stopped the car at the T-junction and turned briefly to look at her. 'I'll treat you to dinner after this, kiddo.'

'On one condition,' she told him, 'that we don't discuss this case. In fact, I refuse to talk about anything depressing.'

'It's a deal,' he said as he swung the car into Jack's road. 'Blimey, for a minute there, I thought you were going to insist on paying.'

'With the nags I've backed lately? You've got to be kidding.'

Jill considered herself a fairly optimistic character. She'd seen it all, little surprised her, and it took a lot to get her down. Yet, as they got out of the car and walked up the path to Jack Taylor's house, she was thoroughly depressed.

It seemed unlikely, but she wondered if Max guessed at her feelings because he gave her shoulder a squeeze and said, 'Take it from me, Jack makes the best cup of tea in Kelton.'

She must pull herself together as, sadly, she didn't have the luxury of sitting on a check-out all day.

Jack answered the door and ushered them inside. He was alone, except for the collie, and he was in the middle of washing up at the old, ceramic sink.

His dog licked Jill's hand with a gentleness that touched her. Animals were far superior to humans, she thought. They were above all this.

'Have you seen your son-in-law?' Max asked him.

'Gordon?' Jack had been about to carry on washing up, but that stopped him. 'No. Should I have?'

'We've just come from Hannah and Gordon's house,' Max explained. 'Gordon left. He was a bit upset by what he heard and we wondered if he might have come here.'

'Ah.' In that short word was a wealth of

understanding. 'No, I haven't seen him.'

'I expect he's gone for a walk to calm himself down.' Jill didn't want Jack worrying unnecessarily.

'Probably,' he agreed. 'How's Hannah?'

'She's OK,' Jill promised.

Jack, for once, was lost for words.

'I think we all need one of your special cups of tea, Jack,' Max said.

'I think you're right, lad.'

Jill watched, eyes widening, as Jack reached for a bottle of whisky.

'Do women drink whisky?' he asked Max doubtfully.

'This one does,' Jill told him.

'Really? My, how things change.' Shaking his head at the state of the world, Jack poured generous measures of whisky into large mugs. 'Let's see if this helps, shall we?'

He put the tea on the kitchen table and sat down.

Jill, very gingerly, took a sip from her mug. Surprisingly, it tasted good.

'Hannah's told you everything then?' Jack guessed.

'She has,' Max said, 'but I'd like to hear your version.'

'My version? That'll be the same as Hannah's. She might not tell me things for years, twelve years in this case, but when she finally spills the beans, you get the lot. She wouldn't lie to me,' he added hastily.

'So tell us your version of events,' Max suggested, taking a swig of his drink.

'If you like,' Jack agreed. 'My Hannah went off to university, with proud parents looking on, and found herself like a fish out of water. She'd lived a simple, decent life in the village till then. She met that bugger Johnson and–' His knuckles were white as he gripped his mug more tightly than ever. 'She were putty in his hands. Next thing, he's buggered off back to America and she's in the family way. So she gets rid of the baby.'

He broke off and stroked his collie.

'That were her decision,' he said at last. 'It wouldn't have been mine, and I don't know what her gran would have thought of it, but the world's different now. Right or wrong, that's what she did.'

He fell silent.

'Go on, Jack,' Jill urged him.

'She hears nothing from him until he realizes she's standing as the Tory candidate. Then the evil bugger – pardon my French, Jill, but that's what he were – follows her here and tries to blackmail her. He phones her and sends her notes.'

'Did you see the notes?' Max asked.

'Yes. Saw 'em and burnt 'em!'

Jill suddenly recalled seeing a spiral of smoke rising from Jack's incinerator when she called here with Ella.

'Memories and truth remain,' she quoted

softly, and he looked straight at her.

'You were here,' he remembered. 'You and Ella were here the day I burnt them.'

'That's destroying evidence,' Max told him.

'I'd have burned that bugger along with 'em if he hadn't been dead already,' Jack assured him. 'And before you ask, Sherlock, no, I didn't kill him. Nothing would have pleased me more, but I didn't do it.'

'I know.'

'Oh? How's that?'

'We've been checking a lot of CCTV footage and your smiling face was caught on camera in Rochdale,' Max told him.

'Was it? Well, I'm buggered. You lot aren't as daft as you look.'

But not clever enough, Jill thought, as Max began asking him about McQueen, Khalil and Tessa Bailey. Max was convinced there was a connection; Jill wasn't.

All the same, it was coincidental that, three weeks after Bradley Johnson's body was found, Thomas McQueen was filled full of bullets. And Bradley Johnson, they knew, enjoyed a spot of blackmail. If he'd found out who had killed Khalil, and if he knew McQueen had been mixed up in it–

Round and round they went in ever-decreasing circles. She was tired, hungry and thoroughly depressed, and she wasn't sorry when they left Jack's house.

'Dinner,' Max said, taking her arm and

guiding her to his car.

'And not a word about any of it,' she warned him.

'Scouts' honour.'

'Oh, yeah, like you were ever in the Scouts.'

'I was! I'll have you know that my sheep-shank had to be seen to be believed. As for my Hunter's Bend and Buntline Hitch, remarkable. King of the knots, I was.'

She smiled at that and slowly began to relax.

It was cold in the car and the heater blew out icy air before Max switched off the fan.

'Where to?' he asked her.

'The Red Chilli in Bacup. And don't spare the horses.'

The Chinese restaurant was always Jill's choice when she was famished. It was impossible to leave the place hungry. Added to that, the food was exquisite and the service first-rate.

An hour later, with her appetite sated and with copious amounts of wine consumed, she felt much better. True to his word, Max hadn't mentioned the case.

And then he took a phone call.

When it was over, he snapped his phone shut and returned it to his pocket. 'Well, well, well. Who'd have thought it?' He put up his hand. 'Sorry, I forgot we weren't talking work.'

'Now what's happened?' she asked, wary. 'We haven't got another corpse, have we?'

But he didn't look concerned. 'It'll keep till tomorrow. We're not talking work, remember?'

Damn him, he knew she wouldn't rest.

'Come on. Tell me.'

'Peter Lawrence was arrested in the early hours of this morning,' he said.

She sagged with relief. Peter Lawrence was arrested on a regular basis.

'Drunk and disorderly?'

'Nope. Breaking and entering.'

'Blimey.' She had to smile. 'That's a new one. Into a pub or an off-licence?'

'Neither. West Mercia Constabulary caught him trying to gain access to a narrowboat in Worcestershire.'

'What? You're kidding me.' She couldn't believe it. 'But I didn't mention anything about boats. All I did was try and get him to come up with names of Claire's friends.'

She simply couldn't believe it.

'The owners returned to it to find him,' Max explained.

'Really? Who are they?'

'I don't know.'

'Who the hell might Claire know who owns a narrowboat?'

Of course, it could be nothing more than Peter Lawrence finding himself in Worcestershire without a bed for the night and trying his luck on the river. No, that was too much of a coincidence.

'I need to get down there to see him,' she said.

And she had no intention of leaving until she had a name from him. He must know something.

Chapter Thirty

Jill often arrived at HMP Styal with time to spare, but today she was in a rush. All the same, as she'd skipped breakfast, she ate a Cadbury's Flake and had a quick look at the day's runners and riders. If she didn't have a winner today, she may as well admit defeat. Gambling was a mug's game anyway.

Not that a mug would have backed Manor Boy and netted themselves three hundred quid, she reminded herself. However, that had been her last decent win.

None of the horses leapt off the page at her. Her dad had told her to back Swansong but, despite his claims that it was a dead cert, she wasn't convinced. Her dad's luck was no better than hers right now. But if she didn't back it, the animal was sure to romp home leaving the rest of the field furlongs behind. She may as well squander a tenner on it. Maybe twenty, just in case.

Minutes were ticking by and, without much hope, she phoned through her bets. Six fine racehorses or six worn-out nags? Time would tell.

Ten minutes later, she was with Claire Lawrence.

'Your husband was arrested yesterday.' Jill came straight to the point.

'Again?' Claire wasn't interested.

'Yes, breaking and entering. In Worcestershire of all places.' She brushed an imaginary speck from her shirt before saying casually, 'Apparently, he was trying to get inside a narrowboat on the river down there.'

Claire was interested now. She didn't say anything, but her fingers were wrapping themselves around a strand of hair in an extremely agitated fashion.

'I wonder what he was looking for,' Jill said carelessly.

'A drink, I expect.'

'It's a long way to go for a drink. Even for Peter. Anyway, he was arrested before he had a chance to find anything and he wouldn't say what he was looking for.'

Those fingers slowed slightly.

'I've had a chat with the police, though,' Jill continued, 'and now they're curious. Very curious. They're talking to owners of every boat in the area.'

Claire said nothing. For a full twenty

minutes. When Jill spoke, she merely hummed tunelessly.

'I can't waste time here,' Jill said pleasantly. 'I'm on my way to Worcestershire to have a chat with your husband.'

Claire merely shrugged.

'Don't worry, I'll let you know as soon as the police find anything.'

There was no response from Claire so Jill left her to her worries and headed down the M6 to Worcestershire.

Traffic was backed up where the M5 joined the M6 but, other than that, Jill's journey went smoothly and she was soon sharing a room with a sullen Peter Lawrence. A young constable sat alongside Jill as they tried to get him to talk.

She wasn't hopeful. Jill had assumed he'd been found trying to break into a specific narrowboat. He hadn't. He'd been walking along the River Avon checking on half a dozen that were moored there. All six had been unoccupied but the owners of the last one had returned from an evening at the pub and called the police.

'So what made you think of boats, Peter?' she asked him.

'Nothing really.'

'It's funny that. Something made me think along the same lines.'

'Oh?'

'Yes. And do you know what, we both thought of boats for exactly the same reason. Because of something Claire said.'

He scuffed his feet back and forth on the floor.

'She told me she'd like to live on one,' Jill went on. 'Something in the way she said it made me think that maybe, just maybe, she had experience of boats, that perhaps she knew someone who lived on one.'

He shrugged.

Unlike the interview suite at Harrington, this one was hot and stuffy. Peter Lawrence was sweating.

'So we assume you were breaking into the narrowboat with the intention of stealing whatever you could find,' the constable said. 'That's a serious matter, as you know. When we heard from Lancashire that you might be looking for someone, we thought maybe you had a valid reason to be there. It seems we were wrong.'

Lawrence thought about that.

'Something has made you think of boats,' Jill said. 'As unlikely as it seems, Claire must have a friend who had access to one. Why don't you save us all, you especially, a lot of time and tell us that friend's name.'

'I don't know her name,' he snapped.

Great.

'But Claire mentioned someone?'

He nodded.

'What did she say?'

'I found a phone number scribbled on a fag packet in her coat,' he said on a long sigh. 'Ages ago it was. I thought it was some bloke. Anyway, according to her, the number belonged to her best mate.'

'And she didn't tell you a name?'

'Not that I remember. She was sad, she said, because this mate was going off with some bloke she'd met.'

'And he owned a boat?'

'Yeah.' He thought for a moment. 'She won't still be with him, though. This mate of Claire's, I mean. She was a prostitute, same as Claire, but the bloke knew nothing about that.'

Even if the relationship *had* lasted, the couple could be living in Australia by now.

'All I know,' Lawrence went on, 'was that he lived on a boat in Evesham. And Claire's mate – she said she was the sort you could trust with your life.'

And with her daughter's life.

This girl, whoever she was, must have been a rare find for a woman like Claire who didn't trust enough to make friends easily...

The drive back to Lancashire took three and a half hours, and Jill went straight to head-quarters where she was just in time for the evening briefing. The first person she saw was Grace, who was trying to get a coffee from the machine.

'Anything?' Jill asked her.

'Damn thing. It's taken me half an hour to get a cup.'

'I meant anything from Worcestershire?'

'Nothing. And don't raise your hopes, Jill. It would be virtually impossible to hide a kid like Daisy for so long. We launched a massive search at the time. No, someone would have seen her long before now.'

Jill knew she had a point.

'How confident are you that Daisy's still alive?' Grace asked.

She wouldn't bet her cottage on it. 'Seventy-five per cent,' she answered and Grace whistled through her teeth.

'If you're wrong, you're going to be in deep—'

'I know,' Jill cut her off, not wanting to consider the possibility of being wrong and the consequences for all concerned.

But she wasn't alone. Peter Lawrence had been convinced enough to go to Worcester-shire...

After the briefing, she went to her office, pushed aside all thoughts of rivers in Worcestershire, and checked her emails. She fired off quick answers to half a dozen and then picked up the sheet of paper on which she'd scribbled all suspects for the murder of Bradley Johnson. What bothered her most was that she knew every one of them.

They were her neighbours.

Phoebe had a motive. Her husband had been sleeping around and might have been on the verge of leaving her for all they knew. She'd had opportunity, too. Yet why would she go to the trouble of killing him in Black's Wood? It would be too risky. Why not do the deed at the manor and trot out the well-worn story of him disturbing a burglar?

But she didn't think this was a family matter. The Johnsons were one of those close-knit families who, although they had a wide circle of acquaintances, were short on close friends. Phoebe kept to herself and the boys stuck together. They were a family who always thought they had to be on show. They wanted to stay private, to keep their petty arguments to themselves.

Damn it, it was always the same. Every case she worked on, the doubts plagued her. She'd got it wrong before, big style, and that mistake had been partly responsible for costing a man his life.

Was she wrong to dismiss Phoebe?

What about Hannah Brooks? She had a motive. Johnson was threatening to end her career and, with it, in all probability, her marriage. She had even admitted to seeing him on that fateful afternoon. Why the admission? Because someone had spotted her? Either way, it would have been easy enough for her to wait until Ella had continued walking, then follow him into the wood. Her grandfather had owned dogs all his life so Hannah would have walked through Black's Wood countless times. Just like her grandfather, she would know every tree.

Gordon Brooks had an alibi. But so what? Just because work colleagues said he was at the office all day didn't necessarily mean that he was. If he'd got wind of Hannah and Bradley's relationship, he might have been driven to murder. But was he such an accomplished actor? Yesterday evening, he'd been genuinely shocked, angered, hurt and every other damn thing one might expect. Hadn't he?

'Yay!' Grace burst into the room, completely abolishing Jill's train of thought. 'We've got John Barry!'

This was a real breakthrough as Tom McQueen's minder – or driver – hadn't been seen since his boss had been murdered.

'You'll never guess where,' Grace said grinning. 'Just down the road at Manchester airport. He was about to board a plane to Ireland. I'm going to have great fun with him,' she added gleefully.

'Me too, I hope.'

John Barry had taken over the role of chief suspect the second McQueen was found dead. He'd have killed Khalil. Possibly, no probably, on McQueen's orders. Then, perhaps they argued. Perhaps McQueen didn't recompense his hired guns highly enough.

John Barry would have taken exception to that and decided to teach McQueen a lesson.

There was a flaw to that argument. With McQueen dead, Barry couldn't expect a pay rise. And how the hell did Tessa fit into the picture?

If she really didn't know the circumstances surrounding her boyfriend's death, why leave her for dead on the back streets of Harrington?

They would worry about that later. Now that Barry had been found, they could, hopefully, arrange an identification parade and see if Claire would identify him as the man sent to rough her up, the same man sent to get Daisy.

Jill's phone rang and she saw from the display that her mother was calling.

'Hi, Mum!' Even her mother had to make more sense than this tangled mess.

Chapter Thirty-One

Max was getting annoyed, seriously annoyed, with John Barry, and he was a step away from strangling the bloke's lawyer.

Joe Hale, defence lawyer to the lowlife, was doing no more to earn his money than advise his client not to answer Max's questions.

'On the evening in question, January the twentieth last year, Tom McQueen's car was seen on Maltby Hill, less than five hundred yards from where Muhammed Khalil's body was found. Were you driving the car?'

'I was asked that same question a year ago.' For once, Barry answered without consulting his lawyer.

'Yes, and you told us then that you weren't driving it. Perhaps you've had a rethink.'

'Hey, look, I can't be expected to remember that far back. If I told you I wasn't, then I wasn't. Perhaps Mr McQueen was. Hell, even Mrs McQueen drove the car occasionally.'

'Muhammed Khalil worked for your boss. McQueen was dealing – crack, I gather – and Khalil tried to do the dirty on him. Khalil got greedy and pretended he'd been robbed of your boss's precious crack. In reality, he sold the goods himself.'

'Crack?' Barry smiled at that. 'That's a very serious allegation.'

'It is.'

'You must be thinking of the wrong man. My boss knew nothing about drugs.'

'Khalil panicked,' Max went on. 'He heard McQueen was after him so he packed a few belongings and walked out on his girlfriend. He was on the run from McQueen – or one of his sidekicks. The next thing, we find him with a bullet through his head.'

'It's not safe out there, is it? I'm always saying the government should put more coppers on the streets.'

'As well as supplying the area with crack, McQueen had a penchant for prostitutes. Who drove him on those nights? You?'

'Wrong man, Chief Inspector. My boss had a beautiful wife.'

'He did, but he screwed prostitutes.'

'Oh, I can't believe that.'

'Where exactly have you been since Mc-Queen's body was pumped full of bullets?'

'I've told you time and time again,' he said patiently. 'I had a holiday booked in Scotland. It was booked six months ago. I go up there for Christmas and Hogmanay every year.' He smiled slyly. 'Don't tell me you haven't managed to check that out yet.'

They'd scrutinized every last detail and, sod it, it all checked out, just as John Barry claimed.

'And you didn't hear of your boss's sudden demise? I can't believe that.'

'Not a whisper.'

Max's patience had worn well beyond thin.

'So you return from Scotland, and go home to unpack. Then, within twelve hours, you're heading off to Ireland.'

'That's right.' John Barry leaned back in his seat, massive arms crossed against bulging chest muscles, and eyes twinkling with devilment. He was confident they had nothing on him.

Max had the sinking feeling that he was right.

'And you didn't think to check in with your boss,' he pushed on.

'No. Why should I? I was on holiday.'

'I believe my client is due a break,' the oily little lawyer said.

'Spinal cord preferably,' Max muttered.

He suspended the interview and went to get himself a coffee while Barry was fed and watered. He got two coffees and took them along to Jill's office.

'Is that for me?' She reached out for the plastic cup. 'You must be a mind reader.'

'God, I wish.' He dragged a chair across the room and dropped on to it. 'There's no possibility that he's telling the truth, is there?'

'John Barry? Never in a million years.'

'He was definitely in Scotland the night before and the night after McQueen was killed,' he pointed out.

'But you know as well as I do that, as soon as he knew what was going on, he'd have made sure he was a good distance away.'

'Hm. But he made the booking six months ago.'

Jill frowned at him. 'Surely you don't believe his story.'

'No, of course not.' And yet– 'I can't understand how he can have had anything to do with that sodding shooting.'

'He wouldn't have been working alone,' Jill said easily. 'We wouldn't expect him to be. He was seen with McQueen too often. It had to look like an honest, working relationship.'

Max felt defeated. He was no closer to solving Khalil's murder than he'd been last year. Every lead they followed took them straight back to square one. They had nothing.

'And now the lying bastard is having lunch courtesy of the taxpayer,' he said darkly. 'Bloody marvellous.'

His coffee finished, he tossed his empty cup in the waste-bin and got to his feet.

'I'll go and see how much more of his story we've managed to confirm.'

'I'll come with you. I need to stretch my legs.'

Several officers, Fletch and Grace included, were busy on their phones, but there was nothing new.

'We're missing something vital,' Max said to no one in particular. 'Something's been bugging me about McQueen's murder from the start.'

But what?

He thought back to that afternoon, to his meeting with Barbara McQueen, to their time in the coffee bar, to her calling the taxi's office, to her stopping for those cases of wine...

'Grace, have we got Barbara McQueen's phone records yet?' he asked.

'The landline, yes. The last I heard, we were still waiting for her mobile details. Why?'

'Just curious,' he said, still not sure which direction his thoughts were taking. 'Hurry it along, will you? Check the calls she made on her mobile the day he was killed.'

Why exactly had he gone into the house that day? If she'd managed to get a taxi, and if she hadn't insisted on stopping for that wine...

Yet she couldn't have known he would be in Harrington that afternoon. He'd only stopped the car and decided to go for a coffee on impulse. And she couldn't have known he would be walking round that corner.

All the same, he'd made a damn good witness that day. Walking into the house with her like that, he'd seen her outpourings of shock and grief at first hand.

Chapter Thirty-Two

On Friday morning, Jill was in interview room three alongside Max. Barbara Mc-Queen, sitting opposite, looked confident and immaculately groomed. Her hair was just so, her clothes – red trousers and white shirt in linen – looked expensive, and there wasn't so much as a single chip to be seen on her red-polished fingernails. She wore a lot of jewellery, all gold, all expensive.

Jill's mind was wandering. John Barry had agreed to take part in an identification parade and Claire Lawrence had been brought up from Styal. Any minute now, the identification officers should let them know the result.

Jill was in no doubt that the man sent to threaten Claire was Barry. But would Claire identify him? Most witnesses found it an intimidating experience, harrowing even, and a lot were reluctant to openly accuse someone of a crime. Claire, still not entirely convinced that Tom McQueen was dead, was more frightened than most.

'I owe you an apology,' Barbara McQueen told Max softly. 'I was distraught that afternoon – the afternoon we found my Tommy. I didn't know what I was doing. But that's no excuse. I should never have accused you of brutality. I know you were only trying to protect me.'

Trying to protect the crime scene more like, Jill thought.

'I understand,' Max replied, equally pleasant. 'Talk me through what happened that day,' he said.

'Well, as you know, I went to the spa in the morning. I had a good long swim, a massage and a sauna. Then I had a manicure before going to the hairdresser's.'

Jill applied lipstick each day. And that was it. Mrs McQueen was always immaculately turned out, but Jill couldn't believe that the time, not to mention the money, involved in achieving the effect was worth it. If she had to spend her days being worked on to that degree, she would go mad.

'What time did you go to the spa?' Max asked.

'I was there by ten o'clock.'

According to their reckoning, Tom McQueen had been killed sometime between ten and midday.

'And it was after you came out of the hairdresser's that we bumped into each other, is that right?' Max asked her.

'Yes. And you kindly bought me a coffee.'

'And then you tried calling a taxi,' Max reminded her.

'I did. Except, as you've discovered, I was calling the wrong number. I was phoning home and there was no one there...' She paused to dab at her eyes with a tissue. 'It's an easy enough mistake to make. I have the house phone, Tommy's mobile, the hairdresser, the spa and the taxi on speed dial,' she explained. 'It's all too easy to get confused and call the wrong one.'

Was it hell. Once maybe, but if you weren't getting anywhere, you'd check you had the right number. At least, Jill would.

'I'm sure it is,' Max agreed smoothly. 'The

thing is, you told me the number you were trying to call was engaged. Now, as we've ascertained that you were phoning your home number in error, I wonder how that happened?'

'I've no idea,' she replied.

'According to our records, no one used that phone. There was no reason why you should have received an engaged tone.'

'There must have been a fault on the line,' she said.

The moisture in the eyes, the shaky voice – it was all an act. A damn good one, admittedly, but Barbara McQueen was a fake. She'd married Tom for his money, Jill would bet her cottage on that.

Max wanted them to be all sweetness and light on this first interview, but Jill was beginning to think that was a waste of time. Max could tread softly; Jill wanted some answers.

'Your husband had sex with prostitutes,' she remarked casually. 'I suppose you knew that.'

'A lot of men do.' Yes, she was very cool. 'What about you, Max? Do you indulge?'

'Well, DCI Trentham?' Jill prompted, giving him her sugary smile.

'No, I don't,' he said finally, scowling at Jill. 'I've always assumed they're a last resort for men who don't get it at home.'

'Oh, they are,' Jill lied. 'I bet Tommy was a bit embarrassed really. A half-decent, young woman at home and the poor bloke wasn't getting anything. Did he take kindly to that, Mrs McQueen?'

'He got plenty.'

'Really?' Jill didn't have to fake her surprise. 'I would have thought you might have fancied someone younger. And someone fifty to sixty pounds lighter. Still, there's no accounting for taste, is there?'

'You don't know anything about me and Tommy.'

'True. Married to a gem like Tom and now you stand to inherit a small fortune. Well, a large fortune, in fact. The gods are really smiling on you, Mrs McQueen.'

'You think the money's any consolation for losing my Tommy?'

'Yes.'

'How many times have you called a phone number in error?' Max asked her.

'Loads.'

'Care to give me a few examples?'

She smiled at that. 'Sorry, but I've never taken notes.'

'You get all sorts of nasty diseases from sleeping with prostitutes,' Jill put in, pleased to see that Mrs McQueen was having trouble keeping up. 'Protection gets forgotten or ignored. Have you been to the clinic to get yourself checked out? That would be a rather unpleasant legacy, wouldn't it? No soreness? Inflammation?'

'You're so coarse,' Barbara McQueen said with real disgust.

'So I've been told.' Jill shrugged. 'It was just a bit of friendly advice. If I found out that my husband had been having it away with crackheads, I'd get myself checked out p.d.q.'

Barbara looked at her the way someone might look at slug slime.

'How did Tom pay for sex?' Jill went on, unconcerned. 'Did he treat them to some crack? I suppose he did. It would cut out the middleman, wouldn't it? There'd be no point his giving them cash, only for them to buy crack from him. That would be plain silly.'

'I don't know what you're talking about.'

She knew. The innocent, scatterbrained wife who spent half her life at the hairdresser's didn't exist. Never had.

Well, perhaps she had existed on that memorable train journey all those years ago, but something, marriage to Tom perhaps, had sent her packing.

'He gave crack to young kids, too, didn't he? As young as eleven. Still, get them addicted young, eh? Far more profitable. Did he fancy sex with those? The eleven-year-olds, I mean?'

'OK, you've enjoyed your little joke.' Barbara's expression was glacial. 'If you want to know anything else, you'll have to wait until my lawyer's here.'

Damn.

Barbara refused to utter another word and Max had no alternative but to suspend the interview until her lawyer arrived.

'Nice going, Jill,' he muttered as they left the room.

'Sorry.'

'And what was all that prostitute crap?' he demanded. 'What in hell's name does that have to do with anything?'

'She's lived with Tom McQueen for years without poisoning him or shooting him,' Jill reasoned. 'Something's happened. Recently. Something has driven her to murder.'

Max rolled his eyes. 'Shagging the odd street girl was the least of McQueen's crimes.'

'True. But if you were Barbara, practically living in beauty salons and designer shops, spending your husband's ill-gotten gains, what would suddenly drive you over the edge?'

He stopped walking to consider that, but he had no answer.

'If it were me,' Jill told him smoothly, 'I'd be pretty annoyed – absolutely furious in fact – if I discovered he'd slept with someone else.' She slapped a hand to her forehead. 'Oh, sorry, you already know that, don't you? I'm sure you can remember how – displeased – I was when you left me at home to spend the night with Miss Young and Attractive.'

'Oh, for Christ's sake!'

Damn it, she'd vowed never to bring that up again.

'I'd be even more annoyed – yes, more annoyed – if I found out he was regularly shagging crackheads. And if he passed on an STD, I would probably kill him.'

Max was weighing up her logic.

'On the other hand,' she said with a careless shrug, 'he might just have refused to buy her a new pair of Jimmy Choos.'

Jill had known she was at fault for making Barbara demand her lawyer, but, having vented her anger, she felt much better.

Max carried on walking.

'Coffee?' he asked her.

'Please.' And now she didn't feel quite so good. 'And I'm sorry I dragged Miss Young and Attractive into it. I was trying to make a point, but that's no excuse, I know. I apologize.'

A reluctant laugh escaped him. 'Jill Kennedy utters an apology. How much more surreal can this day get?'

'Don't tempt fate.'

With coffees from the machine in their hands, they went to the office where the sight that met them told them surreal had only just started. Fletch, all food abandoned, was lying on the floor, chanting, 'Thank you, God! Bloody thank you!'

'Are they bringing out a three-foot Mars

bar, Fletch?' Max quipped.

At the sound of Max's voice, Fletch sprang to his feet and stood by his desk. 'No, Max. It's even better.' His face was tinged red with embarrassment. 'While John Barry was in Scotland, it seems that Mrs McQueen called him several times.'

'Did she indeed?'

'We think so, yes. We've spoken to the hotel's receptionist – not the regular one, but the one that stood in for holidays. She claims to have taken as many as four calls in one day from a female calling herself Babs. Always from a phone booth apparently.'

'So they were in this together?' Max murmured.

'It looks like it.'

'At least we know Barry's lying,' Grace said. 'I'm sure she would have mentioned the small fact of her husband being shot to bits in passing.'

'We'd best have another chat with him,' Max said.

They were on their way to see him when they heard the news. Claire, now heading back to Styal, hadn't recognized anyone at the identification parade. Or so she said.

Jill wasn't surprised. Frustrated, but not surprised.

'I suppose it was a nice day out for her,' Max remarked.

Chapter Thirty-Three

This time, on Jill's advice, Max decided to play the nice cop with John Barry. It went against nature but, as Jill had pointed out, they needed his cooperation.

'We need your help, Mr Barry,' he said. 'And if you cooperate with us, we'll forgive your lies.'

'What lies?' he scoffed.

'Lies about not knowing your boss, Tom McQueen, was dead. We have access to phone records,' Max reminded him, 'and we know just how many times you spoke to Mrs McQueen while you were in Scotland.'

'Oh. OK then. Yeah, she did mention it.' He wriggled uncomfortably in his seat. 'I would have told you but, with the benefit of hindsight, it looks bad. I would have come back, but – well, to be honest, there didn't seem much point. There was nothing I could do, was there?'

'Perhaps not, but you must have realized we were looking for you,' Max said drily.

'It never crossed my mind,' he said, all innocence.

His lawyer bent over and whispered something in his ear. 'The thing is,' Max went on

pleasantly, 'we're interviewing Mrs Mc-
Queen and she isn't being very talkative.'

A nerve twitched in his neck.

'Eh? What's she doing here?'

'What did you find to talk about while you
were in Scotland?' Max asked, ignoring his
question.

'This and that. Why? What's she been saying?'

Barry's lawyer looked worried, too. The
fact that his client had conversed with Mrs
McQueen had clearly come as something of
a surprise.

'This and that? Could you be more
specific?' Max asked pleasantly.

He would love to throttle the man with his
bare hands. Then again, his hands wouldn't
fit around that thick neck...

'I can't rightly remember.'

'Explain this to me,' Jill said casually. 'If
Mrs McQueen were to intimate that you
murdered her husband, why might she
think we would believe her? You weren't
anywhere near England at the time of the
shooting, were you?'

Max winced at that, but John Barry's
reaction was of far more interest.

'What?' A vein pulsed in that thick neck of
his. It was almost possible to hear his brain
trying to make sense of that. 'She told you –
no, I don't believe it. You're lying.'

More brawn than brain, he looked as if he

didn't know what to believe.

'She's said all sorts of things,' Jill murmured. 'But why might she think we'd believe you murdered her husband?'

'Because she's crazy, that's why. How could I do that? I wasn't anywhere near. I was in Scotland. I was hundreds of miles away. You know I was.'

'It's very – what shall we say? – convenient that you were, as it turned out,' Max told him.

'What sort of woman is Mrs McQueen?' Jill asked. 'Is she the sort who would let you take the rap for her husband's murder, do you think?'

His lawyer opened his mouth to speak, but John Barry was too furious to stop and think.

'She's an evil bitch, so yeah, she would. What's she said? It's all lies.'

'You're quite sure that she can't provide us with any evidence?' Jill asked. 'There's nothing she could have – twisted?'

'Evidence?' His small, beady eyes darted from one to the other. 'Of course she can't give you evidence. There's no evidence because I didn't do it. She's a lying, two-faced, evil bitch. Oh, no. She's not laying the blame for any damn thing on me. It was her. Not me. Her, I tell you! I wasn't even in the country. You know I wasn't!'

Fletch was right; there was a God.

'Her?' Max repeated.

Barry's lawyer put a restraining hand on his client's arm, but it was immediately shaken off.

'None of it has anything to do with me. You have to believe me. You were right about seeing Mr McQueen's car – when that Asian lad, Khalil, was murdered, remember? McQueen shot him. It was McQueen.' Barry's words were tripping over themselves. 'Mrs McQueen found out and she asked me to get her a gun. Said she was frightened. Said she was scared that a bunch of Asians would come for her when Tom was away.'

'You got her a gun?' Max asked.

'Yes.'

'Why didn't she ask her husband to get it?' Jill asked him. 'Why you?'

'I don't know.'

He was lying. There was no way that McQueen would have used a gun on Khalil. Or anyone else for that matter. McQueen wouldn't dirty his hands.

'Carry on,' Max prompted.

'The next thing I know, she's killed Mr McQueen,' he said. 'I didn't want to know. Hell's teeth, I hadn't expected her to use the bloody thing – and especially not on her own husband.'

'She phoned you in Scotland to tell you?' Max asked.

'Yes.'

'Did she say why she'd killed him?'

'Oh, yes. She'd found out, you see, that Tom had been screwing around with Khalil's old lady. She's a whore.'

'Oh, dear.' Jill smiled at that. 'I bet that didn't please her.'

'She can talk. She's nothing more than a slag. She'll have sex with anyone.'

'Ah, yes. We heard something to that effect. Something about you forcing yourself on her. Is that right, John? Did you have sex with her?'

Max had no idea what Jill was playing at, but John Barry was on the point of a coronary.

'Me? Force myself on her? The fucking lying bitch! We had sex, but it was her who gave me the come-on.'

'Was that before or after Mr McQueen was murdered?' Max asked.

'Before. I haven't seen her since.' He shook off his lawyer's restraining arm again.

'So you had a – relationship?' Jill pushed on. 'How long for?'

'Four months. Maybe five.'

'Carry on,' Max urged him.

'Well, when I was in Scotland, she kept on and on about this bird of Khalil's. She wanted to know everything – what she looked like, where she lived, everything. It was me who told her to forget it, but she couldn't. She kept saying no one two-timed her and got away with it. She began threatening me. That's when I was in Scotland. She said if I didn't tell her where she could find Khalil's bird, I'd end up like Tom.'

'She'd put six bullets in you?' Max asked.

'Yes. She's one crazy bitch. And you can tell her I said so.'

'So you're claiming that Thomas Mc-Queen killed Muhammed Khalil?' Max asked, hardly daring to breathe.

'Yes. It's the truth, I swear it.'

'And you also claim that Mrs Barbara McQueen murdered her husband?'

'I do.'

'And you also maintain that Mrs Barbara McQueen then attacked Muhammed Khalil's girlfriend, Tessa Bailey?'

'Too right I do. And if she says anything different, she's lying.'

'I see,' Max said. 'And she was acting on your information? You were the one who gave her Tessa Bailey's address? Is that right?'

Barry's face was scarlet with rage. 'I didn't want to, but I had to, didn't I? Besides, I thought she was just planning on having a slanging match with her.'

'Really?' Jill mused. 'But she'd killed her husband, hadn't she? She doesn't appear to be the type of woman who wastes time on conversation.'

'That's what I thought, I swear. A slanging match.'

'How often did you have sex with Mrs

McQueen?' Jill asked.

'Too often. Lying, two-faced bitch. She's like a bloody dead thing in the sack, too. And you can tell her that from me!'

That vein was still throbbing in Barry's neck.

'Are you sure there's no evidence she can give us that will put you in the frame for murder, John?' Jill asked him, and Barry slammed his huge fist down on the table with so much force, Max was surprised not to see splinters everywhere.

'There is no fucking evidence. She'll give you nothing. She can't!'

Max suspended the interview and he and Jill stepped outside.

'What do you think?' he asked Jill.

'I think he assumed he'd be stepping into Tom McQueen's shoes. Bed, bank account, the lot. I bet they planned Tom's demise together, and then he was expecting to move right in.'

'You reckon?'

'Yes, and now he's feeling aggrieved. Cheated. He's not pining for Barbara's company. He wanted, and expected, a share in Tom's fortune.'

'Do you believe his story?'

'Bits of it,' Jill replied. 'I don't believe for a minute that Tom McQueen shot Khalil.'

'No?'

'Never in a million years. He wouldn't do

358

his own dirty work.'

'Hm. That's what I thought.'

Max was famished. He was convinced, though, that they were finally getting there. Barbara McQueen's lawyer hadn't arrived yet, so food would have to wait.

He had a quick word with Fletch to make sure her lawyer was stalled and then they went to talk to her.

'Oh, isn't your lawyer here yet?' Max said, acting surprised.

She sat there tight-lipped.

'He'll be here in a minute.' Max switched on the tapes and introduced those present.

'I've left instructions for someone to tell him that we'll be charging you with murder and attempted murder. That'll have him racing to your side.'

'You what?' She couldn't decide if he was joking or not.

'The game's over, Mrs McQueen. John Barry is just along the corridor,' Max said, 'and he's told us everything.'

'John? Here? But I thought–' She broke off.

'You thought he was in Ireland?' Max guessed. 'Sadly not. He missed his plane.'

'Oh, and he asked us to relay a message to you,' Jill said. 'He said you were – what was it? Oh, yes, like a dead thing in the sack. He's told us all about it. About your husband killing Muhammed Khalil, about you find-ing out that he had been screwing Khalil's girlfriend, about how you killed your husband and then went after Tessa Bailey.'

'You're a liar!' She went for Jill with lightning speed, her long fingernails missing Jill's face by a fraction.

'Calm down!' Max shouted.

He found it almost impossible to believe that Barbara McQueen was the same laughing, fun-loving woman with whom he'd shared that train journey all those years ago. He'd thought her an airhead, but what the hell had she done? Sat in the hairdresser's, reading the latest copy of *Hello!* while plotting to kill her husband? What had happened to her?

Tom McQueen had happened, he supposed. Perhaps anyone married to a man like that would be dragged down to that level.

'We've got it all on tape,' Max told her. 'Now, perhaps–'

'I couldn't give a damn what you've got on tape. You're lying.'

'No, Barbara,' Jill told her.

'The bastard!' she whispered. 'The lying, two-faced bastard!'

She took several deep breaths and she was calm. Dangerously, icy calm.

'On my mobile phone,' she told Max, 'you'll find recordings I made of those lying bastards – Tom and that bastard, John Barry. I knew they were up to no good so I started leaving my phone lying around when they were together. You want Muhammed Khalil's killer? Get my phone.'

'John Barry?' Max guessed, and she nodded.

'Is that a yes?'

'Yes. All the proof you need is on my phone. A hundred grand Tom paid him for that little job.'

'I see.' Max had been right about one thing. She was an airhead. 'We were beginning to think you'd killed your husband and Muhammed Khalil,' he said.

'Of course I didn't kill Khalil,' she scoffed. 'I didn't know him. Never heard of him until I heard those bastards talking about him and that slut he lived with.'

She really was a total airhead.

The same thought must have occurred to her. Belatedly.

'I'll get a deal, won't I?' she said. 'Now I've told you who killed Khalil, they'll be lenient, won't they?'

'I wouldn't count on it, Mrs McQueen.'

Just then, when it was far too late, her lawyer arrived.

Chapter Thirty-Four

Jill's glass was empty, so she went to the kitchen for the bottle of wine. Her boiler had been fixed that morning and so far, she thought, bending to touch the wooden coffee table, it was behaving perfectly. It was snowing heavily outside, but her cottage was a haven of comfort and warmth.

Max had called in on his way home and everything felt – civilized.

She knew, though, just how much work would be involved in getting this case to court.

'Fancy having hard evidence to send John Barry down,' she mused.

'Brilliant,' Max agreed. 'Fancy recording their conversations. What a star!' The idea amused him. 'That's what Harry does. Unbeknown to me, he'll record us having a conversation about going to watch the Clarets and then, when I deny all knowledge of any promises made, he'll play back the recording.'

Jill smiled at that. It was typical of Max's son to know that evidence was vital.

She topped up her glass.

'It's good news all round,' she said with

362

satisfaction. 'The best news, though, is finding Daisy. God, I really feel for that kid.'

Daisy Lawrence had been found in a rundown flat in Worcester. Claire had left her in the hands of her best friend, Natalie Drinkwater. Natalie still worked as a prostitute, but, like Claire, she was off drugs. She took her responsibilities seriously and looking after Daisy had been her top priority. She shared a flat with two other girls, girls who were more than able to avoid suspicion and, more importantly, the police. They'd kept Daisy safe, if nothing else. The narrowboat had gone a year ago, reclaimed by its owner, one of Natalie's customers, and since then, the girls had shared a tiny, two-bedroomed flat in Worcester.

'All that education she's missed,' Jill said. 'It's criminal. She'll never catch up now. She was a bright kid, too. Still, she's happy and healthy enough, I suppose.'

'What's going to happen to her?'

'What do you think? Red tape, more red tape, and yet more red tape. Enough red tape to keep her bound up until she's an adult probably. Claire's clean though, and she's no longer living in fear of McQueen so – well, we'll have to see. I've promised her that, so long as she stays clean, I'll help fight her corner.'

'Do you think she will? Or do you think she'll be straight back on heroin?'

The truth was, Jill didn't know.

'We'll just hope for the best,' she said.

'I still can't believe anyone would do that,' Max said, shaking his head. 'Why the hell would someone deliberately get themselves locked up at Styal? Why would someone hand over their daughter? It's insane.'

'She was scared of McQueen,' Jill said simply. 'She thought her own life and, more important, Daisy's life were in danger.' She looked at him. 'So what would you do if you believed Harry or Ben's life to be in danger?'

'Bloody sort it,' he answered without hesitation. 'In Claire's position, I would have contacted the police.'

'But she had no faith in the police.'

He merely grunted at the truth of that.

Jill tucked her feet beneath her and thought again how warm and cosy her cottage was. The wind was howling and, although she didn't look out, she assumed it was still snowing.

'How was Meredith's health and temper?' she asked him. 'You were in his office for ages.'

'Tell me about it. He's far from happy.'

'Isn't that typical? Honestly, there's no pleasing the bloke. Muhammed Khalil's killer is accounted for, as is Tom McQueen's. Tessa's stabbing – that's solved.'

'You're forgetting something,' Max reminded her.

Jill wasn't. She knew full well that they were no closer to catching Bradley Johnson's killer.

'At least we know Bradley Johnson's murder wasn't connected to McQueen,' she pointed out.

'We know we've found no proof of it being connected to McQueen,' he corrected her.

'No. I never thought it was. Johnson's killer is much closer to home.'

Jill had always believed that. Yet, despite the hours spent on the case, they were no nearer naming a suspect.

'Perhaps it will always be a mystery,' she said.

'No.' Max would hate that thought as much as she did. 'We'll get our man eventually. We always do. Well, nearly always.'

'Phoebe's selling up,' she told him. 'The For Sale board went up this morning.'

'Is she your number one suspect?' he asked curiously.

'No. I'd stake my life on it being tied up with Hannah Brooks. Jack Taylor – is it definitely him on the CCTV? It couldn't be someone who just looks like him?'

'We're sure it's him. Why do you ask?'

'Because he's the only one who fits my profile.'

'But you said he wasn't a killer.'

'That was before I knew all the facts, before I knew that his granddaughter was on the verge of losing everything.' She took a sip of her drink. 'One, he knows every inch of that wood. Two, he viewed Bradley Johnson with contempt. Three, he would do anything to protect Hannah. Four, he has nothing to lose. After all, he's seventy-eight, and his best friend is dying.' She grinned suddenly. 'He even has a dog.'

But cameras don't lie.

'Still, if he's on CCTV, that's my theory shot to pieces,' she said with a shrug.

'Hm.'

'What does that mean?'

'Nothing.'

'Yes, it does. Out with it, Trentham. You've had a thought.'

'Not really.' He emptied his glass and stood up. 'Time I was off, kiddo. Now then, what about tomorrow? Shall we go in my car or yours? It's stupid to take two.'

Jill's brain was ticking over and getting nowhere. What did he mean? What had she forgotten? Whatever it was, she couldn't go anywhere with him. Tomorrow, she would be celebrating her parents' fortieth wedding anniversary.

'Remind me. What's happening—' An awful thought struck her. 'Where are you going tomorrow?'

'Liverpool. You?'

'She invited you?' Jill groaned. Her mother had spent hours on the phone reciting the menu and talking about her outfit, but she hadn't said a word about inviting Max.

'She did, bless her. The boys, too.'

Jill groaned again. 'That's even worse. She'll have a couple of G&Ts, and then make a drunken speech about wanting to see her poor daughter married off and those two unfortunate boys with a mother.'

'Probably,' Max agreed, looking highly amused at the prospect.

'You don't have to go, Max.'

'I wouldn't miss it for the world. Besides, she's expecting us. I couldn't let her down, could I?'

'You could. Easily.'

Jill's stomach turned over. She'd thought it bad enough that her mother had bought an outfit in shocking pink, that her father was still vowing to walk down to the working men's club and that karaoke was booked.

'It won't be as bad as you think,' Max told her.

'Ha!'

'So shall we all go in my car?'

'Why not?' They may as well arrive together and really give her mother something to talk about. 'Did she warn you about the karaoke?'

She laughed at the expression on his face.

'I can always pass on your apologies, Max.'

Chapter Thirty-Five

Max drove away from Jill's cottage and then decided he should stop at the newsagent's for cigarettes. He had a feeling it was going to be one of those nights.

The way the snow was drifting, the roads into Kelton Bridge would soon be blocked. He should drive home while he still could.

He sat in his car outside the newsagent's and lit a cigarette. Snow swirled into the car as soon as he wound down the window.

Maybe they wouldn't be able to get to Liverpool tomorrow. The motorways would be clear, at least he assumed they would, but he had to get into Kelton Bridge before heading off for the motorway.

His cigarette finished, he restarted the car and drove slowly off.

He really wished he could go straight home. Sadly, he couldn't. He wasn't that sort of bloke. He wouldn't be able to rest.

Lights were on in the houses, just visible through the snow.

He pulled up outside one particular house, switched off the engine and lit yet another cigarette. There were times, he decided, when he loathed his job.

What had Jill said? That their killer was someone who held Bradley Johnson in contempt, someone who was very familiar with Black's Wood, someone who had nothing to lose...

Spot on, Jill.

Love and hate, good and evil. There were very fine lines between those.

Bradley Johnson had been an evil man. He'd preyed on vulnerable women, demanding money in return for his silence. His luxurious lifestyle had been paid for by other people's grief. Yes, he'd been an evil man. As Jack Taylor had said, the world was a better place without him.

Whoever had killed him deserved a medal...

He tossed his cigarette butt out of the window, got out of his car, locked it and walked slowly through the driving snow to the front door.

How he wished he could walk away and forget it.

He hammered on the door and a dog barked somewhere inside. It was a high-pitched, excited bark, one that could easily be mistaken for that yappy little ankle-biter belonging to Olive Prendergast.

A light came on in the hallway. A bolt was dragged back. The door opened and there stood Archie.

'You've picked a bad night to be out, lad,'

Archie greeted him. 'Come inside, quick.'

The collie leapt all over Max as Archie closed the door behind them.

'Jess, damn it. Get down,' Archie scolded.

The dog took no notice whatsoever and leapt up at Max's face as if it was on springs.

'Sorry about Jess, but she'll settle in a minute,' Archie told him. 'Come in and grab a chair by the fire.'

Max, very reluctantly, did as he was told.

'Will you have a drink?' Archie asked him.

'No. No, thanks, Archie.'

Archie carried a wooden rocking chair closer to the fire. A heavy chair.

'What brings you out on a night like this?' he asked Max.

'Work, I'm afraid.'

'Ah.' Archie's hand automatically went to his collie's head.

'That's what I'm paid for,' Max said.

'Of course it is, lad. It's late to be working, though.'

It *was* late. Max could be halfway home by now. He wished to God he was.

The TV had been on when Max walked into the room, but Archie had switched it off and now, the only sounds were the ticking of a clock on the mantelpiece and an occasional hiss from the fire.

'You told me you'd given up the radiotherapy,' Max said, his heart somewhere down in his shoes.

'That's right. I decided it were a waste of time and the doctors didn't argue.'

Max nodded. 'So those hospital appointments – you showed me the dates, Archie, remember? You didn't keep an appointment the day Bradley Johnson was murdered, did you?'

Archie looked at him for long moments, his hand stroking the remarkably quiet collie. Perhaps even the dog sensed the sudden tension in the room.

'I didn't, lad. No.'

If Max had done his job properly, he would have checked with the clinic. On two occasions, he'd been on the verge of doing just that. And why hadn't he? Because he had so wanted to believe Archie's story.

'Hannah Brooks is your goddaughter, isn't she? Your best friend's granddaughter?'

'She's a good woman,' Archie answered. 'She's been foolish in her time, but haven't we all? Making mistakes when we're young is how we learn. That's what life is all about.'

'If you hadn't killed Bradley Johnson, Jack would have done it, wouldn't he? You couldn't let him do that, could you? He had more to lose. You? You know you don't have long. You've nothing to lose, have you?'

'Nothing at all,' Archie agreed. 'And I'll tell you something else, I don't regret it. If he walked in here now, I'd do it again. I wouldn't bloody hesitate. Men like that are

371

bad. Like rotten apples, you have to get rid of them before their badness spreads to the others.'

'Who was he supposed to be meeting that day?' Max asked curiously.

'Jack. Poor Hannah hadn't known what to do so, as always, she'd gone running to her granddad. Jack told her to leave it with him. He told her not to worry, that he'd see Johnson and sort it out. The poor lass has been half out of her mind with worry. For a while, she thought Jack had killed him.

'So Jack saw him – met him in the street one day – and said he'd hand over the money on Hannah's behalf. Do you know what that evil bugger Johnson did? He knocked Jack down in the street. Hit him, caught him off balance and knocked him to the ground.'

'Why on earth didn't you call us – the police?'

'No point,' Archie said flatly. 'What would you have done, eh? I couldn't take that. No one comes to this village and knocks down a man like Jack. Johnson were a bloody newcomer and he should've shown some respect for them as have lived here all their lives. Lived honest, decent lives, too.' He shook his head. 'He knocked him to the ground.'

Taking a big breath, he went on, 'Anyway, Jack told him he didn't want word of Hannah's mistakes getting out and ruining her future, so he'd pay the money. And the greedy bugger believed him.'

'When we found him,' Max said, 'he had an empty money belt on him. He was expecting to fill that with Jack's money, wasn't he? You're right, Archie. He was evil.'

'He was, and we can all rest easier knowing that he's gone. Jack's been a good friend to me, and to many others, too. No one knocks him down and gets away with it.' He pushed himself up out of his chair. 'You'll have to excuse me, lad, while I use the bathroom.'

'Of course.'

'You stay here, Jess,' Archie murmured, bending to stroke his dog. 'You're a good dog really, aren't you? Your heart's in the right place, girl.'

Archie left the room, his step slow and laborious on the stairs. The collie slunk over to Max for fuss. The more Max stroked her, the more boisterous she became.

'Your heart might be in the right place, Jess, but you're a pretty hopeless case. If you were mine, I'd–'

The short, spine-chilling bang made the dog yelp.

'Shit!' Max raced up the stairs, taking them two at a time. 'Shit! Shit! Shit!'

The door to Archie's bedroom was open, as was the top drawer in the dresser. Archie lay on his bed, one leg dangling lifelessly over the side.

The collie sniffed at her master, confused

by the sight of him lying so still. She sniffed at the blood and began to whine.

Clasped in Archie's lifeless hand was an old service revolver, one that should never have worked.

'Shit!' Max said again.

Jess was licking her master's hands, as if she could make him get up and stroke her head. All the while, she whined.

Max could have wept with her.

'Come on, Jess.' Max dragged the dog from the room while he took his phone from his pocket. 'Let's get you downstairs.'

Max had seen a lot in his time, but it didn't alter the fact that his hands were shaking so much that he was struggling to tap in the number. He listened to it ring out, and wondered if he'd managed to get the right person.

'Yes?'

'Jack? It's Max. DCI Trentham. I'm at Archie's.'

'Oh.' There was a pause. 'Oh, I see.' A longer pause. 'Is he gone?'

'I'm sorry, Jack. So very, very sorry.'

'Can I come over,' Jack asked gruffly, 'or is the place crawling with coppers?'

'Yes, come on over. There's no one here but me.'

The connection went dead and the silence was overwhelming.

How Jack did it, especially on a night like

this, Max would never know, but he was there in under five minutes.

He said nothing as Max opened the door, but his gaze went towards the first floor.

'Archie's in his bedroom,' Max told him.

'Can I see him?'

'Of course. That's why I called you.'

'Thank you.'

As erect as ever, Jack headed for the stairs. He hesitated at the bottom, took a deep breath and then, as slowly as Archie had, he climbed them.

Even the sight of her sister didn't cheer Jess. She was pacing and whining, and doing her damnedest to get upstairs to her master.

Max kept both dogs in the kitchen, and he paced with them.

Jack spent no longer than two minutes upstairs and, when he joined them in the kitchen, he looked as calm as he always did.

'That's it then,' was all he said.

'I'm so sorry, Jack.'

'It weren't your fault, Sherlock. It were that evil bugger, Johnson.' He reached into the cupboard for two glasses, then went to another cupboard for a bottle of whisky. 'Archie were prepared for it. He'd been polishing that old revolver up every day. I didn't think the thing would work – it's that old.'

'If only it hadn't,' Max murmured.

'No, lad. Archie was planning on using it

anyway,' he told him. 'He still had a few good days when he could take Jess out for a good long walk, but they were getting few and far between. He'd seen what cancer did to people. He always swore he'd prefer to take a bullet.'

Max shuddered.

'Here,' Jack said, thrusting a glass of whisky at him.

Max hesitated. He was responsible for Archie taking his own life. It didn't feel right to take his whisky, too.

'Go on, lad. The last thing Archie wanted were people moping around all miserable when he'd gone. He respected you. I do, too,' he added gruffly. 'Come on, lad. Archie'd want you to drink to him.'

It still didn't feel right, but Max, in need of a drink, took the glass.

'To Archie,' he said, chinking his glass against Jack's.

'Rest in peace, mate,' Jack said solemnly.

They emptied their glasses in record time, neither saying a word.

'How come the place isn't crawling with coppers?' Jack asked at last.

'Because I haven't called it in yet. I wanted you to see him first.'

Jack looked surprised at that. 'Thank you. Yes, thank you. I appreciate that.'

'I do have to make that call now.'

But they had another drink first.

Chapter Thirty-Six

Jill wasn't sure which was worse, her father refusing to set foot in the place and celebrating his wedding anniversary at the working men's club, or her father, very much the worse for wear, standing on stage singing 'My Way'.

'What do you think of Mum's outfit?' her sister asked her.

'It's not quite as shocking as I imagined,' Jill replied, and Prue grinned.

'It is pretty awful though, isn't it?'

'Yep.'

Against all odds, it had been a good day. There had been no bickering between her parents, just a few very sentimental speeches, and it was good to see them surrounded by so many friends. Her parents might spend half their lives hurling abuse at each other, but they were a devoted couple. Their world revolved around their family and friends.

'Do you know,' Jill said, 'I never thought I'd say this, but I'm really proud of them.'

Prue smiled as she watched her father performing on stage. 'Yes, me too. If only we could have talked Mum out of that outfit.'

They both laughed at that. Their mother's

dress sense left a lot to be desired.

'Is Max OK?' Prue asked curiously.

'Yes. Why?'

'He keeps escaping and wandering outside.'

'He's smoking again,' Jill explained.

But she knew it was more than that. She knew how much Archie's suicide had shaken him. It had shaken them all.

Except Jack. Jack had been prepared for it. She could even imagine the old boys saying their goodbyes weeks ago.

Jack had accepted it. He'd taken Archie's dog home with him, and now he would get on with life as best he could without his dearest friend. After almost eighty years of friendship, the circle was broken.

While Prue reprimanded her daughter, Jill went outside to find Max. After the crush inside, it should have been good to be in the fresh air. It wasn't. It was freezing.

She was right; he was smoking.

'I just stepped out for a breath of air,' he told her.

'You stepped out for a cigarette,' she corrected him. 'And you've spent more time out than in.'

He looked pale and unsettled. It took a lot to get to him; he'd seen too much to be easily upset.

'You OK?' she asked him.

'Yes, I expect so.'

'Archie was prepared for it, Max. Jack told

you that he'd vowed to take a bullet rather than a slow death from cancer.'

'I know.'

'And he respected you,' she went on. 'He knew you had to turn him in. He understood that. He was ready for it.'

'Turn him in?' He tossed his cigarette butt across the car park and leant on the railings. 'I had no intention of turning him in.'

'What?'

'I wish I'd kept it to myself,' he said on a long sigh. 'I could easily have pretended to have checked that appointment with the hospital. God knows, the NHS is in such a shambles, they don't know who keeps appointments and who doesn't. There was no need for him to – do that.'

Jill felt her world shift slightly. Max did nothing by the book, nothing at all, but he was a firm believer in justice. As much as he believed that people like Bradley Johnson didn't deserve to walk the planet, he would not, under any circumstances, allow anyone to take the law into their own hands.

'You would have let a guilty man walk free?' she asked in amazement.

'What was the point of doing anything else, Jill? Archie hadn't got long and no one was in any danger from him. What would have been the point of letting the taxpayer pick up the tab for sending him down? It would have been a complete waste of everyone's time and money.'

Jill couldn't have agreed more. 'But we're not allowed to think that way.'

'Christ,' he said, reaching for another cigarette, 'when the day comes that we're not allowed to think, we've really reached rock bottom. Anyway, it's all over now bar the sodding paperwork.'

He kicked out at a stray piece of gravel.

'I'm so bloody annoyed with myself, though,' he muttered. 'I should have known Archie would do something–'

'Come off it, Max. How could you be expected to know he had a gun in the house? A bloke like Archie? No way could you have expected that.'

'I should have kept my big mouth shut. All I was doing was saying "Look at me... I'm not as daft as you think." It was my own personal ego trip. If I'd kept my stupid mouth shut, Archie could have ended his days in peace and Jack wouldn't have to live with – that.'

'Jack was prepared for it. They both knew the score.'

Max wasn't convinced and Jill guessed he'd need time to come to terms with it all.

'Mum wants to know when you're going to have your turn at karaoke,' she told him, changing the subject.

That brought the first genuine smile of the day.

'Sadly, I would need at least half a bottle of Scotch inside me and as I'm driving–' He shrugged. 'Anyway, I wouldn't want to steal your dad's limelight.'

She snorted at that. 'People would pay you a fortune to steal his limelight.'

He considered this for a moment, threw his cigarette butt away, then draped his arm around her shoulders.

'I could do with the money,' he said at last.

'Me, too. The horses I backed yesterday should be reaching the finishing post about now. Having said that,' she added, ever the optimist, 'there are still those I backed this morning. Maybe I've won a small fortune.'

'Let's hope so. I really need to buy that beach bar in Spain.'

Jill had heard it all before. All the same, the idea was appealing.

'Shergar fixing the drinks,' she said wistfully.

Max nodded. 'Elvis cooking the burgers.'

'Lord Lucan waiting on tables.'

'Jack Taylor making the tea.'

'Hey, nice one, Max!'

This Large Print Book, for people
who cannot read normal print,
is published under the auspices of

THE ULVERSCROFT FOUNDATION